TRAGEDY QUEENS

Stories Inspired by Lana Del Rey & Sylvia Plath

Edited by
LEZA CANTORAL

CONTENTS

INTRODUCTION

Archetypes are real.
Muses are real.
Writers are the channels of these spirits
&
if that sounds like witchcraft that's because it is.
These stories gave me chills.
Sylvia Plath & Lana Del Rey
course through the veins of these dark, sexy, mind-bending,
fantastical, romantic,
&
haunting tales.
Authors from different genres came together in their love
&
passion for these muses.

Leza Cantoral

THE BLACKLIST: KATHRYN LOUISE

Richard's a hugger.

He sticks my head against his chest, wraps his arms around me and sways, forcing me to move with him. His shirt is sweat-drenched, reeking of menthol cigarettes and aftershave. "I hope you don't mind. I don't want to end up on the blacklist or anything."

I force a smile. "Of course not."

It takes their breath away, meeting me, seeing me for the first time. They seem compelled to touch me, as if to confirm I'm real, not just some Internet born fantasy.

Richard's hand lingers on the small of my back. He examines me, then, eyes moving up and down my frame. "Your pictures don't do you justice."

I'm not flattered but I pretend to be. "Thank you."

Like his hand, his eyes linger a moment too long. They're a piercing blue, ice white, cut with red veins, lined by wrinkles. Richard doesn't look like a predator. He looks more like a cruise ship passenger, with his sun-burnt skin, white hair, khaki shorts and Hawaiian shirt.

He wears a convincing enough smile, plays polite and offers to take my bags. I decline. With a shrug, he turns and leads me down a hallway, the walls of which are dotted with wedding pictures of strangers and dog portraits bearing his watermark.

The hall leads to his studio, which is little more than a home office with a backdrop hanging on one wall, a stool, and some studio lights. It's dim, cut by streaks of diffused light that highlight the dust in the air. Even minimally furnished, it feels cramped with just the two of us.

Richard closes the door behind him, grabs my bags and asks, "How was your trip? How was Portland?"

He says nothing of the weight of my luggage. I relax once he sets it down. "It was good. Fun. I met and worked with a lot of talented people."

"You worked with Brian Stax, right? I love his stuff."

He's digging, hoping I'll share a bad story. I don't care to indulge him. "Yup."

"I can't wait to see what you did together."

Something moves behind him, drawing my attention. He turns, offering me a better view.

It's a bird. A parrot of some kind, too large for its cage. Light blue with a white face and breast and orange beak.

"That's Ruby. She's a quacker."

Ruby flaps her wings. "Ruby!"

I step past Richard, toward the bird. "Is she nice?"

"Sometimes."

Ruby cocks her head as I approach, stirring in her cage. Her feathers are the same shade of blue as Richard's eyes.

As if summoned by my thought, he appears behind me, his breath hot on my neck. It startles me. He laughs, and Ruby echoes the sound with a cackle, more unnerving than cute.

"I didn't know parrots could laugh," I say, catching my breath.

"She can do more than that! Watch this." Richard presses his face against the bars of the cage and makes a sound like a cat's meow, or tries to. It sounds nothing like a cat. Not even Ruby is convinced. He tries again, to no avail.

He turns to me, embarrassed, then stares past me, at a cat I hadn't noticed. An old thing, with greasy fur, it glares at him from its perch atop the couch. Richard glides past me, grabs the beast by the neck and holds it up.

The cat yowls. Ruby mimics this, too.

Richard drops the flailing cat and turns to me with a grin. "Did you hear?"

I nod, because I do not wish for him to try again.

He seems disappointed by my reaction. "She knows more but only talks under certain conditions."

"She and I have that in common."

The joke does nothing to diffuse the tension.

Ruby's voice cuts through the budding silence.

"Take off your clothes!"

We both turn toward the bird.

Richard laughs and hurries over to the cage. "She's getting ahead of herself. Paperwork first, then pictures." He puts his hands on my shoulders and turns me around, directing me toward a stool, which squeaks beneath my weight when I sit, drawing another laugh from Ruby.

Richard grabs a piece of paper off his desk and hands it to me.

Looks like a standard modeling contract. I sign without reading and pass it back.

Richard frowns. "No, honey, I need your real name. This is a legal document, not Instagram." He taps my signature on the page and hands it back to me.

I bat my eyes and force a smile. "Lola Love is my real name."

He doesn't believe me but he won't press it. Hard to argue against a fake name when you're willing to lie about age. "All right then, Lo-la."

Ruby squawks and repeats my name. "Lo-la."

Laughing, Richard pats me on the shoulder. "You hear that? She likes you!"

I shoot the bird a glare as Richard walks away, humming The Kinks song of the same name. He sets the contract on his desk and fishes a wallet out one of his many pockets. "Remind me your rates?"

We've discussed rates three times. "$100.00 an hour."

"And for nude work?"

"$150.00."

Smirking, he pulls two bills from his wallet and tosses them my way. Both hundreds. "A tip."

"For?"

"Taking the time to indulge an old man. May we start with some portraits?" He gestures for me to sit on the stool.

I nod and do as he asks, pocketing the cash while he prepares his digital camera. He tests to make sure it's synced to the lights, then circles me, once, twice, three times. Finally, he comes to a stop before me and hits the shutter, blinding me with a flash. He reviews the photo immediately, frowning, then turns that look on me. Before I can ask what's wrong, he comes toward me and tucks a strand of hair behind my ear. "There, that's perfect."

It's a test, this gesture. One I let slide.

"Thank you."

It's not the response he expected. "You seem nervous."

"I am, a little. I haven't done this in a while."

"Would a drink help? We only have so much time and I want you to feel comfortable."

May as well take him up on the offer. "Only on the condition that you join me."

"Of course."

He keeps a bottle of whiskey in his desk drawer, which he pours into waiting glasses.

Smiling, he hands me a drink. I down it in one and hand it back. His grin grows, and he trades me the empty glass for his full one.

Whiskey makes the job easier.

Richard pours himself another, lifts his glass in salute, and takes a sip, wet lips smacking.

I join him. "Are you married, Richard?"

He thinks I'm flirting with him. With reluctance, he wags his fingers, displaying a gold wedding ring. "Thirty years now."

"And where's your wife right now?"

"Out."

"Out where?"

"Oh, I don't know. Wherever it is women go when their husbands give them a little money and tell them to get out of the house. No need to worry about her. She'll be out for a while. We're isolated out here. Nearest neighbor is about five miles away, so we'll have plenty of privacy."

Good to know.

I set my drink down and angle myself toward the light. "Should we get started?"

Nodding, he trades his glass for his camera. "Yes, yes. Back to business."

We work in silence for a while but Richard can't hold his curiosity for long. "How long have you been modeling?"

"Since I was 14."

"You naughty girl, you."

"I didn't... it was innocent stuff."

He winks. "I'm sure it was."

I'm not sure how to respond to that, so I hold my tongue, focus on my modeling. Richard can only pretend to be interested in my facial expressions for so long. Already he's getting bored.

He lowers his camera, checks his watch and nods, as if he's decided something. "You can take off your clothes now."

"Take off your clothes!" Ruby echoes.

I strip.

Richard happens to walk behind me at the moment I bend over to take off my underwear.

The shutter snaps and I freeze.

"Oops. Didn't mean to do that. I'll delete the picture, of course."

Ruby snickers.

I ignore her, gritting my teeth. I'll delete it myself, later.

I stand, never taking my eyes off Richard. I don't like having him behind me. He maintains eye contact with me while I take off my shirt, not even offering me the illusion of privacy. Once I'm nude, he lets his gaze fall, and I can *feel* his eyes as they move up my frame.

"You seem comfortable in your skin."

"I am."

"Do you enjoy getting naked for strangers?"

"I enjoy posing nude."

"There's a distinction there?"

"Yes."

That makes him laugh. Ruby joins in too.

"I suppose you think what you're doing is art?"

"Don't you?"

"No, I don't consider myself an artist. I'm just a guy with a camera."

Clearly.

"Why work with models if you don't intend to make art?"

He shrugs, and circles back to stand before me. "It's a hobby."

Silence for a moment or two, save for the shutter. He's working up the nerve to ask me something, I can tell. Takes me by surprise when he finally does.

"Have you ever been sexually assaulted?"

I suppose he expects me to flinch. I don't. "I have."

He doesn't feign shock or sympathy. "By a photographer?"

"Yes."

"Yet you still model."

An accusation, not a question.

"Why wouldn't I?"

To this, he has no answer.

He lifts his camera and we resume shooting.

"Tousle your hair."

I do as commanded and he snaps a photograph.

That's how it goes. He gives me permission to move, but interrupts to redirect often. "Put your hand on your chest, just under your breast. There. Perfect." Click. "Maybe cup your breast? Yes, that's good." Click. "Lovely." Click, click, click. "Okay, can you put your hand back on your stomach? Yes, like that." Click, click. "That's a lovely pose." Click. "Lower your hand."

He has an erection now. I try not to stare.

"A bit lower." Click. Click, click, click. "Now touch yourself."

I freeze, my hand resting on my stomach. "I'm sorry." I regret the words as soon as they leave my mouth. I've nothing to apologize for.

"Touch yourself."

"I—"

The phone rings, saving me. Richard lets it ring twice more, then swears under his breath, sets his camera down, and stalks out the room, closing the door behind him.

I wait until he starts talking, then I put my clothes back on. I believe the stories I've heard of him, but I need proof. I can't act without it, not unless he goes further and I'd prefer to avoid that.

I pick up his camera and open the photo review, scrolling through the images he took of me. I've no interest in these. It's the other girls I want to see. I'm betting Richard doesn't clear his SD card before each shoot. I'm not disappointed.

Here's a redhead. Young. She looks wary in the photographs but there's nothing to suggest he crossed a line. This one is under-age. This one, too. And a third. Seems he has a type.

This one's a bit older, maybe 32. Probably getting ready to retire. I can't recall her name but I know her face. She travels a lot. Works with anyone who will pay. She's been around a long time. Knows a lot of people. He wouldn't have tried anything with her. Probably uses her photos as bait.

Traveling models talk, let each other know whom to avoid. That's why the blacklist was created. Brennan had been trying to help others, to challenge the culture of silence around sexual violence in the industry. But the blacklist only helps those who have access to it. Richard prays on those who have no one to talk to.

Newer, younger models.

Models like Diana, who had told me about Richard. There are pictures of her here, too. Seeing them fills me with fury.

Richard likes to insert himself. His thumb in a model's mouth, his hand around their neck, gripping their hair and pinching their nipples. There's a shot of him looming behind Diana, a camera in one hand and the other on her ass. Judging by the look on Diana's face, it wasn't consensual. She's not alone. There are at least three others in here. Victims then, survivors now. A part of me wants to delete the pictures, but I can't. They need to be seen by the right people.

Best if no one sees ones of me, though. I delete them, then go to the door to listen. Richard is still talking. Sounds annoyed, but there's guilt there, too. The wife, then. He'll try to keep this short. I'll have to be quick.

Ruby laughs as I pass her cage.

Best to ignore it. It's just a bird. Just a creepy, laughing bird I suspect mimics both Richard and his victims.

I go to his desk, riffle through the drawers. Find Polaroids, none of them pleasant. Six in total, one of each girl.

These are his trophies.

Nausea hits like a fist. I push it down, chase it with the rest of Richard's drink. The whiskey helps, but not much. I close the drawer, go to my purse and pull out a cigarette. I trade my lighter for a handgun.

A Smith and Wesson .38 with a pink handle. The best and only gift my father ever gave me.

I holster it, then creep to the door and open it a crack. With my back pressed against the wall, I can see Richard at the end of the hall, his head hung in silence while his wife speaks in his ear. I can just make out her voice. Something about the dry cleaners, a movie, and Richard being a selfish prick.

It's time to end this conversation.

I kick the door. Richard startles at the sound, and turns to find me watching him. I stifle a giggle and walk away, back to the stool, where I prop my leg and wait.

Richard doesn't keep me long.

He comes storming in, red faced, hands balled into fists. His beady eyes fall on me and he falters, stopped in his tracks by the sight of me.

The shock doesn't last long. He looks pleased now, eager even.

I can tell what he's thinking. It's there in his eyes. He thinks he's won. That I'm ruined, weak and easy prey. He's wrong. I'm not defined by the bad things that have happened to me, I'm fueled by them.

Richard points to my cigarette. "Put that out."

"I will when I'm done." The words come through exhaled smoke. I flash him a wicked smile and take another drag.

I don't mind Ruby's laughter this time, but Richard does. His eyes flick to the bird and back to me. If looks could kill, we'd both be dead. "You got dressed."

They always seem surprised when we flaunt what little agency we have. "I did."

Richard looks at his watch. "We've got roughly forty minutes left."

Ruby picks that moment to chime in with something new. "No more!"

I nod to the bird. "Who taught her to say that?" Richard frowns but doesn't answer so I continue, prodding, moving toward him as I speak. "Was it Diana? Carol? Sierra? Darleen?"

It's his wife's name that gets him. He charges, fast, so fast, and backhands me. I go down, stumbling over the stool, mordant laughter falling off my lips.

Ruby laughs along with me.

Richard isn't amused. He looms over me, hands in shaking fists at his side, eyes narrowing as the moment stretches. I touch my face where he struck me, and my voice comes out as a sob between breathless laughter. "It felt like a kiss."

The look on his face makes me laugh harder. He takes a step back at the sound, then seems to remember he's bigger and stronger than me. He's smiling as he yanks me off the floor by the arm and undoes his belt. The movement lifts his shirt, revealing soft flesh covered in curly white hairs.

I grab my cigarette and put it out in his belly button. Screaming, he drops me. Down I go again, like a rag doll.

We move at the same time, Richard and I. He yanks off his belt, brandishing it like a whip. I draw my gun and level it at him.

Ruby cackles. I'm starting to wonder whose side she's on.

Richard seems to be deciding whether or not he should laugh too.

There's doubt in his eyes I intend to quell. "I've killed before. Brooklyn Madman. The Rhiddler. Brian Stax."

He recognizes that last name. Doubt is replaced by fear. "What do you want?"

Ruby chimes in before I can speak.

"Take off your clothes. Take off your clothes."

"You heard the bird. Strip."

"Wh-why?"

I raise a brow. "Because I asked you to and I'm holding a gun."

That's all the convincing he needs. He strips, starting with the cargo pants. His hands are shaking, his eyes lowered and cheeks flushed red with shame. Richard is not comfortable in his skin. He stands there shivering, his right hand covering his junk, left hand wiping congealed sweat off his brow.

Slowly, I get to my feet, keeping the gun trained on him. I stalk over to him, loving the way he flinches as I get near. I circle him, like he did me, and whisper in his ear, "What about you? How many lives have you stolen?"

"I don't know what you're talking about."

I run a hand through his hair. He turns away, and that's when I know for sure I'm stronger than him. "Don't know how to lie either, it seems. Let's try again. How many lives have you stolen, Richard?"

"None! I'm not a killer."

"I never said you were." I circle around and whisper in his ear, "I've seen your photographs. How many were there?"

He understands now, but has to force the answer. "Six."

"Six?" I mouth the word, feigning shock.

"It was consensual! They signed contracts, all of them."

"They didn't agree to be raped." The words come through gritted teeth.

He flinches at the word. "I didn't rape anyone! They wanted it, at the time. If they're saying something else now it's because they want attention or money, or maybe they just hate men or something, I don't know. I'm not a fucking rapist!"

I take a quick step back and shoot him in the foot.

He falls, screaming, eyes wide with shock, and rolls into a fetal position, right arm reaching toward his injured foot.

I did warn him.

I extend my foot and bring it down on his hand, pinning it to the floor. He screams, and Ruby echoes the sound, thrashing about her cage.

A horrid sound. Good thing no one can hear it.

Right now he looks like he'd like to hit me again, but the gun deters him from acting on such dumb impulse.

I crouch beside him, grab his face and turn it toward me. "Does your wife know what you did to those women?"

I'll stay and kill her too if I have to. Richard can see that in my eyes.

He shakes his head. "Darleen? No. Oh, God, Darleen!" He starts sobbing, then.

I smack him on the cheek. Try to get him to focus. "You hit her too?"

"I'd never hurt her!"

I press the barrel of the gun to his forehead, burning him.

He flails in pain. "Stop! Stop! Please stop!"

Ruby rattles her cage. "No more! No more!"

She's right. It's time to end this.

Richard is starting to beg. "Please... I'll turn myself in. That's what you want, right? Justice? Just let me go and I'll turn myself in."

That makes me laugh. "Vengeance makes a nice motif, but it didn't bring me here. I target people like you for the same reason you pick people like me. No one will care about your death."

"Wait, no! I'm sorry, I—"

I do as promised and put a bullet in his skull before he can utter another word. Blood and brains and flesh explode in an angry red flash, painting my face in warmth. Richard goes still and silent. I've no need to check his pulse to confirm he's dead.

I lower the gun, hands and body shaking with adrenaline.

Ruby's been in a frenzy since the first shot. I watch as she flies into the walls of her cage, as if she could break through them. Finally, the cage falls to the ground. The door pops open and Ruby finds her freedom.

She circles the room a few times before landing atop a coat rack, where she studies me and says my name. "Lo-la."

I can't have her repeating that, even if it is a fake name. Better to let her go. I open the window, watch as she flies away, then turn and consider Richard's corpse.

Killing is easy, disposing of a body takes work.

I start by going through his clothing, setting aside the cash and car keys I find in his pockets. That done, I gather his clothing and toss it into my suitcase, which is mostly empty, save for a few pieces of lingerie and a hacksaw.

What comes next is brutal but necessary. Knowing what he's done makes things a little easier. With the faces of his victims fresh in my mind, I do what I have to do, letting my rage fuel me as I work the saw.

I say their names as I cut him down to size. "Diana." He loses an arm. "Carol." He loses the other. "Sierra." I start on his legs. "Brennan." She may not have been one of his, but that doesn't matter. I cut his legs into three pieces. "This is for me," I say as I take his head. I pack him up in my bags, a souvenir.

I'm breathless by the time it's done. Tired and sore and ready to get the hell out Richard's house. I don't want to be here when the wife gets home. Don't care to know whether she'll call the cops once she learns what he's done.

I take the contract and whiskey bottle with me, though, and leave the Polaroids on the desk for Darleen to find.

Richard's cat laps at a puddle of blood, purring. I leave her to it and drag my bags out the room.

I toss Richard in the trunk of his brand new truck and open the garage door. The road is clear in either direction, though I suspect that's not unusual out here. I light a cigarette, take a moment to appreciate the view before pulling out my phone. I open the black-list, scroll till I find Richard's name, and read the next entry.

'Dangerous photographer operating outside San Jose, California. Goes by Cash. Real name unknown. VERY inappropriate. Offered me drinks and pressured me when I said no. Pushed my limits multiple times and touched me without permission. His pics were shit, too.'

There's more.

Multiple allegations of physical assault and rumors of a past stint in prison for battery.

San Jose is only three hours away. I can make it there by sundown, if I leave now.

I hop in the car and tuck my phone away. I'll post a travel notice in the morning, see if I can't catch Cash's interest. For now, I'm happy just to find a signal on the radio. Lana Del Rey's 'Born to Die.' How appropriate. I sing along as I wash the blood off my face with a wipe I found in the dash, hands and voice shaking. "Feet don't fail me now, take me to your finish line."

I turn the music up and back out onto the road, smiling as I cry and sing along.

CRAZY MARY: PATRICIA GRISAFI

Day 34

I have not been able to move. For days, like Tracey Emin in her soiled, award-winning bed, I have stewed in my piss and spit, all the while feeling like an art exhibit in my own shit museum. Over there is the vodka bottle, set against the suitcase half packed with socks and sweaters. And there is The DaVinci Code—we've all been passing it around here because the bookstore had one copy in English, and it's a hot commodity. Bookmark halfway through because after my train ride back from Milan, I stopped wanting to find out what happened.

Five Chanel lip glosses are lined up on my desk. When I found out Gina swore by the one that looked like psychedelic ballet slippers, I bought the whole collection at the farmacia. Gina, with her strawberry blonde curls and pouty sneer, had been slowly poaching the classmates who ate lunch with me in the lemon tree grove near school. One by one they had moved with their mozzarella and tomato sandwiches over to the wooden benches at the far side of the grove. I know if I wear the same lip gloss she does, they will come back.

At least I still have Eating Disorder Katrina in Milan, who is living with three American boys, the flat stacked with rotten vegetables and the sheets teeming with filth. The last time I visited

I kept worrying I would pick up pubic lice or a skin disease, so disgusting were the linens.

And then there is my boyfriend David. His goddamn beautiful face weaving through the crowds, his dumb American jeans and sneakers, the canvas bag he carried his paints in. I knew once he left me at the train station in Rome, that I would only ever fuck him when he called me and never when I called him.

I slip a little on the slimy cobblestones outside the Museo dell'-Opera and catch my breath. It feels like it will never stop raining, coating every surface in a slick veneer. I shake my umbrella and step inside the monastery-like quiet. I know she is waiting.

Mary Magdalen always knows what to say about men.

"Girl, tell me about it. If I called him, he was always busy giving speeches or making tables. And now, all these years later, men use their hands and recreate me how they want to. I have long hair and perky breasts if they want. I might even wear a hair cloth if they've got a fetish for penitence. Here, Donatello cut me into wood and damned me to cower in this well-lit corner with my hands folded in prayer. Mostly, I'm drawn into these sexy little shrouds, though, with my eyes open to the sky and my lips parted for a dick that exists somewhere outside the frame."

I nod my head.

"Yeah, Mary, I get it. Men are the worst. I have to admit, I'm really moved by how Donatello made you look like such a convincingly sad old hag. It makes me want to cry, to really lose my shit right here in front of these reverent tourists. I mean, I'm a tourist too, aren't I? Even though I kind of live here now?"

"You are living the best of lies," Mary says, "in the dirtiest of cities. You have never wanted anything out of life except to be loved. You will never find that, but you will have nice dresses and quality leather goods."

When I leave the museum, I decide to go shopping. I buy two pairs of boots.

Day 37

Apparently, there has been so much inter-collegiate fucking that a new, rather insidious and antibiotic resistant sexually transmitted infection has become a problem. Shania, one of Gina's new friends, whispered this to me while I glop foundation on my rosacea in the University's second floor bathroom.

I balance the pot of cream on my thigh while Shania smokes her pen like an imaginary cigarette and laughs with nervous eyes swinging back and forth.

"I might have to get tested," she says.

"Um, okay," I say.

"That color is not your skin tone."

"Um, okay," I want to take the blunt end of my foundation brush and stab her in the throat.

"I'm serious. It's way too yellow. Also, can you believe this is happening?"

I reach for the eye shadow, which is perched on the radiator. Might as well re-do my whole face.

"Well, how many people have you slept with so far?"

"I don't know. Maybe three? What about you?"

"I have a boyfriend."

"Maybe he's screwing around."

I haven't spoken with David in a week. He's been busy painting, he said. I was prepared to be deeply understanding but mostly felt like a discarded gym sock, especially when he called me terrified that he had picked up a foot fungus at the community pool and then proceeded to ignore me after I helped him procure a special foot salve.

The last time we spoke, David took me up to Fiesole. I stupidly wore high heels for the trip. Halfway down the hill I had to take them off, so bloody and sore were my new blisters. We passed used condoms and a hypodermic needle, feral dogs and fields of golden flowers. I sat on a wall of crumbling stone as he drew my leg dangling down to the swollen foot. We had an ice coated in sticky black cherry syrup at a tourist trap before he put me on the bus.

"See you next week."

Day 38

An Italian boy grabs my arm as I walk home from the bakery one night. He puts his face right into mine, so that his nose grazes the socket of my eye. I don't understand what he is saying, so fast are the words vibrating off his tongue. My face shakes with the waves, and I jerk back hoping to fall flat on the cobblestones. I pray that I will just hit the floor. I don't even care that there is a pile of dog shit next to my foot.

He lets me go and laughs. His friends laugh. I turn and walk away so as to not let him know I am fucking out of my mind with terror. I make sure I sway when I walk, like it's no big deal, like I get grabbed all the time and I'm cool with it.

Out of his sight, I throw my pastry on the ground. I hunch over like an old woman.

Day 40

Slime on the concrete again, the sky a dull brown. On the way to Mary's, I see a rat the size of a large cat crawl down into the Arno, that filthy stream. I peer over the bridge, see the rat squirming its way into a pile of sticks.

"Mary, you get a bad rap," I shrug, staring into her hollow, peach pit eyes. "Some people think you're a whore. Others try and reclaim you, make you an idol for marginalized women. They try and give you saintliness, sanctification. But you never actually existed. If you did exist, you were at least three different people. Maybe more. I get the symbolism. I get the mythology. I take art history classes. I'm a feminist."

Mary sighs.

"People are multi-faceted. How would you like it if you had to be everything to everyone?"

"I'm pretty much nothing to no one."

"Just as much of a burden."

"Hey, what do you think of Titian's portrait of you?"

"I think I look fat. If you believe the stories, I hung out in the woods for a really long time. You don't get glowing skin and pudgy cheeks from living in the forest and eating insects and roots. Plus, the guy Titian painted it for was a real pervert. He hid the portrait in his study, behind a velvet curtain for 'private worship.' Boy that got old real fast. It's pretty insulting to be someone's holy pornography."

"Uh huh. I think I look fat too, I've definitely gained weight. David said—"

"You don't have to always make everything about you," Mary says sharply. "There are other things going on in the world."

Day 59

I pin photos of pit bulls and Marilyn Monroe on the faded rose wallpaper of my bedroom. I will be out of vodka soon. My host family hasn't checked on me. I think they think I have been going to school because I bang around in the room a lot and turn on the shower and eat their food. David hasn't called. Shania hasn't called. Katrina hasn't called.

When I recently visited Katrina in Milan, we took a taxi to the outer limits of the city, to a club full of red lights and round couches. She was happy to meet Italian boys while I hugged myself against the wall. Each boy, she said, was so nice. They were all just so nice, so happy to meet us, so interested.

How does one perfect a stone face?

"I have a boyfriend," I told everyone who looked at me. "He's an artist. His stuff is really good. He's going to be famous. We're going to get married."

"You are so pretty!" some guy said.

"See? They love us!"

Katrina's smile was bright.

And the night spun about us like Rapunzel's hair.

All the time, choking.

Day 68

David calls.

"Oh, hi!" I hadn't expected to hear from him.

"Um, hi."

"I've been so busy!"

"Oh? Okay."

"I went to visit Katrina in Milan."

"How is she?"

"She's great! We had a great time! Milan is awesome!"

"I'm glad to hear it."

"How are you?"

"Busy. I've been painting a lot."

"Oh yeah? How is the painting?"

"I think it's okay."

"I'm sure it's awesome. When can I see it?"

"Uh, soon. I'm just really busy."

"Okay. Cool! Maybe we can get dinner?"

"Yeah, okay. Maybe next week or something. I'm just really busy."

Day 78

I always end up in the cemetery. You can take the city bus up the hill—and there is a spectacular view—and then you could wander amongst the dead for a few hours. I always liked cemeteries, even as a kid. They were peaceful, magnetic. Some of my best memories are washed in cemeteries.

When you can't get to a cemetery, an old Church is best. Even if you don't believe in God, there is something comforting in feeling the worn benches, sucking in the wasted hopes of people who came here praying for their lives to be better, for their hearts to heal, for their children to walk, for their parents to sing. You can feel the itchiness at the altar, the worry in the wood. Light a candle and you can smell sorrow in the sulfur.

There is a perfume with a scent like Church sadness. I don't remember the name, but I bought a bottle along with some burgundy nail polish and coal black eyeliner.

Day 79

I run into Gina and Shania underneath a ridiculously picturesque archway in downtown Florence. They giggle over glass bottle Cokes. They look like Cold War domestic fetish pin up girls. Gina's lips shine in the light, that intangible iridescent pink.

"Hi!" I say, wanting to grab their drinks and shatter them on the ground. Grab their heads and shatter them on the ground.

"Oh, hi," Shania says.

"What are you guys up to?"

"Just hanging out."

Gina's face slams into the cobblestones and pulp spreads out underneath. Blood splutters around her golden brown hair. Spikes shoot from the sky and fix her to the ground by the wrists. A man's foot cracks down on her neck and crushes it like an overripe melon. Gina snorts, the blood thick from her nose flowing into the neat margins of the cobblestones.

"Have you done the homework?" her severed head asks me, patiently annoyed.

I laugh.

"Hey, I love your lip gloss! What is it?"

"I don't remember," Gina's head says.

"I'd love to talk, but we're meeting some friends at the Duomo. See you later!" Shania says. They walk off down some filthy alley.

Alone in the archway. The nearby restaurant smells great. The desire to stab myself in the temples is intense.

Day 90

I throw The Da Vinci Code out of the window. If a student dies alone in Italy, does America hear her sputter?

I know David hates me, but I slump down the street and under the archway to his flat and climb the stairs and shrug off my sweater and cram my body onto his dick and then stare at the ceiling wondering whether that was a loss or a gain. His roommates argue in the kitchen—they are lovers—Nancy has eaten the last of the prosciutto and Rita is angry about the lack of consideration. The door slams and all I hear is the hiss of the radiator.

Day 99

I turn 21. David and some of his friends take me to an Irish pub in the Santa Croce section of the city, which feels absurd. He gives me vibrant orange lilies as a gift, and I am overjoyed that he has remembered my favorite color. I drink an obscene amount of alcohol because it seems like the thing to do. I am convinced that I will die. I expect to be worried, but I'm not.

That night, David drags me back to his apartment. I vomit all night into individual plastic bags that I pile into a neat stack in the corner of his bedroom. The next morning, I stumble into a taxi cab carrying the bags of vomit and the wilting orange lilies because David says there is no way I can throw my puke bags out in his apartment and there aren't any garbage bins on the tiny street. The driver gives me a look so foul I want to curl into my long hair like it's the thorny branches of a dark wood and sleep for one hundred years.

The next day, I walk into the train station and approach the druggist.

"Ho bisogno di un farmaco, ma non ho la prescrizione. So che il nome chimico, però. Non so come si chiama in italiano."

The pharmacist looks at me askew, and I grab a scrap of paper and write "Fluoxetine Hydrochloride 20mg."

"Oh, si," he says. And twenty minutes later I have a box of Italian Prozac that I clutch like a golden goose.

I know it won't work for at least a few weeks, but I'm desperate. I swallow at least four pills with a bottle of San Pellegrino hoping that would speed things up but knowing it wouldn't. I should have never gone off the damn drug. Maybe everything would have been different. Maybe I would have felt strong enough to tell David to go fuck himself. Maybe I would have made different friends. Or any friends. Maybe I would have crawled out of bed and gotten some honey-colored highlights.

Day 108

Mary Magdalen smiles benevolently through her chiseled frown.

"Hey, girl. I had a dream last night," I tell her.

"Oh, yeah?"

"Yeah. Usually when I go back on my antidepressants I have these crazy dreams."

"You know, when I was your age we just put on a sack cloth and went into the wilderness and waited to die."

"I mean, wouldn't you have taken Prozac if you could have?"

"What's the point? Life is suffering."

Mary shrugs.

"Can I tell you about my dream now?"

"Sure, I guess."

"Well, I was running through a house, and a rabid dog was chasing me. Hackles all up. Mouth foaming."

"That's the fucking worst," she says.

"Tell me about it. Anyway, I slammed the basement door in this mad dog's face. But I had to hold him, too. I grabbed at these quills of fur that were piercing through the door. I kept holding them so tightly, like if they slipped through my hands I would somehow die. My knuckles got all bloody."

"Well, you can't get rabies from fur," Mary Magdalen says logically.

"I know! But what do you think that was all about?"

"I don't know," she pauses. "I hate hearing about your dreams. They're so boring. You can be really selfish. Get over yourself. A lot of people have it worse."

Day 132

Katrina in Milan became sick from her eating disorder. She was admitted to a hospital. I found out from David's brother Jerry, who had been dating her in secret and had made his way to Florence after a disastrous visit.

"I flew out to see her and she sent me packing. I saw how she was living. Not like a human," Jerry says shaking his head. We were crammed in a small corner of a tiny pasticerria near the touristy part of town; I was sipping a cappuccino, Jerry an espresso. I was surprised he even wanted to see me. Maybe he was feeling vulnerable, his grand romantic gesture squelched by the florid, grim reality of mental illness.

"I mean, the sheets, the rotten food. It was like a swamp in there."

"She seemed to be having such a good time, too."

I stare into my coffee.

"Was she seeing anyone?"

"Um, I don't know. I think for a bit she was cozy with some guy we met at a club. I didn't know you guys were dating."

"Oh."

"Hey, did David say anything?" I ask suddenly.

"Huh? About what?"

"Me."

"Huh? Oh, I mean, he said you're having a good time, yeah?"

"It's amazing!"

"Yeah, David loves it here. He's so inspired."

"It's so beautiful, and the food is amazing, and the people are amazing, and I'm so happy. I can't believe it will be over soon."

Day 150

I hadn't gotten a haircut the entire time I was in Florence, but the minute I step into the airport I purchase a nail care pack and hack off five inches in the bathroom. I don't care who stares or shrieks or smiles or anything. All that dead, haggard hair has to go.

I sit crossed-legged on the floor of the terminal and rifle through the tabloids and newspapers while munching on a Toblerone. Jennifer Lopez married Marc Anthony. Lindsay Lohan was rumored to have had a boob job. Someone mutilated a statue of Mary Magdalen in what was called an anti-Catholic hate crime but there were no suspects. The damage was minimal—only a missing pinky finger—and the museum already called in restoration experts to work on repairs. Catherine Zeta Jones had a stalker who threatened to "slice her up like meat on a bone and feed her to the dogs."

David was going to Bruge to see a Hans Memling triptych and I didn't know when I would see him next. Katrina stopped answering my calls weeks ago. Maybe she was still in the hospital. Maybe she was dead, wrapped in her dirty sheets, rotting like all the other forgotten meat in her apartment. Shania and Gina were taking the train to Paris for a three-day shopping extravaganza.

I sleep soundly on the plane after swallowing three Benadryl. It is the best sleep of my life.

As I walk into the terminal at Newark, I see my mother and father waving frantically.

"Well, you've gained weight!" my father says. "And what did you do to your hair?"

I wrap my fist around Mary's finger, smooth in my pocket. I smile serenely and tell him it's the latest style in Florence.

New Jersey stares at me, gray and drizzling.

"I'm so glad to be home, it's been…"

My parents' faces turn to me, hopeful and expectant. They want to know about how I've grown, what I've learned, if it was worth it. They want my gratitude because anything else would destroy them.

"Wonderful."

That's what Mary would do. Give them what they want.

PIPEDREAMS: DEVORA GRAY

"Love is a chopped-up rubber hose filling this car with exhaust fumes," he says to you and tucks a strand of hair behind your cold ear. The air conditioner is blowing full blast. The hose he speaks of is tucked into the back passenger seat while the old sedan rumbles in his grandfather's dark garage.

He says, "We agreed to this—you and me. Yes, I'm going to make this sound vile. The things that will come out of my mouth will shave off layers of who you think you are. You'll hate me. Maybe you'll fear me. In the end, you'll be free of the thing that terrifies you most."

He slaps you hard when you go for the window crank. The ease in which he does this reminds you how comfortable his hands felt everywhere else. You get flashbacks of finger-fucking at a Sonic drive-thru, the foot job he gave you in a Jacuzzi full of Austrian tourists, and you are at once excited and calm. You notice how you're breathing. God, it sounds loud, fast. You better slow it down. Control your shit.

In the time it takes to remember why you're here, you might both be dead. He's that committed.

You were driving buses for the elderly and infirmed when you met. He was a dark-haired boy loading a wheelchair-bound Pops the War Veteran onto a lowered silver plank. When he looked at you, the world felt less scary. Ever since your father took communion from a shotgun, life had been an escape into wrinkled affirmations taped to your bathroom mirror: dog-eared, highlighted self-help books and weekend seminars on how to LOVE YOURSELF. You read, but you've never been a reader, avoiding Hemingway, Virginia Woolf, and Hunter S. Thompson. Anne Sexton was a loser. Sylvia Plath is your goddamn Antichrist. Art to you is a pretty floral design on wallpaper, Hallmark cards with lots of glitter, and Grandma Moses paintings. You are happy. You smile at your passengers. You wonder how much time they have left and wish one of them thought the same about you.

At least that's what you believed before the dark-haired boy—shall we say surly with a touch of swagger—climbed into the van and positioned the Navy hero amid straps that would prevent his plastic leg from slamming into the safety glass. Pops wouldn't mind a wild ride if you took a sharp turn while repeating your Deepak Chopra 'Mantra of the Day,' but his attendant would take it as a personal affront.

The sunlight caught the red in his hair, another surprise of Norman ancestry. He leaned toward you without chagrin and said, "Try not to kill him."

He was your favorite passenger, the guy that didn't ride the bus.

Now as you sit in the passenger's seat, the faded blue velour feels softer. The edges have been worn smooth as canvas by sliding blue jeans and hairy thighs. You can't see the red in his hair. By mutual agreement, he turns on the headlights. The slowly twining curls of smoke are far more sluggish than cigarette smoke. Even they are affected by the cold.

As if he were reading his child a Grimm fairy tale—the real kind, not the watered down variety where everyone lives happily ever after—he tells you it wasn't your fault, that you had no chance of escape, that genetically, the best thing you had going was youth and a wicked collection of books. You knew how it was going to end, and this should be your ultimate consolation.

The exhaust doesn't smell like you thought it would. It's not a natural gas vehicle like the city-issued bus you learned to drive, after a piss test that said you didn't need additives to make your life bearable. The air is getting heavy. The dizziness could be from your burning cheek or the hand he's pressing up your old cheer-leading shorts.

"Look at me. Focus," he tells you.

You focus. Here's the face you love, not the one you see when you close your eyes, her cheeks puffy and white.

You hadn't planned on telling him how your mother and father died. All you said was that you doubted you'd live past thirty. Kids who've had a parent commit suicide are 66% more likely to put a bullet through their temple, swallow a handful of Ambien, or hang themselves in the closet. You got two for the price of one. Natural selection at work. Being versed in the arts of self-warfare, it is natural to think of putting one step in the hole to avoid the unavoidable fallout.

Telling him was the decent thing to do. You didn't want him to get his hopes up, build a picket fence, and raise a kid cursed to walk on eggshells when the bipolar swing set threatened to over-take the playground. Who wants to come home from school and pull a corpse from a bathtub after said parent has exited the family in a less than maternal fashion?

He just nodded and asked if you were willing to rewrite your history. You couldn't imagine anyone who wouldn't give that serious thought.

In the car, he takes your other hand and blows hot breath into the chilled palm. "Did we miss anything?"

"I don't think so."

"You can't think of anything you'll miss out on?"

———

The term bucket list had always taken on a hollow ring. You could see yourself playing on the beach the summer you were five. You held a blue plastic bucket with a white handle. You were making a castle in the surf. This was before they both got sick of each other. The sun shining down, warming your skin, it made the cold of the sand tingle up the soles of your feet. You closed your eyes, remem-ber? And heard the waves coming to you, welcome and meaningful.

Past the age of twenty-five, a person can't blame their parents any longer. Unless of course, one or both of your parents is an *artiste*. A painter, a musician, a writer, they're all the same: drama queens, adrenaline junkies, and sublime narcissists. Selfish pricks, the whole lot. Had you been born with the same talent, you would have invested it in something more foolproof than short-term life insurance—like an acting career that peaked when you were thirty, after which you would have picked a stable man. You would have saved money into your middle-age years for things like braces, Disney vacations, and the occasional big screen TV. You would have produced stable children that loved you and did not need to prove themselves your opposite.

This was your parents' life. They left wreckage in the carpet fibers and blood behind the walls. What talent they had was steeped in bitterness, a constant tally they kept between the sheets. Who did what for whom? The obligations rang as pennies thrown into a dry well. You are saving yourself from this wedded, monotonous, and antiquated suffering. You love the dark-haired boy too much to curse him with your ghost.

Children? Had you wanted children? Maybe—when you were small enough to love something innocent and not hold your breath: a Cabbage patch doll that smelled of baby powder, a pink teddy bear whose tummy held a music box, a blue nosed Pit bull you had to give away when the neighbors complained of his breed.

Heartbreak. Sheer, utter failure at any true happiness that lasted more than the time it took to call an ambulance.

"No. There's nothing else I want to experience." When you told the dark-haired boy about your intentions, he didn't react the way you thought he would.

"You've made up your mind, then?"

"Oh, yes. It's easier this way, not that I haven't enjoyed every minute with you." This is hard to believe. No one in their right mind considers suicide as a road that is less than horrific to its bystanders. You're not supposed to get used to it. The stages of grief don't apply. Just the same, acceptance is needed for a modicum of success.

"Do you want to be alone with it?"

"I'm not volunteering you for anything!" You're not that kind of girl. You don't need to hold someone else's hand. Killing oneself is not something done on a buddy system.

"You think I want to be here alone?"

You *had* thought of that and decided to leave while the going was good. Why be a television series that doesn't know how to let go of its story? Are you in love? Yes. Are you committed? Yes. Are you hopeful? Terribly so.

This is the problem.

As intolerable as it is to speak of such things to a beloved, the thought of leaving your body for him to find is steeped in angst. That he has also considered leaving the party early is not a surprise, not for someone who doesn't believe in death. Still, he's beautiful. He's kind. He's wrestled in Mongolia, fished in the Congo, and gotten holy-roller stoned with the atheists in Tangier.

"What are your reasons?"

"The why isn't important," he tells you. "Why always why? It's a delay. Pause. Commiserate. It makes me come unglued. It makes me feel like I'm skiing backwards. I'm sick of the 'why.' At some point, I knew where I was going. I had some control over it. Then, I don't know. My dad got sick, and I started taking care of Pops. Every night he tells me, 'I love you. I hope I don't see you in the morning.' I know that's where I'll end up: in a chair on a bed that isn't my own. Someone will be changing my sheets. I'll smell, no matter how many times they wash me. I won't be visited, and you won't be around. It's downhill from here. "

Yeah, right. *Why* is a natural repellent. You cast it off and attract other questions in its place. What is the most fitting and peaceful way to transition? Morphine? Razor blades? Sleeping pills? No, thank you. Ultimately, this is the last ditch effort to tell your folks to go fuck themselves. Despite their greatness and lack thereof, the kid of such parents should be able to think and feel about the situation however they want for as long as they wish, *carte blanche*. You will not be taking cues from their playbook.

The dark-haired boy took up your cause without blinking. A man who can hit that kind of curve ball makes doubt a waste of time.

The more you planned the event, the more purpose he gathered. When you made love, every stroke was the length and width of a waterfall. Every whisper was an exclamation. Every moment, one you would not take for granted.

You knew, given its own space, this kind of happiness would never last. Neither of you had any intention of undergoing 20+ years of drudgery, not when you still liked to fuck and feed each other sourdough toast and French press coffee for breakfast at two o'clock in the afternoon.

When your chest starts to tighten, he starts to look different, and you regret not reading *Lolita* or Dostoevsky. Do you know a villain when you see one? The soundtrack he's got going is a mix of *Nine Inch Nails* and *Deftones*. You thought this was a considerate gesture, but fear is no less a playback on pain than holding your father's hand while you pull the plug on his life support.

He closes his eyes, cupping your breast, and says, "Next lifetime, I want to be a monkey."

Out of nowhere, you want to hit him. Just cold-cock him while his hand is down your pants. You do. Your little fist doesn't do much. It glances off the side of his nose. You can't put much weight into it sitting in a car. His head snaps back, and that's satisfying.

"Yeah," he says. "That's what I'm talking about. You're a fighter. You go down swinging."

You want to tell him stupid stuff: how he looks when he's sleeping, the shape of his hand on the blanket your granny made, and all the times you have gone to sleep syncing your breath to his. It's roiling around in your belly, but you know if you said those things out loud they'd water down how you really feel. Instead, you reach for his belt buckle. You've never wanted so badly to make him feel good.

He doesn't say a word. He helps you, lifting up from the seat. The opening of his pants is a dull glow in the dark hollow under the steering wheel. The air has become oily, tepid and dank. Ducking your head, it's warmer. You're glad you can't see the swirls of gas, grateful the humming engine is respectfully reliant.

What is amazing is all the things you're *not* thinking. You don't consider these *violent* thoughts. Death has far exceeded an R-rating, NC-17 is a joke, and if they ever made a true-to-form film of people killing themselves, it would scare the crap out of any manic depressive to the point where the words "cold turkey" sounded like a vacation.

Your own indie film, you see it thus:

OPEN TO: A pre-teen in soiled underwear. The black sludge ejects itself from the misery of her body; white pill remnants are floating buoys on cool linoleum. Where are her parents? Getting lost in debt, blind and oblivious, she's been molested by her uncle since she was four.

FADE IN: A pasty white virgin with too much hair launching himself from his mother's nightstand. He knocks over her Mother Mary statue, too stupid on antidepressants to use the proper hangman's noose. He thrashes as the rope cuts into his jaw. His eyes pop out, a live Saturday morning cartoon of wolves that whistle, and clutches his brother's war medals until his palms bleed a purple-red.

FADE TO BLACK: It's hero time. Disgraced by failure to get into an Ivy League college, a young Japanese man double-fists a filet knife. The look of stoic resignation on his face before sinking the blade reiterates the phrase, "Just the tip." This guy, his intentions are crystal clear, and they spill out everywhere in a bright stream over his parents' white carpet.

All of these scenes downplay the urgency of liquids and solids, actual parts of people making their escape. All of them are sorry to have been such a disappointment to dreams not their own. To say that you don't think of violence is the understatement of the year.

Meanwhile, here's your man's penis under you, scooping upward into the vacuum of your mouth. His fist in your hair, making you gag, your eyes are watering past the friction of your throat. You can't breathe. This shouldn't be alarming.

You can't breathe. He's got the back of your head too tight. What small sips of air you're getting, they aren't enough. You're trying your best to please him, please yourself. Accidentally biting down at this point would be a tragic loss of brownie points. It's a Radiohead song crooning from the speaker beside your head. He's humming along, crying, head thrown back and trying to gulp breath without hacking.

You can hear him and the deep sorrow in which he sings, "You are all I need..." and he's saving you because you can't breathe, except in little snorts through the material of his briefs.

All those martyrs, they really should figure out this health care thing. Put all that raw talent to good use. What person taking their Lithium and Nembutal and St. John's Wort wants to end it while their son or daughter practices putting on make-up down the hall? Those bitches. Just because you write it down, every painful moment of ecstasy, and make the descent sound pretty freaking righteous, your readers, your FANS, were not the ones with the front row seats. And just because others don't write it down— those *thoughts* extracted from the essence of pure God matter, resonating as sure and solid as a knee in the solar plexus—does not mean they forget the sentiment.

If there's a maestro in charge of this trainwreck, you've yet to see evidence of benevolence. If anything, you're convinced He gets a kick watching strong women crack open like farm eggs in a weak basket.

We get it already. Life was hard. The voices got too loud. They wanted it all to end. Period. Stop. Rest. They just needed a moment to catch their—

You don't see your mom or her blue lips. You don't see yourself as a 13-year-old throwing fists into her chest or blowing bubbles of snot out her nose past the silent hollow of her windpipe. You don't see your father or the barrel of his shotgun. You don't see the broken shards of glass from their pipes, paraphernalia, and misplaced illusions. Your eyes are closed to better savor a dark-haired boy's final sacrifice, his lusty winking eye puffing up with pride for you. You taste tears and your man's juice, and you swallow his last moment of pleasure.

He's gone limp, satisfied and nearly dead.

Oh, no. No, no, no. This is not how you wanted this movie to end. Where is your climax? Where is the light at the end of the tunnel? When is it *your* goddamn turn?!

You now want a do-over.

Slapping him, spittle flies from both your swollen faces. This isn't payback or foreplay. It's your will to live rising in a hot shock wave. You tingle and shout his name. It hits you; if you don't fight for yourself and your own ending, he will be yet another still body in a story full of deceptions.

Sweat tickles your eyelashes, and his right leg is a fallen tree trunk in a forest of rusty tools hung on plywood. Swearing your affirmation of the day, your fist slams the gear stick into Reverse at the same time you shove his foot down on the gas. You're both shoved into the dash as the car takes off in a rocket boost through the aluminum garage door. It crunches and folds over like a bully's foot stampeding through a fortress wall of Legos. The car shoots down the drive, a streak of silver hurtling into the large oak tree that doesn't flinch as it accordions the back bumper and trunk.

Your door swings open, and you fall out onto summer grass. These fresh gulps of air burn. Something is bent but not completely broken. The garage, the car, the toxins have ejected you. You roll and tumble, limbs flopping weak and malleable. Into a cloudless sky, gripping wet and earth, you are born again into something that may have a better idea of what sacrifice actually means.

You're still laughing as he comes to and retches on the whistling airbag. Chuckling is hard with cracked ribs. The future is hard with so much to undo. Courage is hard in the face of inevitable loss.

But love…

Loving is easier than living with a past that isn't yours and never fit.

He hears you, wipes the back of his mouth, and manages a thumbs-up.

You are not who you thought you were.

AND ALL THE WORLD DROPS
DEAD: MAX BOOTH III

The way the night sky stared down at me on the beach, I was convinced a vast cosmic mouth would widen within the stars and devour me whole. The thought turned me on and I prayed to the bottle of Bourbon held clumsily in my hand that the fantasy would transition into reality. I tried to drink and more liquor dripped down my cheeks than my throat. Fuck it. Wasn't like we paid for it, anyway. You don't need money when you got a gun, and you don't need fear when you don't give a shit about dying.

Somewhere behind me, Layla slammed a car door. "Fuck! We're out."

I laughed in the sand, eyes lost in the stars. "One night and you're already a dope fiend."

"Hey, don't judge me. You've had plenty of practice. I'm just trying to catch up."

She stood over me and for a moment my vision redirected to her ass, visible beneath her bloodstained skirt. It shared a similar paleness to the moon, only her ass contained many more bruises than the little orb hanging outside our planet. She plopped down in the sand next to me and lay down. The sides of our heads connected like misfit puzzle pieces. She'd cut the majority of her hair off with old rusty scissors she'd found in my trunk a few hours prior, manic on dope, convinced the act would help disguise her from Jim, who was undoubtedly still on the prowl. She offered to work the same massacre on my own head, which I refused. My hair was no easy feat. Before the estrogen treatment, I'd started balding. Twenty-four years old and already losing my hair. But the pills fixed that potential horror show. The pills fixed a lot of things.

Layla ran her hand through my hair now, perhaps relieved I hadn't granted her approval to whack it off. "Sylvia?"

"Yes?"

"The longer I think, the more I freak out."

"Then don't think, baby."

Old Hollywood, New Hollywood, Future Hollywood, Who-Gives-a-Fuck Hollywood. Throw it all in a mixer and shake it up, it all tastes the same. It tastes like cum. It tastes like cold coffee. It tastes like the whiskey at the bottom of a bottle, that last swig you take after waking up and looking at yourself in the mirror, the swig that helps you avoid asking, *Is this really it? Is this all there is?*

I once asked Layla that question—*is this all there is?*—and she didn't know how to answer, took her about a flat minute to make up some bullshit Disney gibberish. The important questions, they don't got answers, they just got more questions. Questions after fucking questions. You ask enough questions, and that's all you'll do the rest of your life.

Me, I got sick of asking questions. I got sick of answering them.

There's no room in life for questions.

We would need three things to make this night eternal: more gas, more booze, and more dope. The first two would be easy enough to acquire. The dope might be trickier. Not impossible. This was Los Angeles, after all.

For the gas, all I had to do was press my gun against the clerk's head and tell him to fill up the tank. Layla loaded the trunk with liquor bottles as we had our little fun, and afterward, since he was such a good sport, I let him off with a warning. Well, tried to, at least. Motherfucker had the nerve to call me a crazy tranny as we were burning rubber out of the parking lot, so of course I had to make like a horseshoe and pull a you-ee. I gave him a hole to remember me by, and me and Layla drove like demons fresh out of hell deep into the city where you could find the real good shit.

We found a man in a suit sitting alone in a club and he offered

Layla a line of coke if she snorted it off his dick. We followed him into a bathroom stall and bartered his deal by pressing the cold steel of my pistol against his balls. Told him to pick what he wanted to lose, his testicles or his dope. Of course he was a fool and coughed up the latter. Poor little delusional fuckboy still attached to things that didn't matter. We took the coke and I acted like I was still gonna shoot his junk off and the motherfucker actually started crying, which I figured was enough shame for one night, so we left him alone and ran back to the car, cool as goddamn cucumbers.

We snorted lines off each other's hands and she looked at me and said, "I swear, I think I made you up inside my head."

I leaned over and kissed her and whispered the next line in her ear: "Shut your eyes and all the world drops dead."

She kissed my forehead, hands caressing my ass. "Not ready for the world to die."

"Just give me the word, darling. Just give me the word."

We drove and snorted lines and played the radio loud. Layla took my gun and said she hoped Jim did find us, because she was ready for his ass.

"What are you gonna do when you see him?"

"I'll show you what I'm gonna do!" She stuck the gun out of the window and fired a couple rounds off into the sky.

"You think that's gonna stop the crazy fucker?"

She shook her head. "Doubtful, but goddamn would it feel good."

I took the gun from her and emptied the rest of the clip out the driver's side window. "Goddamn is right, baby." I tossed the gun in her lap and told her to reload it. We had plenty more planes to shoot down. Hell, we might get lucky and clip one of those weather helicopters from TV. Nobody could predict how this night would end. Nobody could even predict it would end.

Truth be told, I'd already shot Jim.

Twice.

In the head.

It put him out of commission for about a dime, just enough time for the wounds to heal themselves. By then, me and Layla had already packed all her things and were on our way out the door. Just as I was following her out onto the porch, there he fucking was, sitting up in the living room where I'd shot him, rubbing his head like he'd only bonked it on a table. He looked at me and I looked at him and recognition filled his eyes and utter fucking fear filled mine. Before he could so much as grunt, I was out that goddamn door and sprinting to my car.

Layla stood waiting by the passenger's door. "Jesus Christ, is he already up?"

"Get in, get in!"

"That bastard. I'm so sorry."

She'd told me about him, about the things he could do, and although I never called bullshit, it was more to spare her feelings. Not for a second was I ever convinced Jim could do the things Layla claimed. Never for a second did I truly comprehend what we were getting into. Not until I shot him in the head, not until he sat up like it was nothing. But by then, it was too late. Maybe if I'd taken her more seriously, we could have planned our escape better.

"Get in the fucking car!"

As we sped away from the house, I watched Jim chase after us on foot in the rearview mirror. For a moment, I was convinced he was actually going to catch up, but halfway down the street he doubled over to catch his breath. I guess being an immortal piece of shit doesn't turn you into a superhero.

Still. Wasn't like him to give up a pursuit so easily.

He was after us, somewhere, sniffing out our trail.

The coke and gas station snack cakes could only satisfy us for so long. The hunger had finally dug into Layla. The weed we'd smoked didn't help matters either. Girl was so hungry her stomach grumbles damn near drowned out the radio. Of course Jim was the kind of fuckhead who never let her eat anything but a salad. Now that she was finally free of his chains, she said it was like all the hunger that'd been building up inside her over the years rose up to the surface at once and demanded her full attention. She didn't just need to eat, she said, she needed to goddamn *feast*.

"Well, shit," I said, "let's go *feast* then," and pulled into the next Denny's we came across. We didn't have much, or any money, but that wouldn't matter. Anybody tried fucking with us and they'd never see another day.

The waitress only barely flinched at our appearance. She was used to the freaks coming in at this time of night, especially here in the heart of La La Land. We'd be more suspicious if we strolled in *not* looking like total deviants. She took down our order: for Layla, a Supreme Skillet with cheesy scrambled eggs and a large chocolate milkshake, and for me, just coffee and toast.

I couldn't remember the last time I'd eaten anything but the bare minimum. The last sentence is a lie. Of course I could remember. Three Thanksgivings ago—the last day I ever talked to any of the pieces of shit sadly related to me by blood. I'd finally had enough of the secrets. I couldn't take any goddamn more family functions hiding my true identity. I'd go to these dinners and parties and people would make conversation with an artificial representation of myself. They weren't talking to the real me. What was the point? It just all seemed like a waste of time, so halfway through dinner, I tapped my glass and announced I had something to say. Now, when we had Thanksgiving, we *really* had Thanksgiving. Family from all over the goddamn country flew out to eat with us. We had one of those long, geeky-ass tables you always see in rich people movies. I was near one end, close to my mom and dad.

Once I had everybody's attention, I stood up and announced that I'd been living a lie, that it was time they all understood my life. I told them someone had made a mistake when I was born, and that I was never meant to be a boy. I told them I no longer wished to go by my male name. I told them my new name was Sylvia, and I would be starting a treatment to transform my body into the person I was meant to be. My dickhead uncle didn't wait but ten seconds before bursting into laughter. The kind of laughter that boils your blood and makes it easy to commit multiple murders with just your bare hands. My dad and mom just sat in silence, looking at me, then each other, then me again. Finally my dad asked me if this was a joke, addressing me by my male name with a certain kind of emphasis that pissed me off so much I lost control and hurled a glass plate against the wall and it shattered and one of the shards bounced back and cut one of my cocksucker cousin's cheeks, not so deep that it'd require stitches or anything but of course he acted like I'd just cut his pathetic goddamn throat the way he cried. My dad told me to go home and he'd call me tomorrow to discuss this new fad I'd taken up. I told him to get fucked and stormed out and drove my car to a Walmart parking lot and cried myself to sleep. The next day I traded my phone to a guy at a club for a bag of dope and never talked to my dad or my mom or my dickhead uncle or even my stupid cocksucker cousins again. Fuck 'em all.

Layla dug into her breakfast food feast and I sipped at the coffee. It tasted like shit and I grimaced and I loved that it was so awful. The worse it tasted, the more I wanted it in my body. I could have added some sugar and cream to it, but that would have made it enjoyable. That would have ruined it. Layla ate like she'd never eaten before. It occurred to me that, despite all the times we'd hung out when Jim was at work, all the times we fucked and got high together, I'd never once seen her with food. She was skinny, sure, but not skeleton skinny like me. One time, when she was in the bathroom, I discovered a box of Zingers stuffed behind her couch. Things were clicking into place. Jigsaw pieces scattered but not abandoned.

Layla asked me where we were going after this, and I told her the only answer that mattered: forward.

With the implication: away from your demonic motherfucker of a husband.

Ex-husband now. Maybe not in the eyes of the state, but once you give the go-ahead to your secret transgender mistress to insert not one but *two* bullets into your husband's skull, you can't exactly consider yourself married anymore.

"I need more than just 'forward'. We need a better plan." The food was already ruining our good time and had Layla thinking rationally.

I leaned over the table. "Which answer would you prefer? 'Forward' or 'I don't know'?"

"But we got to have some kind of plan, don't we?"

"Why?"

"They always have a plan."

"They who?"

"You know." She shrugged, playing with her fork. "People in movies and stuff."

"Baby, those people only have a plan because some white asshole with an expensive suit wrote that they needed a plan out of fear of the audience not liking the movie. We aren't characters in a movie, now are we? Nobody wrote our destiny but us, you and me, right here, right now. We'll drive until we can't drive, then we'll stop and fuck and sleep and drive and keep driving until something shiny grabs our attention. Plans? Plans are for fascists and sewer systems."

"I'm afraid, is all."

I smiled, which immediately made me feel like an asshole. "That's what the dope's for." I nodded toward the bathrooms. "Why don't we go freshen up a little bit before we get out of here?"

She seemed to consider it, then sighed. "No. I think I need a break or I'm gonna get sick. I'm sorry."

I shrugged, pretended like it didn't bother me. "Whatever, more for me." I hopped out of the booth and skedaddled across the Denny's. I briefly studied the MEN'S door before laughing and entering the WOMEN'S. Since beginning my transition, I'd only experienced one conflict with the whole bathroom situation which every news channel seemed so goddamn concerned about. Some redneck dad saw me follow his little girl into the bathroom and figured I was some rapist. He stormed in with his big boy muscles flexed and I broke his nose against a hand dryer. His daughter watched in shock, but not fear. As he lay on the ground, bleeding and crying, I gave her a little wink and she responded with a smile, but only slight enough for me to see and not her dad.

In the Denny's bathroom, I pissed and snorted a line off my compact. My head cleared and I convinced myself I'd go back out there and snap Layla out of her sudden unfortunate mood. We should have never stopped to eat. At best, we should have taken something and eaten in the car. But sitting at a restaurant gives a person too much time to think. The more a person thinks, the worse off they become. More moving, less thinking. That's how you survive. Just move move *move*.

Out of the bathroom, I strode with purpose back across the restaurant, then stopped dead in my tracks at the sight of Jim there in the booth next to Layla. Layla herself shaking, staring ahead at the wall, Jim's hands out of sight under the table, surely threatening something against her flesh. A blade, a gun, shit, who knew, just his presence alone was enough.

Before I could decide what to do, he spotted me and waved me over. I sat down across from them in the booth and we just stayed like that for a moment, him looking at me, me looking at him, Layla looking inside herself, somewhere far away from here. Jim's forehead was smooth and slick, no sign of the previous injury I'd inflicted upon him. A shit-eating grin widened across Jim's face, the motherfucker.

"So," he said, and I pulled out the pistol from my purse and shot him in the face.

His head whipped back and splattered skull fragments and brain matter across the empty booth behind him. The Denny's patrons took one look at our booth and started screaming and fleeing the building. I reached across the table and grabbed Layla's trembling hand and told her to move her ass and she stood on the cushion and stepped on top of the Formica and jumped off, keeping her distance from her shithead ex-husband convulsing in the booth. We ran out the doors without looking back, although if I had, I was sure I would have seen the hole in his face already healing itself. We jumped in the car and booked it through the next three red lights.

In the beginning of their marriage, Layla thought Jim's abilities were cool. It was one of the reasons she married him. Imagine never having to worry about your loved one driving home after a late night at work. Never having to hold his hand in a hospital bed. He couldn't get hurt. He was her bulletproof vest. No other woman had anything even close to what she had. She couldn't tell anybody else his secret—*imagine what the army would do with me,* he'd warned her time and again—but she liked to imagine how jealous her friends would get if she revealed the truth. Back when he allowed her to have friends, of course. Back before the real Jim came out of hiding and everything went to shit.

She'd only asked him how he came upon these powers once, back when they first started dating. He'd told her many times already that he wasn't like all the other guys out there, told her no matter what, he'd never die, even if he wanted to. She giggled and told him he was crazy and he said that didn't have anything to do with it. But it was clear she thought he was just goofing around, so he said he had to prove to her. That's when he bent down and pulled out the knife from his boot and slit his own throat, right there in front of her, and she screamed and screamed as the blood poured down his neck, and she didn't stop screaming even as the gash started sealing itself. Afterward, holding her and rubbing her back, he told her he'd never showed another girl his powers like that, that she was special to him, and he wanted to be with her forever. She was young and dumb and said she loved him, she felt it, she really did. Then she asked how any of this was possible. How did he get to be the way he was? *Well, darling*, he'd told her, *let's just say some things are better left unexplained*, and two months later they got married.

But she always wondered. The mystery of it drove her mad. As the years passed, her need to understand his immortality evolved. Now she wanted to know how it happened so she could reverse it. So she could squat over his corpse and piss on him.

As we got drunk in her living room one weekday afternoon, she told me she had spent hour after hour researching Jim's condition on the internet, but she never seemed to get any closer to discovering the truth. There was nobody on this planet quite like him. Was he even human? Shit, who knew. Layla sure as fuck didn't, and she'd been married to him for years.

What you couldn't kill, she told me, *you either pretended to love, or you ran away from it, ran away as fast as your little feet would let you*, and she was goddamn tired of pretending.

She wouldn't stop asking me what we were going to do and I wouldn't stop telling her I don't know, I don't know, I don't fucking know.

I pointed at the gun I'd thrown in her lap. "Reload that, would ya?"

"Where's your purse?"

"What?"

"Aren't the bullets in your purse? Where is it?"

"Oh."

"Did you leave it at Denny's?"

I punched the steering wheel and pushed down harder on the accelerator. The engine moaned in ecstasy. Roar, baby, roar.

We didn't say another word until we passed the state border and entered Nevada. The sun was just beginning to peek its ugly bastard head over the desert wasteland and blast my eyes with its newly awakened red and I refused to squint. I'd rather die than squint.

"Vegas," I said before knowing what I was gonna say, and it made sense. All our dope and bullets had been in my purse. The only thing we really had now was the gun, and even that was empty, but shit, only reason anybody would know that would be if I tried using it.

Layla ran her finger along my cheek. "I always wanted to go."

I placed my hand on her bare thigh and squeezed. "Start thinking of all the other places you've always wanted to go to, baby, because we're gonna hit each and every one."

She leaned her head back and sighed softly, content. "I think I made you up inside my head."

I leaned over and kissed her on the neck, not giving a good goddamn if we veered off the road, the only thing mattering right then being my lips upon her neck, here and forever, always.

"Shut your eyes and all the world drops dead."

WITHOUT HIM (AND HIM, AND HIM) THERE IS NO ME: LAURA DIAZ DE ARCE

I could see the small imperfections in his back tattoos from this angle in this light. One was of a large, grayish dove that circled an oblong skull. The dove's eye was a little off, and I could see its unevenness best as he breathed. His buddy had done that one at the back of a garage. He said it represented how life was short or some such bullshit. They always fed me bullshit, and I ate it up.

The light was coming in high in this piece of shit motel. He was still passed out on the cheap beer and whiskey he'd bought at the gas station last night. I got up and pulled on his shirt.

It reeked of him, his dried sweat, spilled beer and the dust of the desert. Just yesterday I'd found that smell attractive, but it was losing its luster. Now it smelled like distaste, a gross substitute for a body melting in front of me.

I knew he liked it when I looked like this. When he would wake up he'd find me in his worn shirt, my eyeliner from last night smudged in the right way, my hair half out and teased and a lit cigarette hanging out of my mouth at an angle. He'd look at me, without a second thought, but I know that if I give him that bitch-tired look, he can't stop his dick from twitching. We have a lot in common, he and I, we both like to feel like shit.

He'll probably pull me on top of him and we'll fuck. It wouldn't be lovemaking, that's not what I'd call it. No, we'd rut like animals for a few minutes. He won't wait for me to get wet, he'll just jam is hands between my thighs, pushing his calloused fingers into my skin to pull them apart. He thinks his roughness is hot. He gives himself too much credit. My cheeks will burn, not from flush but from the wire of his beard as he pushes his tongue down my throat. He'll grab my tits, not to titillate me, but for his own amusement. Then he'll jam his withering half-hard dick into me and I'll have to force out a convincing moan, not that he needs convincing.

A few days ago that would have been the thing that kept me. I'd feel fulfilled for a few moments, warm in the embrace, in the attention, in the knowledge that I've won the game. But that's not me today. Today it feels like it's going to be a chore. And this life, that I had hoped wouldn't be routine, has its own slow, stupid rhythm. And now I'm getting bored, just like with the rest of them.

We'd met four months ago in a small, no-name hole North of Reno, but he followed a string of my lovers. Men. I need to taste new flavors and I crave the ones I've yet to taste. I'll play with the flavor on my tongue, but soon the taste is bland and burnt. I look to taste men to fit my moods.

I started out, like most people did, with Vanilla. Not even regular vanilla, vanilla sweetened with Splenda. He was a homegrown, good old boy. The captain of our football team with me, the homecoming queen. Small town clichés. He'd pray apologies to Jesus after we made out. I wanted more, but all he'd let me get away with was nervous teenage hand jobs. He smelled like wet grass and sweat from practice. I still see his perfect teeth, his dimpled chin. His fake masculinity and confidence was the gross aftershave left in a closed-mouthed kiss. When I was with him I wore knee-length skirts and cardigan sweaters to prayer group. As prom king and queen, I learned to smile so prettily to hide my disinterest.

After a messy breakup with my football captain that included him crying at my front door threatening suicide, I moved on to the class clown. He had the pop and lightness of Ginger-Ale. His freckles dotted his face and body, down straight to his pelvis. He was skinny and bare chested, with those same freckles dotting his shoulders and torso. The head of his circumcised dick had a solitary freckle on the tip that I first thought was cute, but became an obnoxious blemish. He smelled like weed, deodorant and fabric freshener.

I wore loose jeans, dark t-shirts and crooked eyeliner to get his attention. I let my hair get greasy and taught myself to smoke weed when I set my eyes on him. He was on the scent like I was a bitch in heat before the week was out. His jokes and his moves (a total of five) got stale. But with him I go to play it as one of the guys.

I was cool, I was funny and low maintenance.

The performance was draining.

And then there is Chocolate, he was an aspiring designer or some nonsense. We went to a lot of clubs, a lot of parties where he bullshitted his talent and his business prowess. I was the in-person model that he showed off like the latest phone.

He put me in skin-tight jeans and dresses with slits up the side. I pranced in heels that I had to abuse myself to walk in. And he fucked me, with eyes open so wide it looked like it hurt.

When I smell strong cologne or hear the heavy bass of a rap song I think of him.

It was Chocolate's investor that took me on. He liked fine things and he had the money to get those things. It wasn't his money that bought me as a mistress. It was the way he looked at me over a glass of overpriced scotch. Like I was already his.

I was.

He was older, married and in his forties, but he looked good. He had the chiseled and styled features of a well-kept vintage. He tasted like leather, cigars, and old Hollywood. He kept me in furs and tailored wear.

We'd cruise to some event. Me on his arm, a starlet's smile on my lips, and a long cigarette on my fingertips. I was a trophy for him. I'd prance and slither like a charming sex kitten hidden in silk. He didn't need to tell me, he wanted other men to want me. He wanted them to covet his property, his car, his clothes, his money and his mistress.

I was a seductive flirt to every man we met. From the balding business partners, to the young, hot, muscled waiters. Their eyes would creep from my lashes, which would slowly flutter, leading them down to my lined and plumped lips, down to my breasts. When they got there I'd take a breath to heave them up and then down, pointing them lower still. And when they got to my hips I'd shift my weight, so that my hip swayed from one side to the other.

The message was clear: imagine this young body writhing beneath you. Imagine the kind of man you could be. I was a living fantasy for the wolves. And if he saw them watching me, saw them scouting his object, he'd get hot for me.

Looking back, the sex was dull. He was only into foreplay if it subdued me. But all I needed was the memory of those eyes on me, of the hungry stares that ate me up. That filled me with a delicious, caramel flavored warmth. Rich, sweet, bad for you.

We traveled, a lot. Hopping from one glittering city to another and staying in penthouses. Each one, a gilded cage where I was on display. I learned to fix cocktails and do my nails quietly. I learned to subtly hint that I needed money for things, and in some ways it was bliss. He was strong in a way I wasn't, in a way that didn't care for people or consequences.

I didn't want to leave, but his wife caught up with us in Miami and chased me out.

The newspapers never got him right. The headlines read "Tragic Murder-Suicide: Heiress Kills Husband and Self After Going Broke." She killed the love of my life. Sometimes I think maybe she should have taken me too. Our death would have been so artistic. So beautiful, my young body bleeding out alongside his refined older one.

Las Vegas made me feel like an empty soda pop bottle.

The men there were as empty as me, none could give me what I needed as I hollowed my day down the strip. The artificial scent they pumped through casinos, the cheap buffets and fake jewelry, the vapid heat that made the sweat disappear from your brow before it's formed made me sick. The most sickening was the cloud of complimentary bathroom perfume that choked the air like a sunken cloud.

I was sick.

I was empty.

Then I saw them.

They drove by in their bikes, clad in leather. Driving though the strip like they owned the place and suddenly I was hungry again.

How self-assured they were, a pack of animals prowling for what they wanted. I could smell it, the oily tar from cigarette and gas fumes. It all cut through the pristine casino and hotel lobbies. It hacked away at the artificially perfumed air, the cologne and the buffets, like a machete. I wanted one. I needed one. I wanted to ride those bikes to the desert. I wanted to fuck and be fucked.

I wanted to feel their older, leathered skin, against my body.

The ride was nice but Reno was suburban hell, but outside, just a few miles and bottles West, there was a little Piece-of-Shit half city with all the essentials. A strip club, three bars, two tattoo parlors and a Walmart. It was like their breeding ground.

My first stop was the tattoo parlor. My skin, despite everything, had remained virginal.

Would I bleed for one of them?

Yes. Yes I would.

"Fresh meat," one of them growled as I walked in. You could see in my shorts and top that nothing had been inked before. It was cute, like he was trying to scare me. It took most of my control not to laugh and bark at him.

I just winked at the one with ink and he was putty.

By the end I had "Margaret" tattooed on my shoulder and two other obvious pieces done.

"Why Margaret?" he asked, dipping the needle into the pot.

"It was my grandmother's name," I lied. I just like that name.

He finished the belladonna flower on my inside thigh the next afternoon.

And I finished him, because I had no money.

I didn't stay. He didn't have a bike.

This one I found when the pieces came together.

The Licorice that is fucking me in this cheap motel. I saw him across the room in one of those bars in that little shithole place. I had my trap set and he was like a fly to the spider, with my torn stockings, fraying shorts and stolen leather jacket. My cheap, poorly drawn drugstore makeup and boxed dye just screamed "Daddy Issues" and he was hooked. Bought me a shot, and then four and then a ride to the closest motel.

He smelled like beer, but that was fine.

He was the heat of summer. An unconcerned, unwavering, and unsympathetic summer. He was who he knew he was. A man in his early fifties still pushing drugs as a means to shift from place to place. A man with fierce loyalty to his buddies and his own set of issues set in stone.

Or he was.

Now I think he's too old to be pushing drugs like he does at this age. And his buddies are fine, I guess, but not worth his sense of loyalty.

What I loved most about him was his bike.

The other love in his life. It wasn't just a machine. It was an experience. On the road, I felt like the me I should be. Every moment racing on the open road felt like flight. I'd let the wind cut between my open fingers and the kicked up dirt would get tangled in my hair. It smelled like freedom and gasoline.

It's late in the afternoon and I make the excuse to go to the ice machine. At the back of the motel I steal a cigarette. Here there's a flimsy wire fence that divides us from the desert. I look out to that landscape and I can breathe. It's void and yet beautiful. It exists for itself, for its emptiness. Sure there are the shrubs, the rock and desert critters, the odd random pieces of trash, but they only make the quiet louder. Its got a hell of a surface, this sandy canvas that we paint with our bike tracks. It's a place impermanently marked by our footsteps. Eventually the wind comes and blows over those steps, making it new. The deserts' changes are make-up, wiped away to reveal the skin of it.

There's that bright blue sky, that golden ocean of sand and I realize I'm miserable. He kept my attention for a bit, but the sweet taste is gone. I've got to find a way to ditch him.

The little hotel corner market has dry shampoo and powdered flea insecticide of all things, and I start to hatch a plan to get rid of him but keep the bike. As much as I don't like him, I love the power of that machine between my legs. I pick them up in cash and head back to the hotel. He's got a stash he only uses for himself, it's not for sale. It's for us, when we want, but I never partake. I tell him it'll ruin my figure, and "baby, you're all the drug I need."

He's in the shower when I cut the stash.

And I wait.

Two days later and he's finally feeling it.

We're riding on his bike down a lonely stretch of desert. The bike starts wobbling and he pulls over to the side and starts retching behind a fallen road sign. Out here, we're alone, and I'm thankful. It couldn't be better. I'd hoped he'd just get sick enough to have an ER pick him up somewhere and keep him out of my hair.

"Give me a sec babe, I need to sit for a bit."

He looks like death.

He's pale, and old.

So old.

I hold my breath and touch his forehead. He responds by puking on my boots. Vomit dots the black toe and I hold my temper to keep from socking him. "Baby, you've got a fever." I don't really know if he does, but I'm sure he thinks he does.

"Our cell doesn't have any bars."

It does, but I know he won't check as his eyes are glazing over with illness.

"Give me the keys baby, I'll get help."

And he looks up at me, weak.

Gross.

He looks like a wounded animal, like a raccoon that's been run over but isn't quite dead yet, just suffering. If I had a gun I would put him out of his misery.

He hands me the keys. So trusting. I blow him a kiss and mount the bike he only started to teach me to ride a few weeks ago. It feels lighter than I remember. I look out at the sunset and turn in that direction.

And it's just me, the road, and the desert.

And I'm free.

Free like the expanse of it.

I think about him for a minute after I leave.

Maybe someone will find him and get him help.

Maybe he'll die and the sand will cover his body as he disappears into the landscape.

The desert righting itself.

That thought fills me with an inexplicable calm, and then I think, maybe I should head to San Francisco.

Maybe catch me a Silicon Valley mogul.

GOING ABOUT 99: CHRISTINE STODDARD

Shadows from the lace curtains cut your face into one hundred black lilies. You were in our bed, propped up too close to the fogged up window. Your mother had embroidered the satin pillow that made it possible for you to sit up because your body no longer could. Your muscles had all the strength of a toadstool trying to bolster a boulder. I didn't mind that the bed smelled musty because you had spent the last week dying in it. But I did mind that your bones pushed through your yellow skin more and more each day. You had always been a substantial woman.

When we first fucked, I took comfort in the depths of your flesh. From there, we made love. Sometimes we made love hard and rough, but we still made love. I adored every pound of you. Friends accused me of having a fetish.

"What's her fetish then? Skinny blonde bitches?" I quipped.

"No, that's what everyone wants," they said while sipping their margaritas at the only lesbian bar in town. "That can't be a fetish."

I told them that the reason their pussies were dry was because they had hearts of stone.

"Why are you so desperate? You could have anyone."

"I'm desperate for her because she's the one I want."

Somehow, I had convinced myself that you didn't want me. I felt certain that I wasn't smart enough. You managed a prestigious archive at a university library while I hosted at a steakhouse downtown. Academics across the country interviewed you for journals and books from elite presses. Meanwhile, I could barely remember to give menus to the flocks of tobacco corporation executives who came to my workplace every day. You had discipline; I had dreams.

But if I hadn't been bumbling my way through another dead-end job in the city that gave my pathetic little suburb the right to exist, I never would've met you.

"Table for one," you crooned as you marched up to my stand. The harmony of your voice intrigued me, especially since it came from such plush, red lips. You were sharply dressed in a black cocktail dress and Kit Kat Club glasses to match. But it was the shock of pink hair that hooked me.

"One?"

"Yes, just me tonight."

It was 2000 and I had been out all year. Just two years before you walked into that smoky steakhouse, the press outed George Michael after an undercover police officer found him having sex in a public restroom. Humiliated, he admitted that he was gay in a national CNN interview.

As a 23-year-old Baptist from the outskirts of Richmond, Virginia, I was not supposed to fall in love with you. I was supposed to fall in love with a weak-chinned boy from school or church and be married by now. Where was my ring? Where was my child?

"Would you like a table or a booth?"

"Oh," you said, slightly startled but quick to chuckle. "Well, a booth then!"

"What brings you here tonight?"

"Nothing special. I'm a regular. I like the skirt steak."

"I've never seen you here before."

You raised your powdered eyebrows.

"I just mean we get so many businessmen. I think I would notice…a woman like you."

We were standing at your table when you looked straight at me and said, "You mean a lesbian?" You laughed it off, but when you later told me you were testing your gaydar, I was flattered.

"Yeah, I guess," I laughed, embarrassed. I pulled out your chair and set down the menu. "Enjoy your meal."

Maybe our history might have ended with our encounter at table no. 7, but I found your note later that night. You had scrawled *Do you like comics?* with your name and number on a napkin. Best yet, you had written it in metallic purple gel pen. Even before I came out, I knew I wanted a woman with style.

"Panache," you later corrected me. You were fingering me in the back of the archives that had become your life's work when you whispered that in my ear. Somehow, you had singlehandedly persuaded thousands of comic geeks from across the country to donate their rare editions to the university library. In less than a decade, you had taken the collection from literally one title to the largest university comic book collection in the United States. All this before age 35.

You were bragging, but I didn't mind. I wanted you to talk to me, to hold me, to run your fingers through my hair. I felt more electricity making out with you among those comic books than I did losing my virginity to Robby Stone the night of my junior prom. The latter had been my hetero test and I failed it. I wept for a month. To this day, I hate Camaro's.

As you lay in our bed dying, I recalled the former roundness of your belly and how I took solace in it. You let me cry there until my mascara ran down my cheeks and I resembled the raccoons that terrorized my grandpa's old apple farm in the holler. You said your weight came from all the cornbread that your mama made you when you were growing up in Charlotte.

Once you ended your cancer treatment, the doctor told me that you were almost too delicate to touch.

"I've touched a lot of ancient paper in the past sixteen years, doc. That's what happens when you marry a librarian."

He smiled, but didn't say anything.

I touched you, anyway. I didn't rest my head on your belly because you had no belly to speak of, but I did hold your hand. I stroked your sunken cheeks. I even rubbed lotion on your skeletal feet. I touched you as gently as I knew possible. I looked after you in ways the nurses could not.

Of course, there was no one to look after me. Even with in-home hospice care, the nurses must call it a day and return to their personal lives. We had no children and, apparently, no true friends. While plenty of people were happy to take part in our wedding, none of them could be bothered to comfort me or even relieve me from simple household chores. One goddamn casserole was too much to ask. The burden of carrying out the most mundane tasks while the love of my life was dying fell completely and totally on me. I accepted that I couldn't rely on my homophobic, racist family, but what about my friends? Where was the so-called LGBTQ community? Where were my flag-waving, oh-so-open-minded allies? When I actually needed them, they could not be bothered.

Once the shift nurse went home, it was just the two of us. The first couple of nights, I attempted to fall asleep once the nurse left, but I could never squeeze in more than a nap before I woke up shrieking. I was terrified that you would die while I slept. So instead, I read to you until you fell asleep. At this stage, you could no longer sleep peacefully. Even though it pained me to watch you twitch and even kick in your feebleness, I kept my eyes on you. These moments were part of the countdown.

I could usually stand these periods of obsessive observation for about an hour. Then I had to pour myself a drink. It always started with one, but it could never end there. One drink became two and two became three and three became four and then I typically lost count. You knew when you married me that I had an addictive personality. You were just always there to temper it. Normally you would cajole me to bed and I no longer cared for another drink. My desire for you ignited every vein, every pore, every hair on my body. I would follow you to bed, knowing in my bones that you going down on me would give me a much bigger buzz than that next gin and tonic ever could.

Yet once you entered hospice care, you could not supervise or seduce me. Alcohol entertained me until it drowned my brains. I needed to drown them so I could forget that we would not grow old together. We would never venture to Paris or Australia together. We would never eat chicken quesadillas at our favorite drive-thru or catch another dollar movie at our go-to dollar movie theater. We would never make love ever again. I wanted to taste your cunt until you squealed and moaned. I wanted to kiss you until you teared up and giggled and cried.

But I couldn't do much more than watch you.

The doctor had practically wrapped you up in caution tape.

On that seventh night of hospice care, I told myself that this was not how you wanted to live and this was not how you wanted to die. I cannot say how many drinks I'd had by then, only that I'd had more than any good Baptist girl was supposed to have. Needless to say, I was not a "good" Baptist girl. I wasn't even a bad Baptist girl. I was a godless girl and I was not sorry for it. I was sorry for not loving you harder. I was sorry that I could not inhale you and possess you or even become you. I wanted to preserve you. I wanted to protect you. I wanted to take all of the faith I did not have in religion and put it in you.

When I left church life for good, we had been dating shy of three months. I swore that I no longer believed in God, but I didn't invest that belief elsewhere. I believed in you in the sense that I supported you. But you were in your early 30s and had already accomplished so much. How much of my support did you really need? I doubted our relationship needed my faith, either. I took it for granted that we sustained each other. For that reason, I didn't think our relationship needed faith. I should've believed in the power of us as much as I had once believed in the power of God. Even atheists need faith in something.

You were still doing your end-of-life equivalent of tossing and turning when I appeared at your side in my wedding dress. It shone scarlet in the lamplight. I discovered the iridescent gown at a disco vintage shop and wore it to the courthouse with twinning silk shoes. You had on the same cocktail dress you were wearing when we met. I had talked you into donning a daisy crown all through the ceremony and reception. It's poignant to think that your black father and white mother were lucky to meet after the U.S. Supreme Court legalized interracial marriage. We met 14 years before gay marriage was legalized, but it wasn't too late for us. We could still walk down that aisle.

I poked you because I wanted you to wake up and see me in my wedding dress. I wanted you to remember how beautiful I had been when we got married. Somehow in my drunkenness, I had even approximated the big beauty queen hair I wore on our wedding day. It wasn't exactly a flawless recreation, but I knew you would get the idea.

I poked you again when you would not wake up. Aware that your sleep was not a deep one, I figured one poke would be enough to wake you. It was not. It took half a dozen prods to rouse you. Though your body remained stiff, you gradually fluttered open your hazel eyes. I couldn't tell what color your eyes were when we first met because you had on glasses and the steakhouse was so dim. But on our first date, we were outside of a coffee shop in the light of day, discussing *Superman* and *Little Audrey*. Sometime during your telling of Lois Lane's feminist revolution, I noticed that your eyes were pools of light brown with green and gray flecks. It was during that same conversation that you got me to admit that I wanted to be an illustrator.

You didn't have much control of your facial expressions in this final phase, so I read your eyes. It took a few beats, but your eyes lit up when you registered that I had on my wedding dress. I almost tricked myself into thinking that you had turned. You weren't going to die. You'd recover. You'd survive. We could go to Paris and Australia and the chicken quesadilla place and the dollar movie theater.

Then you coughed.

"No!" I shouted. It was the biggest noise the house had heard all week. I clamped my hands over my mouth. "I'm sorry," I whispered. "I won't be that loud again. I'll put on some Nat King Cole—real soft, promise."

"Unforgettable," which we played for our first dance, eked from my iPod. The song had never sounded so slow before. But as you lay there, it played slowly and softly for you. Too drunk to mimic our first dance, I simply twirled.

This is the when the alcohol began making waves in my skull. It wouldn't be the first time you saw me stumbling drunk, but it would be the last time. I always used to say that you were my weakness. While that was true, my fixation on you never hurt me the way my slavish dependence on gin hurt me. You encouraged me to draw, to pour out the contents of my imagination on the page. You encouraged me to abandon the church that made me miserable. You encouraged me to embrace my sexuality. All you ever did was encourage me, except when it came to drinking. That was one desire of mine you were eager to stifle.

I'm not sure how long I was twirling, but I could not spin around and around forever. I got dizzy and collapsed into the rocking chair that held my iPod. I thought the crunching noise came from my bones hitting the wood at the wrong angle. That wasn't it. I had crushed the iPod. It was gone. Done. I threw the iPod's remains against the wall and wailed.

Your beauteous hazel eyes had closed again, so I came over to rub your forehead.

"Wake up, my love," I said.

You did not wake up.

"Wake up," I growled. "Wake up. Wake up."

I shook you by the shoulders and you woke up. Maybe I should've seen the terror in your eyes and stopped, but I did not. Instead, I kissed you. I knew I was not supposed to kiss you, at least not with any real vigor—any real feeling—but I did. You could not reciprocate. Your tongue remained curled up in your dry, dying mouth. Your once bee-stung lips were parched.

If I could not kiss you, I figured I could hold you. Thus, I violated another one of the doctor's orders. I swept you up in my arms and cradled you. One year ago, I could not have possibly done that. For fifteen out of our sixteen years together, you dwarfed me. Now I was the big one, the strong one.

If you responded to me cradling you, I did not notice. As much as I loathe admitting it, the night was no longer about you. It was about me. Alcohol had made it about me. By drinking, I had made the night about me. It's tempting to wonder whose brain was more alive then—yours or mine.

I kicked off my heels and stood up with you still in my arms. I stopped marveling at how light you were. Now it was a fact, just like the fact that you were dying. I couldn't be stunned forever. The novelty of this new reality had worn off and my perception adjusted accordingly.

Maybe that is why I began heading toward our pool. It glowed in the backyard, calling to me as it had in all of our years hosting lesbian pool parties. Our email invitations always read "No boys allowed." Funny how friends will come to your Southside house to enjoy your pool, but none of them will come to your Southside house to mow your lawn or do your laundry when your wife is dying.

The pool hadn't only been for parties. Really, it was for us. Sometimes we'd read in our beach chairs and just stare at it as the water lapped the steps. Other times we'd play volleyball or swim laps. The sensation of underwater sex never lost its appeal, either.

Even in my drunken state, I knew we would not play volleyball or swim laps. Sex, too, was out of the question. But I saw no harm in us floating in our inflatable pool raft shaped like a Corvette. It was as pink as your hair had been at our wedding.

Maneuvering into the raft with you in my arms was no problem. For thirty seconds, I seemed to regain my sense of balance. I held you tight and, sometime while floating, I fell asleep.

You and I almost died once during the first year of our relationship. All of the downtown bars were closed, but you insisted on going into the city anyway. You were almost certain that this one diner was still open. Those were the pre-Internet days and you saw no point in calling, so we had to drive there to find out. When we approached the James River Bridge, you let out a battle cry and hit the gas. It was clear at 3 a.m., which made the fact that you were going about 99 a little less unforgivable. Still, I was horrified.

That horror increased tenfold when a homeless man toppled into the street. You swerved to miss him, momentarily losing control of the car. You just missed a lamppost as we ricocheted from one side of the bridge to the other and then shot down the length of it into Richmond.

"We made it!" you yelled, a crazed grin taking up more than half of your face.

I sat in silence for a full minute before confessing that we needed to go home because I shat my pants.

We could not have possibly been going 99 in our Corvette raft when I woke up. Yet we had been going fast enough—or at least clumsily enough—that you had fallen off of the raft. I didn't realize it at first because I didn't understand why I was in the pool. I didn't know where I was and I couldn't remember why I had on my wedding dress. What I did know was that I had been clutching you like the most precious jewel on earth because that's exactly what you were to me. But I had let you go. I deduced this because you were facedown in the water.

This was not a nightmare. This was my life, which had somehow escalated past the terror of any nightmare I had ever had. After days of forcing myself to stay awake for your last breath, I had been asleep when you died.

I paddled the raft over to you and scooped you up. It was only then, holding you as the Blessed Mother held Christ that I howled. Otherwise, I did not move.

I am still in this raft with you in my arms, not knowing what I will tell the police, though I swear I will call them at sunrise. All I do know is that I will never drink again or draw again or love again. I could say that it was your greatness that has made such things impossible, but really it is my worthlessness. When you told me that I was worthy, you were lying. I am less than the scum sticking to the sides of our pool, your deathbed.

THE LAZARUS WIFE: TIFFANY MORRIS

When they'd met at a New Year's Eve party he wore a crooked tiara reading 1959! and was perfectly sloshed on whatever cheap champagne the Anderson family had served. Her gut was rotten and fruity-sour from it, but something Beverly had said must have impressed him because he kissed her at midnight. She didn't even know his name.

Their wedding was eight months later, held on a hazy August day at the First Street Chapel. She'd worn a long satin dress and a veil topped with a floral crown. The ivory flowers hugged her face and her mascara ran just a little when she gave her teary vows. The gritty frosting of their wedding cake got stuck to her back molars, but she felt happy and alive, with her husband's arm in hers while the photographer's flashbulbs popped.

Then their honeymoon: a road trip across the Midwest, where endless fields swayed groggy in the summer wind. These were her first seeds of boredom, her first encounters with his long silences, the way his eyes would go blank and glazed as he drove on roads that bore nothing but horizon. Beverly had dismissed it as fatigue. These were the last things Beverly noticed before she died:

Sputtering firework echoes and buzzing patio lanterns, their red, white, and blue lights casting strange shadows over the wooden deck.

Their American flag flapping.

Sizzling burned hot dogs and the taste of coconut rum at the back of her throat.

Canned laughter that swam into her ears and rooted there, a parasite. A flash of Ruth Pullman's red cherry print dress.

Her knees buckled as she grasped for balance.

Then falling. Then sleep.

There was nothing to it.

Well, no. Not nothing. Not exactly.

There was purple stardust in there, like when you rub your eyes too hard.

There was that. Then a gaping, sucking, howling darkness.

She stood up in a daze and saw that the party had scattered into trails of foamy cocktail spills and napkin detritus. Her head was still swimming. Had she blacked out? That had never happened to her before.

Harold paced, his loafers clopping on the concrete. His voice rose just enough for the paramedics to hear as they pulled into the driveway.

"My wife!"

He managed to choke out just a hint of a sob. When she turned to him, to reassure him she was okay, Beverly saw her own body, collapsed. It was ghastly, seeing her body splayed like some doe out in the woods, full of buckshot. Like she was flora and fauna at the moment of her last damned breath.

An It instead of a She.

"Harold?!" she screamed.

He didn't look at her. His lanky, frantic body was clamoring alongside the medics. They broke her ribs trying to revive her. It was the crunch of fresh gravel, over and over and over, crunch, compress, crunch, their curled fists on her chest. Beverly screamed at them until they stopped. They readied the stretcher and put it under her limp body. Her hand fell over the side as they hoisted her into the ambulance. She grasped at her own cooling flesh, clawing feebly, trying to jump back inside her skin.

Harold ran to their car, a candy-red number he'd bought when he received his promotion last year, and revved the engine. The twin headlights stretched into the growing darkness before turning into the street.

Beverly walked back onto the deck, light as air, and stared at the yard. The reflections from the dancing lights filled the swimming pool with their shimmer. A sense of endless time creeped around her like curling vines. She wanted to shiver but felt nothing at all.

Harold lit a cigarette and sucked the smoke into his lungs, the ember glowing bright in the darkness. He hadn't cried once since he'd returned home.

Beverly stared from the corner of the room, longing to touch his warm body, the curls of his chest hair peeking out from the light purple sheets.

"Harold!" she exclaimed. "Can you hear me?"

He exhaled smoke into the dark. She couldn't smell it. She walked over to their bed and kneeled at his side, a nurse tending to a sick patient.

"Harold. Harold! HAROLD!"

She snapped her fingers in front of his face. He took another deep drag of his cigarette. He coughed, full of phlegm. It was thunderous beside her ear.

Beverly sat on the edge of their bed. The sheets didn't rustle. A sharp hysteria rose through her and crackled like electricity.

Had she really died? Beverly reached out to touch his leg. He didn't respond, just shifted and sighed mechanically in the dark.

She wanted to sob, felt herself wrench and retch. She pulled herself up and crawled into bed next to her husband, listening to his breath lull into sleep. She wished she could sleep, touch him, whisper to him that she was here, she was home, with him this whole time. Forever.

She sank into the soft sheets, wishing she could smell his skin. She stayed there all night and watched the dark turn into day.

Beverly tried to follow him to her funeral, watched as he dressed in his best black suit, his black silk tie. She wanted to straighten it for him, like she always had, before they left for parties. She stood behind him as he stared into the mirror, his face expressionless. Beverly reached her hand up to tousle his hair, but he moved just out of range. She followed him down the stairs where her sister, Rose, was waiting for him. Beverly stared down at her and raised her hand. It felt foolish to wave. Her sister paused, staring at the spot on the staircase where Beverly stood. Beverly froze. Her sister turned and followed Harold out the door. Beverly hurtled down the lush carpet and threw open the front door. The Fourth of July wreath, wrapped in red, white, and blue ribbons, was still hanging there.

There was only glaring light outside.

She stepped forward, into the nothing.

She blinked, her eyes adjusting to the light. She was in the backyard, standing next to where her body had collapsed. Beverly sighed as she climbed the deck stairs and went back inside.

The catering company would be there soon.

After the funeral everyone met back at the house, where they served Manhattans, Harold's favorite drink. Maraschino cherries glared bright in the dark amber glasses. Beverly watched as her friends gathered, dabbed at their eyes with handkerchiefs, nibbled at the tiny sandwiches and crackers with pate. She milled between the black-clad bodies.

"—loved her Bananas Foster. Never got the recipe from her."

"That time in Reno. My goodness. I've never laughed so hard."

"Sorry for your loss."

"…Just…wonderful. She lit up any room she was in."

Beverly couldn't help but feel jubilant as she weaved herself between the bodies and spotted her sister's sullen, swollen face. Rose was sitting in the corner, gingerly wrapping and unwrapping a napkin in her hand. Beverly walked over to her.

"Can you see me, Rose?" she asked.

Rose continued to stare at the floor. Beverly felt sadness climb her spine. She walked into the kitchen, away from her mourners, and stood among the caterers. They were smoking cigarettes and waiting for their shift to end. It was just another day for them. For her, too.

Neighbors dropped by hourly in the days following the funeral.

A week passed, according to the calendar, where Harold crossed off each day with a steady-handed X. The calls and visits were starting to slow. The next Friday had only one word written on it: Honolulu.

Beverly puzzled over that word, turning it over and over in her brain. Did he have clients there? She had always wanted to go. She placed her hand on her chest as she imagined herself in a swim-up bar, Harold in tow, both golden with fresh tans and smelling like coconuts, listening to the waves and wind in the palm trees.

Honolulu.

Beverly listened to their conversations when guests dropped by, tired of Harold and his boring, silent, nothing nights, eating frozen dinners, falling asleep in front of the television. The awkwardness of the conversations gave her an amused schaden-freude as she watched him try to navigate other people.

It was different the day that Eugene and Ruth Pullman dropped by. Harold had just finished his lunch, the same plain peanut butter sandwiches he'd eaten every day since she died. He fixed them drinks. Eugene refused, Ruth accepted. Harold downed the drink he'd poured for Eugene, then poured himself another. The Pull-mans sat on her couch as Harold opened up to them.

"I swear," Harold said. "It's like I can still smell her. You know? That pineapple and powder smell she had."

Beverly smiled. Perhaps she'd made herself known, somehow.

"I called her my pineapple upside-down cake."

Beverly cocked an eyebrow. He'd never called her that. Eugene looked at Harold. Pity spelled itself across his face.

"I'm so sorry," Eugene said. He shifted in his seat, his leg bopping in slight tremor.

"She's everywhere," Harold said. His voice cracked.

Beverly was sure she spotted a small gleam in his eyes. Was he about to cry? Was he drunk?

"Maybe you ought to go stay with family," Ruth suggested. "Just for awhile."

"Say, that's not a bad idea, Ruth," Eugene said. "Do you have family nearby?"

"In Delaware," Harold replied. "It's a bit of a hike." He paused. "But that's a good idea."

Oh no, Beverly thought. She'd be alone in this endless time, wandering her empty house, watching the clock and knowing it meant nothing for her. At least Harold gave her some measurement of time, some frail meaning to her longing.

"I'm sure the company would understand," Eugene said solemnly. "The whole office is in mourning for Bev."

"Speaking of the office," Ruth suggested, looking at the clock. "Don't you have to get back?"

"Oh, that's right," Eugene said. He looked at Harold. "Lunch break. Ruth offered to stay behind and fix you up a casserole, if that's okay."

"Oh, no…no, thank you. I don't want to trouble either of you," Harold said.

"I insist!" Ruth said. "Really. It's no trouble."

Eugene kissed his wife on her forehead and stood. He grabbed his hat from the coffee table and held it in one hand.

"I'm just so sorry," Eugene said. "I can't put it any other way."

Harold stood and shook his free hand.

"You're a good friend," Harold assured him. "I'll see you when I get back from Delaware."

Harold and Ruth smiled at each other as the door shut behind him. They listened, ears perked, for the sound of Eugene's engine, then the car pulling away. Beverly watched them, a tightness growing within her as Harold walked over to Ruth.

"Hi, honey," he said.

He placed her chin in his hand and kissed her. Their mouths devoured each other, heated with passion. Shock tightened Beverly further and sent her reeling. A wave of static fell over her as she tried to make sense of what was happening.

He hadn't kissed Beverly like that in years.

Ruth came up for breath and tousled Harold's hair.

"That must have all been so nerve-wracking," she purred. "I'm glad the capsules worked."

Harold pulled back from her, his face wrinkled in disgust. He turned away from her.

"I don't want to talk about it," he muttered.

He picked up his cigarette pack and gently knocked it against the table, packing his cigarettes down the way he liked them. Beverly wanted to vomit but couldn't.

"She was so drunk," Ruth giggled. "But she went quick."

Beverly stood, frozen, something worse than nausea consuming her.

"Drop it," Harold said. A venom in his eyes.

He'd get that way, something dark and faraway in him. Sometimes she'd look into his eyes and he'd give her a 3AM feeling, that liminal time of shade and specter, where loneliness unfolded into fractal geometry.

"Aww, I'm sorry, baby," Ruth said.

She placed her hand on his thigh. Harold ignored her, rubbing his temples with his cigarette in hand.

The world swam and crackled before her as Harold stubbed out his cigarette and grabbed Ruth's hand from his thigh, pulling it up to his mouth, kissing it.

Rage consumed Beverly. Harold had made a fool out of her; she had died a cheated woman. Murdered over a sad cliché. And Ruth Pullman! She was far too young for him, and worse, she was dull. Dull, but young and uncomplaining. Beverly gritted her teeth and became a current of hot air. Beverly reached for the nearest object, a pretty green vase they'd received as a wedding gift. She pulled it off the shelf and hurled it toward them. Even in her rage, she moved with feeble strength, arms heavy, like moving underwater. The vase fell and shattered into emerald shards.

"Harold!" Ruth exclaimed. "Did you see that?"

Harold jumped up and walked over to the mess.

"A vase fell from a shelf," he snapped at her. "Don't get hysterical."

Ruth's crimson mouth pulled down into a pout as she stretched her legs out on the sofa. Beverly's sofa, a tufted buttery-velvet one that she'd picked out with her mother. She glared at Ruth as Harold did the same.

"This place gives me the creeps now," Ruth said. She hugged arms to her chest.

"Yes, well," Harold said. His voice was sharp. "I'm sure Honolulu will put it out of your mind."

"One week!" Ruth squealed. She smiled and sat back, calmed a little.

What a fool, Beverly thought. What a foul, naive fool. She wanted to claw Ruth's china blue eyes right out of her doll face and shove them down Harold's throat. She watched them kiss on the couch, Harold's hands sneaking under Ruth's dress, Ruth's lurid moans drowned by kisses.

Rage and jealousy began to transform into a new feeling. It washed over her, cleansing as water. If she could grab a vase, she could grab other things. She smiled as she imagined the life draining from Harold's eyes. Her hands around his throat, his last gurgling breaths, eyes frantic, searching for his invisible assailant.

She glanced back at the disgusting lovers.

She had a week before they left for Honolulu.

Beverly had Harold by the throat, her flimsy hands wrapped around his pulsing jugular.

"Fuck you," she whispered.

She thought of the hidden moments between Harold and Ruth, flirting and fucking right in Beverly's home. Only right that he should die in their bed, where his lies were born. She'd come back from the grocery store and there he'd be, home early from work, the taste of scotch on his mouth. He'd say that he'd gone home sick and she believed him. It all made sense now. He hadn't respected either of them enough to shell out for some seedy motel.

Harold stopped breathing for a moment. A sleepy, confused choke rose from his slack mouth.

This was it.

Beverly smiled as her shoulders shrugged with laughter.

She pressed harder.

A loud snore sounded from his mouth. She wrapped her hands tighter.

Another, softer snore.

Defeat tugged at her as she unwrapped her hands and looked into the shadows of their bedroom. She was able to smell again. The dry, musty breath of her sleeping husband.

She could give up. Wait until nothingness came back for her, until she met her heavenly reward. If any. But a man like that...it would be a public service to put him down like a rabid dog. And foolish Ruth would suffer and wail, too ridiculous to realize she'd been saved from Beverly's fate. And Beverly would be saved from an eternity of seeing Ruth's vapid face, hearing her shrill voice.

The need created her and gave her form. It was Wednesday and Harold was getting nervous, jumpy. Beverly had been practicing her vengeance; shattered plates, slammed doors, running and laughing as she stomped throughout the house.

Only rage made her real.

It was Thursday. Tomorrow, Honolulu. She stood on the deck, glowering at Harold as he barbecued hot dogs, only five feet from where she had died. He whistled tunelessly as the smell of burning meat filled the air.

He might as well have been dancing on her grave.

The smell of something rotten carried on the wind, pungent under the barbecue fumes. She looked at her arms, less flimsy now, bruised purple and sloughing flesh. It was time. She might have had infinity to do this, but she needed him dead. She refused to be trapped here, to watch her husband screwing another woman and being nothing for the rest of his soulless life.

Beverly punched at the wooden rails of the deck. Harold ignored her. He had always ignored her, hadn't he? She felt the rage thunder within her again. She thought of the sunset in Hawaii that she'd never see. She thought of his dull eyes, how they had fooled her into thinking he'd loved her, how young and dumb she'd been to fall for this unremarkable man, a pile of flesh that encased a monster.

She thought of their wedding day as she reached out her rotting hands and grasped Harold from behind. He jumped, then gave a cry and shrugged violently as he tried to shake off his assailant. Beverly wrestled him to the ground. Her fury gave her body strength and form.

"Harold," she said. Her voice was nothing but a dull whistle.

Harold screamed. All color drained from him as he stared into his wife's ghoulish face. She pulled him over to the pool, thinking of the first time they'd made love, the times he'd told her she was special, that their love was special. He slid over easily.

She sat on his stomach and held his head over the water.

He screamed, eyes and mouth bulging wide, cartoonish with alarm.

Her reflection in the pool showed her ashen face and rictus grin, her eyes transformed into empty, howling black sockets. Ragged seams of flesh hung off of her. She laughed as she shoved his face into the chlorinated blue. She laughed as she pulled him back up to air, as he sputtered the turquoise water, still screaming, his face contorted in horrified confusion.

She brought him closer, kissed his wet, cold lips, and plunged his head back under. His arms struggled against her. He hammered at her with his fists but hit nothing. His legs jerked with desperate violence. His head thrashed in the water as his gurgled screams made frenzied, Jacuzzi-like bubbles rise to the surface. She laughed as this tortured infinity passed between them, his spastic body and her heaviness, her fury, that anchored his doom.

She laughed until his body went slack.

Beverly pulled his shoulders up from the water. His head lolled and bobbed at unnatural angles. No breath came.

She pulled herself off of him and shoved his heavy, lifeless corpse into the gentle ripple of the waves. A splash of water. Dead Man's float.

The night came alive again with the hum of grasshoppers and the buzz of the patio lanterns. Beverly smiled as she watched Harold's body start to sop up water. She imagined the bloat on his decaying face. She smiled at the horror Ruth would feel on discovering it in the morning.

Death instead of Honolulu, It instead of He.

Beverly laughed, feeling impossible tears, at last, rise to her face.

She laughed as her body started to crackle and burn, disappearing into purple stardust, consumed by shadow, buzzing with searing heat and pain. She laughed into the nothingness, ready to become one with the howling dark that awaited her.

STAG LOOP: BRENDAN VIDITO

Amanda found the film in the discount bin at the adult video store. The case insert was missing. Only a pale strip of masking tape scrawled with the words "stag loop" served to identify its contents. She bought it for three dollars, along with a handful of more legitimate-looking DVDs, as a gift for her boyfriend, Logan.

When she returned home, the sharp, icy fingers of winter had dragged the sun into an early grave. The house was muted in shadow; the only sound was the rumble of Logan's snoring upstairs. Amanda followed it to the bedroom. Nyx was curled up at the foot of the mattress, purring ecstatically, and regarded Amanda with her golden-green eyes. Amanda scooped the animal into her arms, turned to face the cheval mirror behind the door, and studied her reflection.

Enough moonlight crept through a slit in the curtains to sketch out one side of her body. The result looked something like a work of scratch art: fine strokes of silver against solid black. Nyx appeared to grow out of her chest, the jagged tracery of her pelt gleaming like polished steel.

"Look at those beautiful ladies," Amanda said and kissed the cat between the ears.

She replaced Nyx on the bed, searched the grocery bag of DVDs, pulled out the one marked "stag loop," and slotted it into the player. Logan stirred. Amanda checked her watch. He was supposed to leave any minute for the graveyard shift.

She crawled up beside him and breathed hot breath in his ear.

"Time to swim up out of those dreams," she whispered.

Her eyes swished to the television. The film was starting. The white flicker of damaged negative was replaced by a lingering shot of a sixties-era living room. The picture was yellowed in sepia and poorly lit. Amanda knew right away that it was a bad VHS transfer. The living room was furnished with a couch, garishly floral-patterned, a coffee table with a white porcelain bowl in the middle, and an ugly Grecian urn off to one corner.

A man with shoulder-length hair entered the frame. He waved impatiently to someone off-camera. After a beat, the actress stumbled into the scene. Her hair was styled in a bob that framed her face in an inverted triangle. She wore a button-up dress and no bra. Her breasts curved under the sheer fabric. Timidly, she approached her co-star and allowed him to undress her. After a mediocre blowjob—Amanda realized that vintage porn was closer to real life than the modern fare—they fucked on the couch. The scratchy background noises gave way to porn groove.

Amanda let out a soft chuckle and recalled her attention to Logan. He groaned, threw an arm over his face, and Amanda rolled back the sheets to expose him to the night air. He was naked except for a pair of boxer briefs. His morning wood was more than a suggestion under the membrane of cotton.

"What are you doing?" he said, voice drunk with sleep.

Amanda kissed him on the stomach. His skin was hard and soft, the light smattering of hair tickling her lips. She moved up to his chest, planting little kisses along the way. He made a noise halfway between a grunt and a moan. His arm slid away from his face and their lips met. They kissed gently at first, Logan still only half awake, and then grew more urgent, passionate. His breath was stale, but it did little to deter Amanda's affections. Over the lip smacking and panting, the stag loop provided a comedic backdrop to their activities.

Soon the music reached Logan's ears, piercing the blinders of his arousal. He laughed, a loud bark that sent vibrations down his stomach.

"What is this shit?" he said, staring beyond her at the television.

Amanda pulled away, lips plump and sheened in saliva, and followed his gaze. Onscreen, the woman had mounted the man in the cowgirl position, with her back facing the camera. She bounced up and down, throwing her head around in exaggerated paroxysms of pleasure. With a species of envy, Amanda noticed the beauty of the woman's back. Her shoulder blades stood out in sharp relief, softly pointed, sliding under the buttermilk skin with each thrust of her pelvis. A beauty mark fringed the slope of her right back dimple. At first Amanda thought it was a discrepancy in the image, a scar on the negative, but then it moved in conjunction with the woman's flesh, startlingly black in that sepia world.

"This porn is ancient," Logan said. "Where did you find it?"

"The adult store," Amanda said, eyes lingering on the screen. "Don't worry it wasn't expensive."

"I was going to say. Amateur porn filmed in the dark looks better than this. This is just weird…and creepy."

"Because it's old?"

Logan gestured toward the screen. "It looks *off*."

"What are you talking about?" Amanda propped her head in her hands. "It's two average-looking people having sex. He doesn't have an obscenely large dick, and her tits aren't big enough to smother a grown man. They're normal."

Logan shrugged. "It's not that. I can't put my finger on it. Maybe it's the yellow tint or the shitty lighting. It makes their eyes, her eyes especially, look empty."

"Maybe she was doped up on something."

"Could be. This was the decade of peace and love, after all."

Amanda playfully flicked Logan's cock. He flinched. "Well I think she's beautiful."

"For a ghost, maybe."

"Why would you say that?"

Logan wagged a knowing finger. "I think I figured it out. The girl doesn't look real, but more like a cheap optical effect than actual flesh and blood."

Amanda grinned. "You're thinking way too hard about this. It's a fucking porno."

Logan sighed. "Yeah, you're right." Then in a sleazy accent, said,

"So how's about we bring our own porno to its natural conclusion?"

Amanda said nothing, only lowered herself back down on Logan, filling the room once again with sounds of their passion.

Meanwhile, on the television, the longhaired man came on his co-star's chest. The picture sputtered to black, to be followed by the second scene in the loop. It was dark, grey-tones. Two men and one woman were writhing on a bedspread veined with wrinkles. A distorted, porn-groove rendition of a church hymn played in the background. As the larger of the two men penetrated the woman from behind, Amanda and Logan were already naked and moving together between disheveled and twisted sheets.

———

After Logan left for work, Amanda found herself once again in front of the cheval mirror. The porn loop continued to play in the background, spewing a funky version of honkytonk piano. Amanda frowned at her shadowed reflection, pulled her lips apart in a grimace.

While alone, Amanda found amusement in affecting different personalities. Now she was testing her capacity to be a bitch. She loved Logan more than anything, but even so, and purely out of curiosity, she held an inner dialogue between the two of them, merely to taste an alternate side of her personality.

In this mental staging, Logan woke from his nap and tried pulling her into an embrace, but she denied him, icily retreating from his touch. Your breath stinks, this version of her said, you have to get to work. But, Logan stammered, a child denied his favorite sweets, we still have time, come on. He looked at the clock by way of evidence. You have a hand, Amanda said sharply, use it.

The real Amanda, head bowed and gazing into the mirror from beneath the hood of her eyes, laughed. She didn't usually have to resort to such caustic remarks, but the potential for verbal violence was definitely inside her. Slumbering. Everyone held an aptitude for darkness, Amanda thought. Better to explore it in her mind, watching the shadows play across her face in the mirror, than exercise it in real life. It was much safer that way, more benign.

Do and say what you can safely to others, and save the rest for the imagination. That was the essence of Amanda's philosophy. This principle allowed her, even for a moment, to become someone else. You may only live once, she mused, but who's stopping you from trying on different personalities?

The woman from the stag loop materialized in her mind's eye. Amanda wondered what she was like, what kind of personality inhabited that beautiful body. She seemed shy, but that was probably just an act similar to what Amanda routinely affected in the mirror. If that was the case, then who was the woman lurking under that veneer? Amanda disengaged herself from the mirror's gaze and rewound the stag loop to the first scene. She let it play for a moment then paused the picture at a frame where the woman *almost* seemed to look into the camera.

Logan was right, there was something weird about her eyes. They stared right through you—empty. She shivered. Keeping the video on pause, Amanda left the room to use the bathroom. Nyx followed.

Amanda watched television in the den until midnight. She alternated between the usual reality and variety programs while Nyx slept on her lap. When she finally mounted the steps back to her bedroom, tired enough for sleep, she saw the porn actress' face frozen on the screen, and realized she'd forgotten to turn off the television. The actress continued to stare with that same emptiness, crystalized in a lurid moment decades past.

Instead of ejecting the DVD, Amanda sat at the foot of the bed, hands clasping her knees, and tried to see beyond the cluster of pixels to the identity buried underneath. She yearned, with a sudden intensity, to know this woman on a deep, fundamental level. She wanted to appropriate her character, taste the exoticism of a porn star of the golden age. Only this time, she didn't want to simply imagine it, as her role-play had compelled her to do, but instead wanted something more, something tangible. To slide into her sheath of skin, wear it like a second-hand sweater, inhale its foreign scent, taste the strange sweat squeezing from its pores.

Amanda shook herself out of the reverie. What strange thoughts, she mused with a smile. She supposed they were born out of boredom. Lately, her days were fixed in the rigidity of routine—waking up early, working from nine to five at the insurance firm, eating a boxed dinner in front of the TV, then bed—and even something as mundane as a vintage porn loop could spur her on an imaginative journey. Private role-play to kept her entertained during life's boring moments. It was an unconventional hobby, but Amanda wasn't exactly one to take up knitting or scrapbooking, and she liked the thrill it ignited in her belly. She turned off the television and crawled under the covers. The sheets still smelled strongly of Logan, the musk of his body and the slightly cloying aroma of his cologne. She extinguished the bedside lamp and closed her eyes.

In the theatre of her mind the porn loop continued to play, feeding her further exhibitions of carnal pleasure. Her imagination became a tableau of sex acts—a series of lantern slides depicting countless variations of fellatio, cunnilingus, intercourse, and sodomy—all of it eerily bathed in a yellow glow. As she drifted closer to the well of sleep, she began seeing flashes of the woman's eyes. I wonder what else is on the loop, Amanda thought as she sunk into sleep's warm, black waters.

She woke two hours later with the distinct feeling that Logan was sleeping beside her. Rolling to face him, she muttered something about his breath stinking and fell back asleep.

Her dream was the yellow of jaundice. The camera of her subconscious was fixed on the floral pattern sofa from the porn loop. A ball of lint, tethered to a strand of black hair, wavered in an unknown breeze. Then the camera focused, the image closing in on the crevice between the back of the couch and the cushions. Amanda was carried into a darkness fringed with loose strands of needlework. It felt as though she were descending into a pit in the middle of a lightless jungle. For some time she incubated in darkness, becoming one with it, it becoming one with her, before a pinprick of light appeared, drawing her attention. Amanda swam toward it.

She found herself under studio lights, in a sixties-era living room. A negligee was draped carelessly over her body, one shoulder suggestively exposed. The woman with the spectral eyes was sitting on the couch. She said, "Care to join me?"

Her hand went out, the nails long and manicured. Amanda felt a measure of reluctance tug at her brain. She stayed rooted to the spot.

"Don't you want to see?" the woman asked. "To feel what it's like inside?"

Amanda opened her mouth to speak, but no sound emerged.

"Just sit beside me. We can take it slow," the woman went on.

A flash of lucidity and Amanda realized this was nothing more than a dream. She was in the playground of her imagination, where anything goes. No choices she made, for good or ill, had the power to affect her in the waking world. She could throw herself off a bridge to feel her stomach lurch into her throat, or cheat on Logan with one of the reality stars she'd gawked at before bed. None of it mattered. Dreaming gave her a free pass to do whatever the hell she wanted. Amanda took a step toward the woman and...

Her eyes snapped open. The bedroom was a uniform blackness. Amanda couldn't distinguish the objects and furniture scattered throughout it. She blinked, hoping her vision would adjust, but a veil had been pressed over her eyes. Distantly, in another part of the house, she heard Nyx meowing, a low, threatened note. The clock in the kitchen ticked off the seconds, sharp and clear in the dark. A floorboard creaked, probably the house settling. Amanda stretched out an arm, hand passing over the space belonging to Logan. It was warm and shallowly indented. The air smelt vaguely of sour breath. Nyx let out a sharp yowl. All these sensations felt incredibly dreamlike.

Comforted by this realization, Amanda submitted herself once again to sleep.

She was sitting beside the woman now.

Something shrieked far off, the distorted cry of an animal in pain. Amanda placed her hand on the woman's thigh. It was warm and downy, like something freshly born.

"You're very beautiful," Amanda said, tracing her fingers across the woman's nubile flesh.

Their eyes met, the woman's lazy with seduction, and Amanda felt herself being drawn into their emptiness.

"I've been here too long," the woman said. "I'm happy for your company."

She clasped Amanda's hand in her own.

"What happens now?" Amanda said.

A mixture of fear and excitement coursed through her veins. She knew on a level of dream logic that she was about to participate in the ultimate role-play.

"I invite you inside," the woman said, with a flourish of her manicured nails. "All I need is your consent."

"Can you show me what will happen before I give you my answer?"

The woman smiled and nodded. Nyx threaded into the room.

Amanda came awake with the feeling that she was being watched. Her eyes had adjusted to the darkness and she could discern the individual shapes of furniture and decoration. But there was something in the corner of the bedroom that did not belong. Whatever it was, it nearly touched the ceiling. It was thin and hunched, its upper half arching toward Amanda.

Still intoxicated with sleep, Amanda tried to figure out what it was. Maybe it was an article of clothing hanging off the hook on the closet door.

Then it moved. A twitch.

The darkness birthed a gnarled, spidery limb. Adrenaline shot into Amanda's bloodstream. She lunged off the bed, blind to all except escape, threw open the door, without pausing to look behind her, and ran into the kitchen. She tripped over her own feet on the way to the knife block, staggered, righted herself, and pulled out four-inches of stainless steel. She stood there trembling, watching the stairs, astonished how she'd gotten here so quickly.

Something shrieked right beside her. She threw a hand over her mouth to catch the scream and wheeled around, thrusting the knife forward.

It was Nyx. She lay on the floor, legs kicking in frenzied spasms. The middle of her body was bare, stripped of fur, the skin pink and bulging as though fat slugs slithered in the space between flesh and muscle. The poor animal loosed a warbling cry. Her head shook, as boneless as a puppet, the needle teeth bared, exposing the corrugated roof of her mouth. The eyelids were pinched closed but the orbs squeezed through anyway, distorted by the pressure and flooded with burst vessels.

Amanda threaded her fingers through her hair and pulled, teeth showing in a tortured mask of terror. Was she still dreaming? What the fuck was happening?

A creak on the stairs.

Amanda glanced sharply up. Nothing. Darkness still boiled in the doorway to her bedroom, but no sign of life or movement.

Nyx screeched until blood sprayed from her throat. Amanda crouched beside her, not sure what to do with her hands. They flapped uselessly in the air. The bare skin on the side of Nyx's body twitched more violently until the ridges of deformed flesh coalesced to form the suggestion of a face. The teeth were the animal's ribs tearing bloodily through the skin, the eyes, some purpled-hued organ bulging closer to the surface. Amanda screamed and slammed her fist into the face. Nyx's ribcage shattered with a dull crunch. She aspirated blood in a series of low feeble breaths, before going utterly still.

Shaking and pouring in icy sweat, Amanda raised the offending fist. It was coated in blood and a sharp fragment of rib protruded from the knuckle. When she looked down to inspect Nyx's corpse, to see if the face was still there, she abruptly found herself back in the sixties living room.

No, not exactly.

She was sitting at the foot of her own bed, watching herself on the television. Onscreen, the porn actress was sitting with Amanda's television counterpart on the sixties couch, and now lifted one hand, unfolding the elbow to reveal a seam in the crook of her arm.

"Come inside," she whispered. The audio was poor, crackled with static. The woman squeezed two fingers into the seam. Skin parted from muscle with a wet peeling sound. An ozone smell wafted from the parted flesh. Amanda, sitting on the bed, could smell it emanating from the television screen.

Onscreen, Amanda stretched out her fingers—they trembled and yellow light glinted and danced off the gloss of her nails—and slid them into the fold in the woman's elbow. The woman tilted her head back, lips peeling stickily so the skin opened lengthwise from the middle, a fleshy zipper. Her teeth, evenly spaced with chinks of empty space, shone and gleamed with saliva. She closed her eyes, the lashes flirting with the crest of her cheekbone, as Amanda pushed her whole hand inside the crook of her arm.

"Be rough with me," the woman said.

Amanda seized the woman by the throat with her free hand. She leaned in, their foreheads touching, and pushed her arm deeper, up to the elbow. The woman's skin bulged obscenely. A moan escaped her lips. Amanda tightened her grip around her throat until she could feel its pulse tapping against her fingertips.

"Harder," the woman gasped.

The elbow seam flowered, the skin receding red, wet and engorged to accommodate Amanda's shoulder and head.

The Amanda sitting at the foot of her bed masturbated furiously.

Amanda's eyes burst open. She was in bed, lying with her back facing Logan's side of the mattress. Her first thought was, why am I here? With sluggish remembrance, the image of Nyx writhing on the kitchen floor sketched itself in her mind. Spurred by the recollection, she lifted her right hand in front of her face. She could feel and smell the dried blood caked between the digits. The knuckles throbbed with a dull pain. A pathetic whimper escaped her lips. In the subsequent silence, she became aware of soft respirations between the sounds of her own breathing. Someone was in bed with her. Her heart revved in panic. She held her breath for a moment—maybe it was her imagination—but the respirations continued, slow and measured. She didn't want to turn and look. Oh God, she didn't want to see. She wasn't even sure she could will her muscles into movement. If she could, she'd run back to the kitchen, but something, some remote part of her mind, told her that she would just wake up in bed again.

The mattress shifted beside her, the bedsprings creaked. Cold sweat seeped out of Amanda's pores. Her breath emerged in ragged, panicked gasps matched by the heavy, but sedate exhalations of the thing beside her. She could feel its hot breath against her neck. If she rolled over right now, she'd be staring right into its eyes. You have to run, she told herself. At least try. For Christ's sake, just try.

A tongue, warm and scaly, ran along the back of her neck.

Amanda shrieked. As if in response, the television flared to life. The woman from the stag loop was sitting on the couch staring at the camera. There was a container of antifreeze on the table and an empty bottle of prescription medication. In one hand she cupped a mound of white pills, in the other she held a stemmed wineglass filled with bright blue fluid. She palmed the pills into her mouth and knocked back the antifreeze.

Amanda rolled over. She had a glimpse of a pale form, naked with limbs horrifically distended, before it sprang on top of her, its voice, the hissing static of the stag loop.

Logan returned early the next morning. The first thing he noticed was the mud on the floor, then the car battery and the axe. The battery had been nearly cloven in two, the ragged wound wet with acid. The blade of the axe also glistened with it.

Fear bubbled up inside him, raw and primal.

"Amanda," he said, bounding up the stairs, two at a time.

After a moment of agonizing silence, she answered, "In the bedroom, babe."

He stepped inside.

Amanda was seated at the foot of the bed. Her negligee was

streaked with blood. She'd cut her hair into a shabby parody of a sixties bob. Her face was variously hued with the white and pink of acid burns. Her lips had been sheared off and blood streamed down her chin and neck like a garish excess of gloss. Despite her injuries, though, there was a familiarity in her appearance. It took a moment for Logan to realize what it was exactly, but when he did, his blood stilled with cold. Amanda had, through self-inflicted mutilation, performed a twisted procedure of cosmetic surgery. She'd burnt away her skin with battery acid, reducing it to malleable clay, and reshaped her facial structure so she looked like the woman from the stag loop. The resemblance, though distorted, was uncanny. Bile surged up Logan's throat. His testicles contracted in fear.

Amanda held out her hand, fingertips eaten away by acid, exposing bone.

"Come over here, baby," she said. "Let's make our own movie."

SP WORLD: LORRAINE SCHEIN

Under a blank, emptied sky that had stopped filling with snow, the red lights of the giant Ferris wheel glowed like blood, and long icicles hung like frozen tears from its swaying cars.

The fair was only open in winter.

How did she know that?

It's cold up here, A. thought. Looking down from her car at the wheel's top, she saw people swarming like bees in a hive, going from one hopeless ride to another.

But why was she here?

That man down there, the roller coaster operator, looked familiar. *He's a handsome man, with big hands*, she thought. *I miss his hands. He wouldn't leave her for me. I am not blonde or English. He wouldn't replace her with me.*

And who was she? A. had slept in her bed and lived in her house and all she remembered was how she wouldn't let A. be with him...

The wind blew A.'s brown hair into her face. A child...and where was her child?

She did remember when she first got here.

"Welcome to SP World, dear," the official Park Greeter had said.

A. wondered what the initials stood for.

"What brings you here, dear? Pills, gas, drunk driving? Poetry, perhaps?" the Park Greeter said with a practiced smile.

She wore a gray uniform with the SP World logo:

a yellow hive embroidered on the pocket.

"Have you read the requirements for an admission ticket?" The woman pointed to the sign over the entrance to the grounds.

ENTRANCE REQUIREMENT:

At Least 2 Attempts And A Note From A Doctor Saying You Should Be Under Careful Observation.

"I'm not sure I qualify..." A. said. "I don't even know how I got here."

"No matter, sweetie. If you are here, it must be for a reason. Go, enjoy yourself!" She gave A. a ticket, then pushed her toward the ticket booth, where a clerk in a cap and brown shirt like a Nazi uniform punched a bee-shaped hole in a ticket and handed it to her.

On one side of the fair was a row of stalls. A large wooden arrow pointed to them. It said THE 10-in-1 SIDESHOW. It looked less crowded, so A. started there.

The first freak show stall had a banner proclaiming:

SEE THE DISQUIETING MUSES!
JUST ARRIVED FROM THEIR EUROPEAN TOUR!

Here were two dressmaker's dummies, standing in front of a painted backdrop that showed a red fortress in the distance. A statue of Apollo stood nearby.

The tall one wore a white toga. Its head was marked with black stitch marks like scars. A seated dummy next to it had a tiny black pin head on a huge stuffed body.

Both were eyeless, seamed. Blank faces, bobbin heads.

We are eyeless, heads stitched up but we see you, they said to her in flat singsong voices. *And we see her playing with the cards.*

Then the Muses sneered at her. "Thirteen poems in your last 3 months. Won't you do it, do it, do it?"

"You must be confusing me with someone else," A. said, and walked to the next stall. The marquee read ELECTROSHOCK SHOW in flashing lights.

This was an exhibit of people getting shock treatment. The viewers were invited to apply the shocks themselves by the barker.

"Step right up and turn the handle! You'll only be helping them, not causing them pain!"

There was a pretty blonde woman on the table, strapped down. A. pulled the lever and watched the blue lightning convulse the woman on the table, arching her back.

Was she better? The blonde was not moving now, and looked very pale. Was she alive?

A. ran from her, panicked. Ahead was a stand of bobbing, colored balloons. A man with a handlebar mustache handed her one for a dollar. He also gave her a long sharp pin, telling her, "If you pop the balloon, you win a prize."

She popped it. "What is my prize?"

The man laughed. "This," he said and handed her the limp shred of red balloon.

She put it in her pocket. Maybe the rides up ahead would make more sense.

She pushed her way through the crowd to the midway, toward the first ride—a lurching Tilt-a-Wheel.

THE MOON AND YEW TREE

A giant tree stood before her, towering almost as high as the Ferris wheel. Cars shaped like crescent moons swung out from its branches as it rotated, raising screaming children into the air. A. worried they would fall out, felt tears well up in her eyes. She decided to save her ticket for something else.

She walked down the path to a sign that said GAMES OF CHANCE.

"Spin the Wheel of Chance!" said the carnival barker. She stopped before it. It was red and black and divided into different sections. One read NURSE COMES HOME EARLY. Next to it was NEIGHBOR SMELLS GAS. Another read WIN STUFFED ANIMAL.

The barker spun it. It whirled and whirled in a blur, but never stopped on anything. The pointer never settled.

It is so odd, A. thought and decided not to play. She walked away as the barker called after her, taunting "What are you so afraid of?" shaking his fist.

BUMP–A–CAR

This was an electrified platform on which small, realistic-looking automobiles whizzed, careening wildly into each other with loud thuds. It was surrounded by a deep lake. The goal was to not let your car be bumped off the platform into the lake.

As A. watched, she saw that some of the drivers thought the goal was to drive your car directly into the lake, because there were wrecked, half-submerged autos in the water with people clinging to their sides. They never called out for help, though, and there was no one on the shore to pull them out.

THE ARIEL CAROUSEL

Here was a carousel with tiny multicolored lightbulbs circling its top and base; its horses were all black. They had no reins or hand-holds for their riders to grasp.

As the sun set, the Carousel creaked to life, piping a fragile yet manic tune as it began to turn.

It sped up with a shudder, but there was no carousel operator to halt it. A. saw that you couldn't get off because it was moving too fast. Its riders became colored blurs as the tempo picked up, one with the horses. The red light shaped like a giant eye above the riders flashed faster, pulsing redder as they accelerated.

The Carousel ran all night and stopped at dawn. It halted so abruptly, riders were thrown off, their sprawled, bruised bodies spewed to the ground.

As she left, she noticed the smell of rotten eggs, gagged and covered her nose. Where was it coming from? A. shuddered. She would never bring a child here.

THE ZOO

THIS WAY TO THE WILD CREATURES EXHIBIT, the arrow ahead pointed.

Several iron cages with tall bars stood in a row. The first one had a crudely lettered note on it:

PLEASE DON'T FEED THE TULIPS!

A bouquet of vicious, ravenous tulips snapped their red jaws at her, rattling and lunging their long stems between the bars as she gazed at them. Even though they looked safely caged, she stepped back. She felt their petals enveloping her throat, throttling her neck like a tourniquet, choking her.

A. gasped, and hurried on.

The next cage was no better—a cluster of growling, vivid poppies whose black tooth-like pistils gnashed together, leaning eagerly forward to slurp at her, drooling.

She ran around the corner to the next exhibit. As she got closer, she heard a loud buzzing and saw the sign:

HALL OF BEES

A giant beehive with no fence or netting around it to protect viewers swarmed before her. Something sticky and molten fell from the canopy above her onto her head, dripping down on her face, to her mouth and her sleeve.

It was honey!

She tried to wipe it off but it was too late. The bees buzzed toward her in an angry swarm. She backed away, swatting at them in terror, but it was no use. Then a beekeeper in a white suit, high-sleeved-gloves and a shrouded helmet with a netted mask drew them away from her, saying, "Beware the queen!"

They followed behind him, a humming, wavering procession.

THE FUNHOUSE MIRRORS

A. entered the Hall of Mirrors in the Funhouse. They were all different sizes and shapes. The first one was long and she saw herself elongated, stretched thin as taffy. In the next, a round mirror, she saw herself squat and stunted, a fat dwarf. Who would love her if she really looked like that?

She wouldn't look English enough.

The diamond-shaped mirror that was next, made her look much younger, first showing her as a child in Tel Aviv playing on the beach, then as a teenager dancing with the handsome British soldiers. A. walked to the last mirror, and saw herself aged, her hair grown gray. Then that image vanished and the mirror's center filled with a silver-scaled fish, expanding till it was no longer a fish but the glistening surface of a great lake that spilled over the frame, engulfing her.

But strangely, A. didn't drown. She was now on the shore of the lake. There were paddleboats on it, and she saw a tall man in one with a blonde woman. They looked familiar.

Though both were paddling, the blonde woman was sinking lower in the boat.

But he was not.

He kept paddling, not even turning his head as she disappeared into the water. Horrified by this, A. shouted for a lifeguard, but there was none.

She needed to get away from here, she needed an explanation, no matter where from.

A. followed the sign that said TO THE FORTUNETELLING TENT.

She found, then entered a canvas tent on the edge of the fairgrounds.

A. sat in the folding chair next to a table. The table held a flickering candle, an incense cone scripting acrid smoke overhead, and a small amethyst crystal ball. A hissing sound came from the tent's shadowed corners.

The reader was a tall gypsy woman with a British accent and big hands. She wore a spangled velvet scarf and a long, tiered skirt.

"And what is your name, dear?"

A. couldn't remember. Was it Sylvia?

"Sylvia, I think," she said. Yes, it must be, because she remembered sleeping in her bed.

"Funny, you don't look like one. But cut the cards, dear," the woman said, handing her the deck, and leaning back with a smile.

A. shuffled the cards, then split them into three piles. They felt sharp as she did so, and when she was done she had tiny red slits from paper cuts on her thumbs.

"Here is your fortune," said the woman, laying down the cards. She turned them over slowly and fell silent, studying them. "Fixed stars govern your life," she said at last.

"These cards represent your past. I see you made a journey here from another land. Perhaps to escape confinement and evil."

"Yes, I'm originally from Germany," A. said.

"Then I emigrated to Palestine to escape the war."

The Tarot reader turned over the cards.

The Eight of Swords. The Devil.

"I see you are involved with a poet—no, wait.

She turned over two more cards.

"Three poets."

"Well, my husband is one."

It was amazing how accurate this reader was.

The cards on the table were The King of Cups, reversed, and next to it the Queen of Cups. Or did the card say The Cuck Quean?

"Now for your future cards," said the woman. "I see a couple entering your life. I see a woman."

The Tower, its turret struck by lightning, with bodies falling from it-- she recognized that one. The Queen of Swords.

But the fortuneteller now turned over many more cards, ones she had never seen before.

The Queen of Ovens

The Two of Orphans
The Priestess of Pills
The Tower of Electroshocks
The Wheel of Misfortune
The King of Infidelity
The Six of Slashed Wrists
The Cups of Pills
The Page of Poetry
The Hierophant-Psychiatrist
The Nine of Overdoses
The Hanged Otherwoman
Bad Judgement
The Ten of Bees
The Lunatic Hospital

"The one you want? He will never marry you," the Tarot reader said, turning over the last card.

The card on the table now was the Magician. . . or did it say the Magic Man? And the Lovers' Triangle, reversed. A picture of a woman and a man. Or was it two women and a man? A. rubbed her eyes. She was getting tired.

"But I'm already married," A. said, confused.

Just then, the woman's velvet scarf slipped off her neck and A. noticed her Adam's apple protruding underneath.

The fortuneteller was not a woman! He was a man with big hands wearing a dark wig and a skirt. His deep voice was now evident as he lunged at her with a growl. A. pushed the flap of the tent open and stumbled outside, shouting, "Imposter! Liar! Seducer! Help me!"

A. rushed outside toward the Ferris wheel in the distance. It seemed to dip down at her feet, beckoning her to mount it. An empty car pulled into place before her.

She handed her ticket to the uniformed ticket taker and climbed into the car. He latched the metal safety bar in place across her lap with a clink, locking her in.

A bell clanged, heavy as fate, in the distance.

A. saw that the front of her car was shaped like an oven, its white door open, and its seat was a mattress.

She thought, *Where is my little girl? I want her to ride with me. Have I lost her in the fairgrounds, is she looking for me, calling my name?*

The child he wouldn't acknowledge.

As the Ferris wheel started to rise, she saw a child hanging by one hand from the car in front of her. *Oh, there she is! My little Shura!* Dangling from the car, trying to climb back in.

I don't want her to be without me. A. stood up, rocking her car precariously, and pulled her to safety beside her. "Mummy!" said the girl, hugging her.

She sealed the car, turned on its oven, laid down next to her child. *I'll give her the pills first.*

The mouth of the oven-car opened, hissing, released that smell of rotten eggs. The Ferris wheel operator below was laughing.

He looked up, his hands on the brakes. He could stop A. if he wanted to.

But she knew he wouldn't. *He wants me to go the same way*, she thought.

"I will never marry you!" he shouted up at her. She knew his name now—knew all of their names.

It is her world, the jealous, lucky bitch, but I can be like her this way. She breathed in the forgetting gas. *Now this will be my world.*

Looking down she thought, maybe Ted will miss me now too.

I am Assia.

And I am dead.

A GHOST OF MY OWN MAKING:
ASHLEY INGUANTA

When I wake up from the storm, I reach for Eli, and instead of burrowing into his warmth, a letter finds my hands: a blueprint, a beach house. I light a candle. "You won't be able to find me," it reads. "The wind picked me up, and now I am every bit of light you see."

In the letter, above the beach house, are pencil sketches of a steeple.

A great big hand lands on my abdomen, reminding me to breathe, that I will be okay without Eli, that we will find a sense of calm apart from one another. Eli and I have been exploring eachothers bodies for months; and our minds, for years. I was starting to feel like I was becoming part of him.

Myself, himself.

His big hand presses to my navel, I close my eyes, breathe. I wake in the sand, covered in a blanket of silver horsehair. It is so cold, every breath stings. The sky is covered in pewter clouds, and even though it is daylight, I cannot find the sun, or a lace imprint of the morning moon.

The air smells like chalk.

Near me is a small fire held by a translucent bowl, a grey ocean, an empty dock, and a house made of glass cards.

I unfold Eli's blueprint, which is resting neatly between my hands. "The wind picked me up, and now I am every bit of light you see."

Nothing threatens a house of cards like wind.

Nothing lets in the light like glass.

I pull the horsehair blanket tightly around my shoulders, place the blueprint in my pocket, and I struggle to stand. I see spots in my vision. I know I need water.

I walk towards the house, and the fire warms me. Up close, its flames look like a painting–orange, yellow, smooth.

With each step I take, I feel the sand below me sinking, cupping my feet. And then, it hits me: I am not in a dream. I am in a real place.

And then it hits me: I wonder how long I will have to stay here. I wonder how long it will take me to crack Eli's code this time.

———

The door to the house is made of glass. Even the doorknob and hinges. Each card is about the height of a door and the length of a swordfish. Most cards are etched with hearts, but some are etched with spades. No matter which suit, each glass card is a pale translucent blue, shining like trays of flat jewels. Inside, the house is empty—except for one intricately carved wooden desk on the first floor.

I knock.

I knock again.

I take out Eli's blueprint. "You won't be able to find me." Its script curls around a steeple. I feel faint. I am tired of him always getting his way. For sending me here.

I walk inside. I go to the kitchen, turn on the sink. It works. There is one glass cup on the counter. I fill it, over and over, drinking the cleanest water I have ever tasted.

———

Eli likes to build worlds like this—ones where I am almost completely alone, so I can open, so I can tornado inwards. I don't blame him. It's what we did together—we shut everything out,

invented our own rules. To understand the jars and their placement, I decide I need height, perspective. I find tools in the kitchen
pantry, and I use wood from the ocean dock to build myself a
ladder. I place the ladder beside my bed, and from this small height
I can see that these jars and wires connect to form a steeple.

I go downstairs for water, and I realize that for the first time in
hours, I'm hungry. I open the refrigerator to find lemons, rose
milk, eggs, and figs. As a test, I drink the entire bottle of rose milk.
It refills.

After I finish my fig omelet, I decide to shower and rest. There
is no need to rush. If there is one thing I have learned from Eli so
far, it's this—finding my way back to him takes time.

In this house of glass cards, I learn to live a simple life. Stay warm
by the fire bowl, which is a star in itself, and sleep, and write.

Sometimes I will think of Eli's blueprint, his message. "The
wind picked me up, and now I am every bit of light you see." He
could take trains across America without a map, without any guide
but himself, and somehow form a steady and strong route. Before
the storm, before he disappeared, he told me my time was coming,
that I would learn to navigate, too, but differently—not by bus, not
by road.

But when I woke underneath that blanket of horsehair, I could
only see what was in front of me. A pewter sky, a large, grey ocean,
and knowledge that Eli once again fastened those thick silk
threads to his fire escape, pulled them inside, wrapped them
around his hands, guiding the reins of an animal that would send
me to a mirror, a place reflecting the collisions of my mind.

And now, as I wake from my nap, that great, big hand comes
again. It brings light and darkness. It brings me bees. I reach my
hand out, palm up, and each bee flies upon it—one by one. They
land on me as soft as stardust, and their wings shine pink and
green like rainbows. After the last bee leaves my palm, the great
hand brings one smooth, glass journal filled with rice paper.

The bees rest in their pastel boxes next to my desk. The glass
journal rests open, on top of the desk.

I don't know what to do with the bees, so I write to Eli.

"Two past missions," I write, "Two. You sent me to the bottom of a warm sea, and I could breathe salt water. I lived in a house of coral. And then you sent me to a castle atop a cliff, surrounded by flocks of birds. To get out of these worlds, something precise had to occur. I had to fit somewhere perfectly. I don't know how else to describe it. I had to fit in speech, in body, in intention. And when I came back into this world, everything was just as we left it —down to seconds on the clock. (I placed my hand onto the coral doorknob, and I remembered the time my cousin Margaret taught me to gallop on horseback, the sense of trust I had in her, the way I truly loved the taste of salt water on my lips, the schools of starfish I helped survive.) The first time you vanished, we were biking in the fog across the Manhattan bridge. I lost sight of you. Do you remember that? How did you learn to tunnel through the fog?"

As I wait for a response, I tend to the bees. One lands on my shoulder, and another pauses in front of me, mid-flight, frozen in air, becoming a work of art, all rainbow and texture. They don't sting. Instead, they teach me generosity, allowing me to harvest their cones. When I say "Thank you," the artwork bees understand, and they fly again, leaving trails of color behind them—bold indigos, oranges, and greens—that imprint and then dissolve in the air. One bee flies to the glass and I follow. It lands on a spade etching, next to the front door. The Ace of Spades.

When I get tired, I make an omelet. I drink rose milk, lemon water. I make a fishing pole out of dock wood and shoelaces, and I catch five rainbow trout. I cook them over the fire and watch the grey ocean move, rhythmically, like music. The fire glows. I lie in the sand, and I visualize myself from above—I am on the edge of something, the edge of some land, and I can rest here.

———

The fire by the sea—it never goes out. I notice this as I make my weekly walk up to it, warming my hands before fishing. Soon, I bring figs to cook, making fig-and-trout kebabs. I warm some rose milk and enjoy the ocean music. The sun never sets here. But sometimes it rains. Maybe one day I will climb silk threads like Eli did; only instead of the moon, I will bring back Jupiter, slide it like a bead onto a necklace. I imagine each of my fingers curling around the threads. Each will have the precision of an archer and the muscles of a horse. Jupiter in my arms will feel like a baby deer; her umbilical cord, the eye of the storm.

Eli has not written back to me in the glass journal. I keep making my way upstairs, filling jars with honey, and then more jars appear, connected by wires. The room expands. I climb my ladder. Below the steeple rests a modest home, the beach house in his blueprint. One bee flies onto my inner wrist, pauses. Its rainbow wings expand slightly, and then a sharp pain moves into me.

A sting from the tiniest of swords.

It's when I jump off my ladder I notice a flicker of silver. It is too small to rip the air, but it sits on top of the air, and then disappears. I run downstairs to check for a response. Boxes of light sweep the surface of my desk. The glass journal slips into one. It vanishes—just like that—sliding into the folds of air, of light.

I try to follow, to fit my hands into each square of light, but my positioning is not precise enough to move inside. What was I hoping for—a miracle?

I tend to my sting, swelling like a tiny cloud. To ease the pain, I close my eyes, imagining a familiar scene around me—my bed, Eli beside me, sleeping—the weatherman on television, reminding us that New York City is in the arms of a hurricane.

But when I open my eyes, I am here—surrounded by cards of glass, sand, and water. No matter what I do, my body weighs into this home like a stone—this is real. I am in a real place. I am here.

When you're alone, every little thing matters more. The ladder, the rose milk, the bees, the coastline, the horsehair blanket, linens. I take out the blueprint. "The wind picked me up, and now I am every bit of light you see." It has been days since my bee sting, but it still pains and swells.

I step out the front door, burrow my toes into the sand. I press my hands to a wall, a translucent blue heart. The ocean rolls, endlessly. This glass home is the beach house, yes.

It is not unlike Eli to rely on mirrors. He believed that our bodies were mirrors of the wind, always moving. He believed some bodies were fragile and others unbreakable. He never told me he suffered broken bones as a child, but he always moved with caution, wrapping his hands in thick silk threads, flipping backwards over a sundial in his apartment. He had no skylights. His sundial was made of a sword and twelve books, all his own writings. Book number twelve was titled The Moon, and the others had no names. He told me this much. The rest I discovered on my own, watching him through the crack of the bathroom door as he cried, whispering "Where did you go," to the air, watching him in broad daylight as he closed his eyes, pressing his palm to one of his journals.

That day, we were walking to the bodega near his apartment for coffee. He said, "Wait," and we sat in the shade, on a stoop covered in vines. He opened a green leather-bound book and wrote something. He was using invisible ink. Only light could reveal its meaning.

I do not have invisible ink in this house. Maybe he was expecting that of me, to make an imprint beneath something. But aren't I already beneath something, separate enough? Maybe I don't want the wind to allow myself to permeate everything. Maybe Eli is content this way, but I miss things here, in this in-between place. I am not everything, but I am not myself. I am starting to forget what it feels like to shake another's hand, to hear my mother's voice, to ride in a subway car, all silver and full of speed.

Maybe the wind dropped Eli off into his East Village apartment, and he's reading my journal right now. Maybe he was here, moving so quickly I could only see him as flecks of silver. Who was he, after all? A poet? A seeker? An artist who can create dimensions by shifting time and thought and matter? And how did he split me from Earth this time, the sacred and private world we created together in New York? And what was he doing out there traveling so fast, so fast, and alone?

Tired, I walk upstairs, lie on the clean bed. I itch my sting and it bleeds. A bee with a deep violet trail lands next to me, rests. The gift of honey and color is nurturing, but within that comfort is the risk of hurt. The Eli I once knew was now a ghost of my own making. Himself, in the past, but here with me.

The Eli I knew walked this world in a state of missing. He missed landscapes of people, maps of people. His mother's funeral was a five of spades, he said, for its sharpness, and his sister's was endless.

"You have to know who you are," Eli said to me before the hurricane hit. "Because if you don't, you cannot know where you are going."

I don't know what I have to find here. I am tired. I am so tired.

I wish I could dive down into the Great Something and touch the top of St. Patrick's Cathedral, the steeple, show Eli that there is a way to grab the moon, that those we have lost will come back. They will all come back.

I run from the fire bowl and into the glass house. The bees— what is the point? The rose milk, the eggs, the beautiful water— what is the point? Yes, they are a mirror of power, of creation, of partnership, of pain—but why? Why?

I close my eyes. I remember playing piano with my father as a kid—my hands were almost the size of his at 10 years old—and the way he smoked his cigarette as he taught me how to find Middle C, how excited I was to learn about music, how terrible I was at naming the notes, how I didn't care and played anyway. I remember the first date I ever went on—with a guy named Pablo. We were both eleven, and we sat in the hallway after school. He wore a silver coat that reminded me of minnows, and he wrapped his arms around me. I remember what it felt like to ride on a tire swing for the first time, age 14, at Cousin Margaret's house on a snow day. I remember feeling like a bird, like a blue jay, like a sparrow.

I remember meeting you for the first time, Eli, and how you listened to me as I stood on stage. I read about a young girl who found a small green deer that could fit into the palm of her hand. When she lost her tiny green deer, some people said she was confusing reality with a dream, but others believed her. Years later, when she's in her 30s, she sees a green ribbon tied to a telephone pole, ends curled. Something makes sense to her then.

I run up the stairs. When I was standing on stage, when I saw Eli in the crowd, his face illuminated like a star, I felt so powerful because there I could create a world.

I lay on the bed, back flat, and close my eyes.

I feel a slight pressure on my shoulders, two hands, and I don't look to see whose they are.

Instead, I breathe.

I keep breathing.

LOOSE ENDS: A MOVIE: TIFFANY SCANDAL

Fallon used to be a fiction writer. She wrote because she loved it; because she was passionate. Then passion gave way to greed. Money became more important than the message.

And that's when it all turned to shit.

At first it was small gigs—commercials, shorts, whatever. Regardless, the work was steady enough and it earned her more than her first five years combined as an indie author. She was able to quit her day job, leave the small town in Oregon, and move to Los Angeles, where she would be closer to all the work she was a part of.

She was Hollywood.

She lived in a happy little place in Los Feliz. The apartment was spacious with large windows that allowed for lots of natural light in a city where it was summer year-round. Her neighbors were actors, models—creative people doing creative things and being successful. It filled her with joy. She had found her people.

She met Dr. Peak at a diner for coffee. Dr. Peak was one of the well-dressed producers she would always see at mixers. He never said much, if anything at all, but he had such an intense stare that people would involuntarily shiver. Most of the work she had come by in LA had been from his colleagues, so when he contacted her with a job offer, she was intrigued. He didn't say much on the phone, but when he said that she was the woman for the job, she felt her heart flutter.

When she got to the diner, she saw Dr. Peak sitting in a booth already. He was dressed neatly in a black suit. She paused at the entrance, feeling embarrassed for how underdressed she was for their meeting. He looked like he could be someone from the FBI and she was wearing ripped blue jeans, an oversized t-shirt, and grungy converse sneakers. Face flushing red, she continued forward because she'd rather be underdressed than late. She sat across from him, tucked her long brown hair behind an ear and smiled.

"Hello, Dr. Peak."

His face remained expressionless, eyes locked on hers.

He raised his left hand and briefly gestured two fingers to the moderately busy diner. As if on standby, a waitress appeared with a mug and a pot of coffee and set it right in front of Fallon. She cupped the mug in her hands and brought it up for a sip, letting the steam hit her face.

"Mmmm, it's fresh." She set the cup down. She wanted to smile at Dr. Peak, but could feel her muscles quiver underneath her skin, making her face feel warm, forcing her to look away, causing her fingers to involuntarily twitch. She gulped louder than anticipated and the surprise caused her to choke. She coughed so hard, tears welled in her eyes.

Still intensely focused on her, Dr. Peak pushed a cup of water toward her. She picked it up with one shaky hand and used the other hand to cover/catch the water dribbling down her chin.

The waitress went to fill Dr. Peak's cup with more coffee, but he raised a hand to stop her, not taking his eyes off of Fallon. The waitress nodded and left.

"I have work for you," Dr. Peak said with a somber face.

Regaining her composure, Fallon took a deep breath and said, "So I've heard, Dr. Peak." She finally pressed out a half smile as she felt her nerves start to calm.

"Jack."

"Excuse me?"

"Just . . . call me Jack."

"Oh, okay." She started playing footsies with herself under the table. Something she did whenever she was nervous.

"In this envelope, you'll see your assignment. Open this when you get home. This is for you and your eyes only."

"Got it, Dr. . . "

His stern expression stopped her in her tracks.

". . . Jack," finished Fallon as she dug her nails into her palms. One meeting with a real important Hollywood executive and all of her nervous tics were coming out in full force.

"You're the woman for the job."

"I'm incredibly honored to be considered. Thank you." She nodded uncontrollably, feeling mortified on the inside.

"You're the woman for the job," he said again, slower this time. Same stone expression.

She finally stopped nodding, and raised an eyebrow. Hearing him repeat the same line made her feel a little uneasy. It seemed . . . ominous. She cautiously reached for the envelope. "I really appreciate you saying that, Jack. Really . . . it's, uh, an honor."

Jack got up and straightened out his suit, set a twenty-dollar-bill down on the table. Seemed a little excessive for two cups of drip coffee, but he didn't seem concerned about waiting around for change.

Fallon eyed the large manilla envelope, thick with papers. After he had walked a few steps, Fallon perked up and called out, "Dr. Pe—Jack?"

He stopped and turned his head to the side.

"When do you need this done by?"

He looked down to the ground. It was apparent that this man carried an enormous burden. "You'll know when you're done." He continued to walk away.

Fallon nodded, "Humph."

She felt the exchange was weird, but it was a job. And it was a job with Jack, so maybe it would be alright.

The waitress came by again and asked Fallon if she wanted more coffee. Fallon accepted and looked at her name tag: Rosario.

"Rosario. I wrote a story once where the main character was named Rosario."

"Oh. You're a writer?"

"Yeah," Fallon looked down, suddenly feeling embarrassed that she said anything. But she kept talking. "Rosario was one of my favorite characters, but I never got around to finishing the story. It was around the time I met these movie executives and I was able to move up in my career. But, you know, I probably still have the story sitting on a hard drive somewhere. I'll get back to it one day, when I'm not so busy with scripts and whatnot."

The waitress nodded and left.

Fallon suddenly felt super embarrassed. She was a writer in LA, and that interaction made her feel like she was *that* writer, the kind that always boasts about projects to sound more important. She took one more sip of her coffee. It tasted like burnt dirt. She eyed the twenty on the table that Jack had left for the waitress.

"How generous."

She grabbed a napkin and wrote *Thank you, Rosario*, placing it under the twenty-dollar bill. It felt weird, but oddly satisfying, to write her name again. She took another sip of her coffee and looked out the window on her left, squinting, almost forgetting that it was still daylight out. She set the mug down, wiped her hands on her jeans and walked out of the diner, large manila envelope tucked under her arm.

At home, she tossed the envelope on her desk and backed away toward the couch. She chewed on her thumbnail until she tasted blood, as questions and doubts circled in her head.

Was she good enough?

Had this city changed her?

What made Jack think she was the person for the job?

Rosario. What a weird coincidence.

Suddenly she remembered all her abandoned projects. Abandoned passions. Stories she started, but never finished. Characters and worlds and dreams never fully developed because she found an opportunity to have writing support her. And that was living the dream. Right?

She slumped her shoulders. All these projects she'd been assigned hadn't been passion work. She'd written commercials for cat litter, herpes medication, and Christian singles. She missed writing fiction, but she didn't have time for it anymore. She had to power through these commercials to keep climbing up the ladder. Eventually she'd get to write for a movie or television show. It was bound to happen. It needed to happen. She just needed to put in the time. And now she had a project from Jack. Yes. She had a project from Dr. Peak. He saw potential in her.

She was the person for the job.

She walked toward the envelope and picked it up. Peeled up the metal tabs and reached for the contents. About seventy-five pages, and on the very top, it read:

LOOSE ENDS: A MOVIE

There was also a post-it note that read in cursive,

you're the woman for the job

A movie script. She was finally assigned a movie script. The moment she had been waiting for. She dropped the packet and looked up to the ceiling with a huge shit-eating grin. "Thank you, Jack!"

Then a heavy click and all the lights went off.

She pulled her head back and looked around, letting her eyes adjust.

She wasn't in her apartment anymore. She looked like she was on some sort of set. She slowly turned, looking for an explanation or an exit. In the distance, someone stood by a fake wall. Fallon called out and they turned and ran.

"Hey! I just want to ask a couple of questions."

Without thinking, she ran after them.

Behind the wall, she found herself in a spot much like the one before. Dark, spacious, and mostly empty except for some flats and facade panels in the distance. Again, she noticed a person standing by a panel. Again, she called out. And again, the person ran. Fallon, once again, ran after them, hoping to get some answers, but once she got behind the wall, she found herself in the same spot as a few moments ago.

She looked around. This was crazy. No one else seemed to be around except for the one person she could never catch up to. She walked in the other direction, thinking maybe she'd find something else. Once she turned the corner, she saw something in the distance running toward her. Something else. It seemed large, and angry, like some sort of beast. It scared the shit out of her, and she turned around and ran.

She ran toward the panels in the distance and saw the person standing there. She frantically waved her arms and screamed for help. The other person turned around and ran. Not wanting to look back and see how close the thing chasing her was, she ran behind the panel and tried to hide in the shadows. When she heard the snarling, she closed her eyes and tried to quiet her breath. She imagined herself as part of the wall, trying to relax as much as possible.

She felt hot breath close to her face, and the second she felt the beast pull back and heard the growl, she peaked with one eye and it was gone. Now both eyes open, she looked ahead and saw her reflection in a window. She was in a maternity ward. Babies laid out in rows in their individual plastic cribs. Each labeled with a unique name.

One name caught her eye. Rosario. She walked over to the crib to peek at the baby. The most perfect baby she had ever seen, wrapped in a pink blanket, was fussing until she saw Fallon. Fallon reached down to pick up the baby. Rosario cooed in her arms and lulled back into sleep.

"Rosario, Rosario. I named a character after you once."

"I know," a voice behind her said.

She was a little girl, no more than five years of age. Brunette hair up in pigtails, a pink shirt with a large flower on the front, pink and purple striped pants, and a purple backpack.

Fallon continued to hold the baby and gave a puzzled look to the little girl. She looked around the ward, no other adult around.

"Excuse me?"

"I. Know," the girl said, sounding a little sassy.

"You know what?"

The girl leaned closer and whispered, "Rosario." She turned and ran out of the ward, the door slamming shut behind her. The loud sound woke up all of the babies screaming and crying. The bundle in her arms felt different. She looked down and instead of seeing a baby, she saw a blanket full of maggots. She screamed and dropped the blanket and the maggots. They spread everywhere. Crawled up her legs, up the cribs, over the babies.

Their names: Octavio. Hector. Linda. Zaida. There were at least twenty babies in this ward, and all the names she came across as she hurried to the door were familiar. They were all characters in stories she had abandoned. The crying grew louder. Cold sweat took over Fallon's body, hands started shaking. She backed toward door of the ward and reached for the knob.

Silence overtook the room. In unison, all the babies sat up and looked at her. Maggots, thick across their bodies and faces. She felt the judgement in their eyes.

"No, no, no."

She turned the knob and left the room.

In the darkness, she heard someone call after her. When she looked up, she saw a figure running after her. Remembering the beast from before, she ran in the other direction. She hid behind a panel, catching her breath, legs feeling like gelatin.

A cigarette landed by her feet. She ran outside into a dark alley. A rat scurried across the pavement, something knocked over a trash can behind her. She looked around and couldn't figure out how she got to be there.

No movie set in sight.

"What the . . ."

Trying to process her new environment, she heard rapid foot-steps behind her. When she turned, she was startled to see a woman standing right in front of her. The woman muttered some-thing under her breath and slapped Fallon across the face.

"Ow! What the hell?"

Fallon, hand on cheek, looked at the woman in shock. Torn fishnets, gaudy mini dress, makeup running down her face, brunette hair a mess. She stood there and locked her eyes on Fallon.

"Do I know you?" Fallon asked, trying to regain composure.

"I'm Rosario."

Fallon squinted to get a better look. The woman looked like the waitress at the diner.

"The tab was paid. My employer left you twenty dollars."

Rosario slapped Fallon across the face again.

"I'm Rosario. Your character, dipshit."

In the distance, two police officers meandered on an evening stroll. When they spotted Rosario and Fallon, they called out and started running toward them.

Rosario grabbed Fallon and said, "We need to leave."

"I don't understand what's happening here."

"I'll explain later, right now, we have to leave."

Rosario reached for a door that appeared out of nowhere and pushed Fallon through. The door slammed shut, leaving them in a dimly lit living room, glowing red. Out of the window, pure darkness.

Another set.

"What the hell, man. What's going on?"

Rosario rubbed her hands together and paced around by the door, staring at the floor the whole time.

"I was a good girl, but I hit a rough patch. I tried to make it on my own. I had it in me because my character had strength and courage." Rosario started crying again. Tear trails clearing through charcoal cheeks of makeups past. Then she looked up at Fallon, walked toward her and put her arms around her shoulders. "I was strong. I was brave."

Fallon flinched.

Rosario continued, letting go of Fallon. "But you left me in the dark. You left me in the rough patch."

Her eyes were wild. She looked crazy.

"I don't understand."

Rosario stood in front of Fallon and cocked her head to the side.

"You. You never wrote my ending. This is all *your* fault."

Fallon backed away. "What? No. No."

Rosario crept toward Fallon.

"Stop it! This isn't happening." Fallon raised her arms to her ears and shut her eyes. This had to be a nightmare.

"You have to fix this." Spit flew from Rosario's mouth. "You left me in hell."

"This isn't real. This isn't happening."

Rosario dropped to her knees and cried into her hands. She looked up at Fallon with pleading eyes, "Please. Please, just please."

Fallon had never seen someone look so desperate in her life. "I — I don't know what to do."

Rosario wiped her nose on her arm.

"Just write my ending."

"Your ending? But it was just a story. Fiction."

Rosario shook her head. "No, no, no."

"Writer's abandon work all the time. This isn't real. You're not real."

Rosario wiped the tears from her eyes and slammed her hand on the floor. "My name is Rosario Hernandez. I grew up in Corvallis, but moved to Portland to try to be something, someone. I met a man. His name was Jack, he was a doctor. He told me if I moved to LA, the world and everything in it would be mine. And I believed him. Everything fell apart after I moved to LA. I lost everything. I turned tricks to make ends meet, met some scary people, real monsters. But I knew that deep down inside that wasn't how my story ended. I held on to hope. I was strong. I was brave."

Fallon's heart raced.

Rosario continued, "My mother always said *when you feel lost . . .*"

" *. . . look to the stars and they'll light your way.*" Fallon's eyes welled with tears. This story that she had abandoned years ago, an attempt to find her own strength after the most difficult year of her life. She loved Rosario's character, but always felt as though she was failing her with each attempted draft.

"I looked to the stars, and felt hope that I'd make my way out. But one day, the stars went out. They sky stayed black. And since then, I've been living the last chapter over and over again. Like every bad thing that's happened to me since I moved to LA just keeps repeating no matter how many times I try to make the outcome different." She pulled a tissue out of her bra and blew her nose. Tissue still covering her face, she looked up to Fallon and apologized.

Fallon stood there, stunned.

"What happens when you try to change what's happening?"

"I always find myself back at the beginning. Stepping foot in Los Angeles, trying to make something of myself . . . "

The beast howled in the distance.

" . . . and *that* always finds me. No matter where I run or hide."

"What is that?"

Rosario amended her posture and scoffed at Fallon. "Don't you know?"

Heavy steps sounded outside of the room. Claws scraped at the door. Fallon jumped where she stood. A sick feeling growing in her stomach.

"It'll never leave. You have to fix this."

"I'm— I'm so sorry, Rosario. I had no idea." As if on autopilot, Fallon caught herself walking toward Rosario to hug her.

Rosario tried to stifle her cries as the scratching at the door became more intense.

She whispered, "Please, just write my ending. Give me something happy, or kill me, whatever. Just please, don't leave me here anymore." She clutched onto Fallon's shirt and continued to cry.

Fallon rested her cheek on Rosario's head and nodded. The scratching stopped. Out of the corner of her eye, she noticed something through the window. Dr. Peak, her employer, standing outside, looking in, smoking a cigarette. Their eyes locked, he nodded, and turned to disappear in the darkness.

She understood what he meant. She was the woman for the job. She had to write Rosario's ending and save her from the hell she had left her in.

"I'll write your ending. I'll write your ending, and I promise it'll be a good one."

She opened her eyes and she was back at her apartment. It was night, and everything was illuminated by the moonlight. She rushed to her laptop, found the last draft of Rosario's story. She scrolled to the end and typed *she conquered her fears, cleaned up her life, traveled the world, fell in love, and lived happily ever after. The End.*

Fallon felt relieved, lighter. Sure, it was a story that would never be sent to print, but she gave Rosario her happy ending. Hands clasped behind her head, she looked up to the ceiling and basked in her accomplishment.

Wet footsteps behind her snapped her back to reality. She turned and there was a gray, sickly-looking boy covered in viscous fluid standing behind her.

"Who the fuck are you?" She slowly got up out of her chair.

"Octavio," and then he screeched so loud, her ears bled.

GIRLS IN THE GARDEN OF HOLY SUFFERING: LISA MARIE BASILE

six

I was born a thousand years into the sadness of my reincarnation.

My understanding of darkness comes early; I have no words for it, no context with which to drown in or master it. But I know it's there; it is my pretty, secret wound. I hide it and pick at it; am preoccupied of it.

I am raised by the darkness, even when things are good, even when I do the normal things children do. I always want more of it. It is buried beneath my bed, in the wall. It is in my bath.

I want that which makes me feel immortal, lithe—a bit destructive. These feelings pulse through my formative years, but I have no articulations for it.

I have an intimate relationship with dark-hunger, that she is my invisible friend. My body and mind cannot catch up quick enough to the condition.

My grandmother, from Sicilia, is a tiny woman with jet black hair; she thinks the devil exists in my father, that he was born of the dark; she says he is the bad one, always will be. Dark and tall and tan and his blood is thick and heavy—not like lemons, but something else.

He wakes early for work and I can smell the trail he leaves behind: aftershave of birch, cotton shirts, masculinity. And he plays guitar. You can even hear him when he's not playing. Of course, darkness makes everything audible. You can always tap into anything you want. It's a gift from hell that says, "you're always sad, you've earned this."

And then he leaves. And so does my mother. I make and remake them both again in other images throughout my life. They become everything, ghosts, nothing, a table, a spoonful of agave, a ritual, a want.

fourteen

I cast a spell for a boy, but he has to have *all* the parts; he needs to have long pale hair, and he has to be on fire inside. I don't have time for anything else. And I want him to be all mine—so mine his organs fail without me. My word is my magic. I want to fuck him but I want him to make love to me.

The stupidity of youth fills me but I don't mind. I don't mind choking on cliché. I want to hold all my want and sorrow in a person who can consume it. Boys make reality more beautiful.

Here he comes, and he is perfect, and for the next five years I will drown in him. He is named after an angel—obviously. I lie about my age, but it all comes out in the water. Nevermind. His mother loves me, takes me to museums and galleries and the theatre. I am a good girl in their eyes, like a daughter, but he and I have our secrets.

We play in the dark. We tend a dark garden.

His hair makes ringlets at the ends, it sticks to his neck when it rains, when he plays guitar, and he is taller than me by a foot or more. Through him I understood that the body is an object, a thing to be abused and hardened and also loved. I don't forget about love; I don't claim a body is a weak thing all the time; sometimes I victimize myself because I like it that way. He wants a special kind of sex, a kind I have to pretend to give. He wants me to beat him up, fuck him up bad, and cover him with black spots. I don't want that; I have no desire to be the one doling out the pain. It's not that I'm innocent, it's that I'm bored by boys who ask things of me. I want to do the asking. The black stone inside my chest says I can.

He has a friend, and his friend had the sort of things I learned to want. His friend is darkness too, and he puts me over his lap. I want that, to be made into a thing, to be possessed by what I have no capacity for. I want to be a table. Maybe a chair. Maybe a vase.

I am rocked in his hands, that black kelp hair, oh his wicked mouth. And we sneak and sneak, we hold hands behind the angel's back, and we fuck in stairwells. In a manner of speaking he is not very kind but I am above the idea of what is or is not good.

That is a naivety I feel particularly disgusted by. He leads me to his father's bedroom and splays me. I understand that what I have been given is an explicit want with no end.

seventeen

I am in a foster home. I am so sad my limbs go numb. This place is sterile and safe and predictable; there are flowers on tables, doilies, Degas. But I am just a boarder, I have a bedtime, I stay up lingering, I perpetually dream otherness—of flowers in fields only I know of, of boys and girls who know my pain and can say they suffer too.

A quiet spell has been cast; I welcome the wound. I know I can relieve myself of want and negative space by chasing the dark, by finding those who understand it too.

Then I find Sylvia—she is an antidote to my sour life.

She fills in the lines.

Tulips. I'll never forget it. I find a space in the school library, back beyond the rows and rows of books, near a wide open window. Summer is full and violent and the other teenagers are kissing or smoking or fumbling in their disgrace. I watch them with a blinding hate and disgust; I want anything, anything, but for them to come near me. I cannot, will not, let them know me or see me or sense me.

All I want is my loneliness and my dreaming and my want to be realized. I want to get out of this other person's life. I want to be distracted by other bodies, then come home at night and keep it all to myself. I want to bring God down to my chest and be inhabited; my magic is my want. Its rituals.

These foul teenagers have no space for the vastness of my life, I think—they toil in the parking lots with their emptiness, I sneak off to New York City and listen to the opera, I dig holes in the soil and plant words that come true (but I always come back by sundown on Sundays).

I have Sylvia. I have a blackness in my heart like my father does, and I am filling it with the world and beauty and sneaky things. Through art, I elevate my heartache. I can live inside the trope. I can live inside my word. I build a world.

Sylvia says:

> *I didn't want any flowers, I only wanted*
> *To lie with my hands turned up and be utterly empty.*
> *How free it is, you have no idea how free—*
> *The peacefulness is so big it dazes you,*
> *And it asks nothing, a name tag, a few trinkets.*
> *It is what the dead close on, finally; I imagine them*
> *Shutting their mouths on it, like a Communion tablet.*

I read it like a birthing; she understands—in her sickness and melancholy, in her being left in a London flat with two small children, in her constant need for death. In her actually achieving it. I think, how can she fit an unreasonable amount of suffering into so small a space? I cut the poem from a book and keep it in my pocket. It's the lock and the key.

twenty six

I have had my fill of the dark, but we'll see. In and out of life, studying literature, studying the night.

We all write and stay up late and smoke cigarettes out the window. I find a home in the east village and revel in the hoax of it all. I am a stupid clichè, maybe always have been. And I have a new lover, he is demented, and obsessed with me; he sneaks through my things, secretly drinks, prisons the light out of me.

Naturally, sex is how I kill him. So I take my sex and put it around town. He leaves and I am left.

I know this game well, you fool, I say. Because you cannot

destroy my blood with my own poison. Because my body will run filters over your trauma. I can make anything a glamour.

I am in love with a sadness, simply because it is easier to translate it than to conquer it. And I am only good at replacing my sadness intermittently, with my body—because my body can transcend, if only for a moment.

Into my body I pour a hundred elixirs and shapes and voids and wildnesses; I can make sacred my misery.

I learn to find men who make me cult-like in my surrender. Whether I am being loved or left, I find myself bending toward those who can supplant what is, day by day, a leaking in me: a sense of self in a world that values normalcy and good homes and nice girls and early mornings.

I am not an early morning girl; I am a destroyer.

I always come back to Sylvia.

Perhaps when we find ourselves wanting everything, it is because we are dangerously near to wanting nothing, she tells me. It makes sense to me; I have nothing to want but the illusions of things, the script, the grandeur, the facade. Because what can be real that also fulfills me? I don't know, I don't know, I just don't know if I want the chaos or the cure.

twenty seven

I am in a church on 14th and I pray for the first time since childhood, since I prayed the devil out of daddy.

I wander in, and when I wander out, the world changes.

I meet Lana; she makes sense to me as though she has always been there, in my chest, playing out. Like a woman stuck in perpetual girlhood, she is the ultimate symbol of woe. Maybe she even makes her face look more sad? Maybe she paid for them to sculpt it? I don't care. She's a comfort to me. She is a vessel; she is a stage show. We place into her what it means to be wholly separate from the world around us.

We like the mirror she holds.

I don't believe she suffers, but I believe she conjures suffering.

thirty

Lana does a photoshoot for Vogue. It's inspired by the idea of *Melancholy Sexuality*, which is something Sylvia knows well about, which is something so simple and clear that the fact that one captures it is reductive and gauche.

But there is a difference between appropriating sadness and being sad, between the romanticizing of pain and pain itself, between death and the daydream of it.

Lana may be heart-aching, and she may be obsessed by a world of beauty and youth, but she is no Sylvia. Sylvia sticks her head in an oven and kills herself, while her children sleep in the other room. Lana wears dresses in Italy.

I wear dresses in Italy.

My life is full of contradictions.

I am been smashed to bits, and I am in love with my own sorrow. I am hurt so badly I want to die. But I also glamorize it; negligee and parfume are a distraction.

But I am not Lana.

I am not Sylvia.

I am just a girl making sense, I am just someone who collects death and beauty. I have to let it pass through me, all of those sad girls, before I can rid myself of it. I have to say, come in, come in, be a friend, be a muse. Let me clean my hands in you. Let me learn how to let it go. Let me watch you suffer. Let me watch you transcend the minutiae.

Let us be preternatural.

Let's walk into the garden.

I wear the mask and the reality. Only now, I understand that my words are a product of the intersection of the two. It is a place that lets me toil without killing me. It is a place I think the other sad girls sometimes go.

We can keep the gate hidden by vines.

GODS IN THE BLOOD: GABINO IGLESIAS

Marta places her elbows on the bar and waits for her beer. She loves how Jimmy, the bartender, miraculously hands her a cold one in a matter of seconds after her elbows hit the perennially damp, scratched wood of the bar. It's one of those little things that make life a tad more bearable.

The few broken souls that decorate the tables are like permanent fixtures. There's Angel, the retired construction worker with the bad leg who drinks and stares at the picture of his dead wife until someone offers him a ride home or the bar closes. On the booth next to Angel are Paquito and Max. Paquito is the cousin of Edgar, the owner. He sticks around so he can drink for free. Max is a huge fellow that came from Texas trying to start a business, lost everything at the casino the second night he was here, and simply stayed around doing odd jobs ever since. Paquito and Max are a couple, but they swear nobody knows. They come in everyday and drink away most of what Max has been able to earn painting houses, washing dishes, taking out the garbage of various businesses, mowing lawns, and washing cars. They are perpetual residents, like the tables and chairs, and that's why they've never requested Marta's services. For that, she has learned to love them. That love is the only thing keeping them alive.

As she finishes scanning the all-too-familiar surroundings, the heavy sameness that hangs in the hot air of the bar pushes down on her shoulders and Marta slumps a little over the bar. It's always the same folks on similar nights drinking their usual drinks at their regular tables. Always the same full ashtrays and the smell of spilled beer and stale piss. It's always the hunger, the inherited monster that lives insider her, the ache to feed on someone's *emi*...

It seems like this will be another one of those long, hot, lonely, boring nights when she doesn't make a penny and her thoughts take advantage of the empty hours to crawl into her head with their own painful agenda. Marta welcomes all of it. As the years pass by, the feeding becomes a more tedious task and the ghosts of those she's fed on scream louder insider her skull. Tedium makes the cacophony seems like the noise of an airplane's motor; something ever-present, but relatively easy to ignore. The feeling always makes her think of her favorite Sylvia Plath line:

> "From that pale mist
> Ghost swore to priest:
> 'There sits no higher court
> Than man's red heart.'"

Marta wonders if she ever knew how right she was.

Thinking about Woolf makes her momentarily contemplate suicide for the millionth time on her life, but she knows the idea is just like an old, familiar toy, more than a serious option.

Marta pushes the ludicrous thought of death out of her head. She's a strong-willed woman. She is something special and contains something insider her that is even more special than her. She will not succumb to negative feelings. She will keep on being strong. As always, the thought of strength brings her the one inevitable, recurrent memory, the one that pains her the most: Mami.

Whenever Mami comes back to her, whenever her memory insists on retelling the story of how they came to be apart, a strange thing happens: she's unable to remember it as an adult, from a mature perspective. Instead, her memories invariably carry a feeling of innocence, of things past and lost, of another time in which she was another person. Even the vocabulary with which she remembers things is somehow different from the one she uses now. It's simpler and straighter, somewhat pure and inexperienced. Marta can always feel the change, like a switch being thrown somewhere deep inside her head. The sounds of the bar dim, the light becomes unimportant, and the brain-movie of those early years begins to play.

Mami had been a typical strong Puerto Rican woman who had married a typical Puerto Rican macho. Marta's recollection of that odious figure she had been forced to call dad is vague: a stumbling figure moving around the house late at night, smelling like horses and rum, muttering hateful words all the time. He would beat Mami before sitting down with his old, discolored radio to listen to the afternoon news while drinking some more and cursing at everything around him.

Marta remembers him spitting on the floor and scratching violently. She remembers how she started going to bed earlier, sometimes when it was even light out, just to seek the comfortable silence of sleep, the sweet oblivion of unconsciousness, the magical bliss of contrived ignorance. But the sounds always woke her up. She never heard screams, just things being broken, callused hands striking soft flesh, and almost imperceptible gasps she knew were cries hiding under a thick cloak of shame. Sometimes she would hear the sound of a door slamming in a futile attempt at becoming an impassable barrier between Mami and the pain the evil, drunken man she was forced to call dad would bring upon her.

In the mornings, Marta would walk three miles to a shack in the outskirts of town where she learned how to read and write. The teacher's name was Gisela. She was a skeletal woman with pasty skin that came from a university somewhere. She was obsessed with teaching them how to read, write, and do basic math. Marta was very glad to have those hours away from home, her chores, and the drunken man. She was always carrying a book and kept them around the houses. Books in the kitchen, books in the bathroom, books in her tiny dresser, books in every corner. Mostly poetry by Sylvia Plath, Gwendolyn Brooks, and Anne Sexton. Mami would often close the book she was reading while preparing a meal or fixing one of the monster's shirts and shake it at Marta, telling her it was very important for her to get an education so that she could aspire to better things. Marta could never fathom what those better things could be.

Of the five kids that showed up to school regularly, only two were girls. Inevitably, they gravitated to each other. The other girl's name was Samantha. It struck Marta as an exotic name that came from some cleaner, faraway land. Mami had said it was a very white, expensive name. She said it with a note of sarcasm that escaped Marta until much later in life.

After months of being friends, Marta confessed to Samantha that she wanted her dad to die. Samantha told her to pray at night and ask baby Jesus for the things she most wanted. Samantha said her mom had told her that baby Jesus provides us with the things we need. She also told her to fear nothing because baby Jesus was in their lives and he would make sure nothing harmed them.

That day she went home and told Mami about baby Jesus. Mami took her into her bedroom and opened the top drawer of the only piece of furniture in the room. She pulled out a weird necklace she called a rosary and explained to her that she used to pray to baby Jesus before, but not anymore. "There are much better gods than Jesus, older gods who actually make things happen," Mami had said with a seriousness in her voice that she usually only used when talking to strangers. "These old gods live in your blood, mija. Los traes en la sangre. They don't want to you to pray on your knees; they want things they can use, not silly words. Soon I will help you meet them."

While she talked, Marta had looked at the rosary. The image at the end of it had struck her as strange. She brought out a necklace with round beads and a semi naked, skinny man hanging from a cross.

For three months Marta tried the praying thing in silence, not letting her mom listen to the prayers she had learned from her friend. She would go to bed and ask baby Jesus to kill the rum-breath beast as the sounds of pain and anger came from her mother's room.

Sadly, baby Jesus never answered. Her father kept at it. He abused her mother and seemed as healthy as ever despite the coughing and vomiting when he drank too much.

Marta told Samantha she thought maybe baby Jesus was deaf. That's when her friend explained that baby Jesus doesn't give favors away for free. Samantha told her maybe baby Jesus ignored her prayers because she didn't go to church. She was not a true Christian. Marta asked her to take her to church so her father would finally die.

Samantha took Marta to church the following Sunday. She told Mami she was going to a birthday party and asked her take her on the bus to Samantha's big house. From there, they got in a car with Samantha's parents and went to an old building that smelled like wet wood. Marta looked up and saw the skinny man from Mami's rosary everywhere. She learned when to kneel and when to rise, when to drop her head in silence and when to pray with all her fervor and ask for her father's demise.

By Monday, Mami knew she had gone to church. Someone had told her. She was angry. "What is it, mija?" Mami asked her. "What is it that you want so bad that you went to that place to ask a fake god for a favor?" Marta explained how she heard what went down every night. Snot ran down her face. A headache unlike any she'd ever head grasped her head in its sharp, strong talons. Sometime during her confession, Mami had also started crying. Then she apologized. "I thought you didn't know. I was sure that I'd managed to keep you from all of it. It's okay, mija. You will meet the gods in your blood soon."

That night Marta looked up at the sky one last time. She knew it was just a vast and empty darkness with nothing else inside it except silence and dead stars. There was no higher power that would make dad's heart pop or his hands go limp before he struck Mami again. Marta began to think that, if baby Jesus existed once, maybe they had crucified him when he grew up because he never did was he was asked to do.

The next night, just before the slaps and cries and abuse started, Mami knocked on Marta's door. "It's time, mijita, come with me."

Marta didn't know what was about to happen, but she took her mother's hand and followed her into her bedroom, that old, smelly room at the end of the house where all the bad stuff went down. Her father was sitting on the bed. "Stand up, Ramón," Mami said. The man looked at her. "Qué te pasa ahora, mujer…" He stood up. Mami walked up to him, lashed out with her right hand, and stepped back. Marta looked on in shock as her father's throat parted slowly and a thick crimson tide quickly began to flow from his slashed neck. She looked at her mother. She was smiling. She looked down at her mother's right hand. Her nails were two inches long, thicker than normal, and entirely black.

"Arrodíllate, mija," Mami said, helping her kneel.

Mami pressed her mouth against her father's mouth and inhaled. "Drink his *emi*." Marta didn't know what she was doing, but something deep insider her guided her actions. She pressed her mouth against her dying father's mouth and inhaled. A surge of energy shook her body. She felt simultaneously hot and cold. She felt stronger, happier, more secure of herself.

After the body on the floor hadn't moved or made a noise for more than ten minutes, Mami ran a knife across the open wound and then placed it in its hand. Then she went to the phone and called an ambulance, crying hysterically and saying her husband had hurt himself.

No one asked any questions. No one bothered them. No one cared that the old drunk was dead. Marta and her mother carried on and never talked about what had happened.

A few years later, Marta would wake up thirsty, but it was a strange thirst that didn't go away regardless of how many glasses of water she drank. The thirst was deeper, stronger than anything she had ever known. Her brain would show her pictures of her father, squirming weakly on the floor. She understood without having to ask her mother: she needed someone's *emi* inside her.

Mami and she spent hours talking on the porch. They were planning to get enough money together to send her to a real school, one of the big ones in town where kids wore shoes and everyone sang songs in the morning. After all, Marta was 14, and Mami said a young woman needs an education if she's to go places.

Marta kept her thirsty nights from Mami, but they were driving her mad. She wasn't sleeping and she struggled to stay focused on things. She would feel a tingling warmth between her legs and in her head and in the center of her chest. When that happened, her nails would grow out, becoming black.

On her way home from the market one Sunday afternoon, one of the youngsters from Marta's barrio saw her walking to her house with a couple of bags of food. He started helping her. With all the bags in the kitchen, Marta had turned to the guy and, without thinking about it, lashed out. Mami walked in halfway through her feeding and told her to finish.

The conversation that followed was the hardest one Marta had ever had to endure. Mami told her she sometimes had to leave the house to feed in the middle of the night and that, for years, there had been rumors about her. Now, with a dead boy in her kitchen before sundown, things were only going to get worse. There was only one way to save Marta from all that would follow: she was going to move in with her Uncle Silvio.

Uncle Silvio was Mami's only brother. He had moved to New York in the 1950s and eventually became a restaurant owner. The morning after she fed on the neighbor's *emi*, Marta learned she had a job and a house waiting for her in New York. She was going to eat three meals a day and probably get an education. Uncle Silvio had even paid for her ticket and would pick her up at the airport when she arrived. Mami said he has a special trick to keep the thirst away. Then she gave her a book by Sylvia Plath and, with a sideways smile, her rosary. They were the first things Marta place on her pile of things to take.

Marta packed every piece of clothing she had in a small valise that Doña Raquel gave her and got on a bus not unlike the one she had taken to school. Mami cried a lot and so did she. They hugged every few seconds while waiting for the bus to come. Then she stepped inside the bus and said "Ay, mijita, lo siento…" and cried some more. She just said "Te quiero, Mami," which was the most difficult thing to do in all her life up to that moment, not because she didn't love her mother, she loved her more than anything, but because what she really wanted to say was: "Mami, yo no quiero irme." Then the driver told her to put her things away and take a seat. Marta obeyed, just like she knew she simply had to obey Mami on this.

As she rode the bus to the airport she couldn't come to terms with her mixed emotions. She was leaving Mami, but a new life awaited her somewhere else, a life that was allegedly much better than the one she had known until then, a life in which maybe she could be a little bit more of the thing that was inside her.

She'd had no idea of the massive amount of people that took to the skies every day. The sheer size of the airport scared her and at one point Marta felt like she would never be able to find the gate from which her plane was departing. Once inside the metallic bird, she noticed it was similar to the inside of the bus, only rounder and more uncomfortable.

After what felt like a whole day without sleeping, the plane bumped a few times and made a dreadful noise that came from everywhere at once. Once the thing had stopped, the man that talked to them through the roof gave them permission to get their things. She collected her suitcase and walked out. She had never felt so lost.

A man with a never-ending forehead and a thick mustache was standing outside, very close to the door, completely dressed in white, with colorful beads around his neck. He was holding a rough piece of carton that said "Marta Vázquez" on it. She approached the man and he hugged her. He smelled like cooking oil and fresh bread. It was all very strange, but uncle Silvio had a warm smile and he seemed to be the only one around that spoke Spanish. He had a car and he asked a lot of questions while he drove. He wanted to know about Mami and about how far Marta had gone in school. He said she was going to learn the language pretty soon and, after a few minutes of silence, spoke of her dad for the first and only time: "No te preocupes por tu mamá, ella va a estar bien. Me alegro de que finalmente se encargara de el hijo de puta de tu papá." She knew he was right. Mami was definitely better now that her father was dead, but she still worried about her, out there at night, desperately trying to become a shadow while feeding.

The tall buildings and the crazy amount of cars scared her, but uncle Silvio kept reassuring her that it would all be fine. He was going to take care of her.

They finally parked on a busy street and uncle Silvio carried her bag up some stairs and opened a door to show her in. He lived in small apartment on top of his restaurant. A very dark lady came out of the kitchen and stretched out her hand, smiling. "Hola, Marta, I going to show you all the language," she had said. The woman's name was Sonia and she was uncle Silvio's beautiful and round Dominican wife. She took care of the kitchen in the restaurant and had sad, deep-set eyes that contrasted with her wide and constant smile. Sonia reminded her of Mami.

They sat down and had some sancocho without much conversation. Later she took a shower in a very small bathroom. After her shower, Sonia led her to the couch that she'd arranged for her to sleep on.

After a long, sleepless night, Sonia woke her up when it was still dark outside and told her to shower again and get dressed. They had a glass of milk each and half an hour later they walked downstairs. Sonia started teaching her the chores she was expected to do around the restaurant as soon as it opened a few hours later.

The next few months went by in a hurry. A week after her arrival, uncle Silvio had given her a white dressed and told her to put it on. Then he had taken her to a tiny room in the back. There were paintings on the walls and the floor and candles along the walls. He said he was going to speak to the gods in her blood, to offer them fruit and rum and the blood of a few animals. This, he said, would keep the thirst at bay. Soon after uncle Silvio started talking in a strange language, Marta lost consciousness. Whatever was inside her had come out to talk to Silvio. When she finally woke up, uncle Silvio told her to take it easy for a while, maybe go to her room and read from her "sad book," which is what she had started calling the Plath book.

A few more months went by and, before realizing it, Marta was peeling potatoes, frying bacon, beating eggs, learning how to make sancocho and mofongo and taking orders from customers at the tables. The climate started to change and she got to know what being cold meant. Uncle Silvio took her to a store that sold secondhand coats and paid for two coats, three shirts and some new jeans for her...

Marta feels a tap on her shoulders and travels from her past to her present in less than a second. She turns around and sees Edgar, the owner. He asks her if she's okay with a curious smile on his face. She throws a distracted "yes" back at him and he moves on. She takes a sip of her beer. The lukewarm bitterness of the cheap drink tickles her throat and she can feel the alcohol reaching for her eyes. She suddenly realizes it's not the beer. She's tearing up, dancing a senseless dance on the threshold of crying. She refuses to do so. It would send down her cheeks an hour and a half worth of hard work and good makeup. She clears her throat and takes a deep breath. Wasting her money and ruining her fake face is not a loss she can afford so early in the night. The thought of what could happen if she lost her face sends her a little further down the road to depression, a little edge she's been walking on for what feels like a lifetime.

She takes another mouthful of tepid beer and sits up a little straighter on her stool. She pushes her chest out. A john has just walked in. He's not one of the regulars. As always, the potential client looks around as if searching for someone. It's a little trick men use to cover up their nervousness. Marta finds it awkward and vulgar. The john walks up to the bar with a pathetic macho strut that screams out that he feels uncomfortable and scared. He asks Jimmy for a beer, pays for it, and sits down at the end of the bar, next to the old red jukebox. The machine is blaring out a song from the Mamas and the Papas and the john taps rhythmically on his thigh and nods every once in a while. Marta hates old songs, but it's all part of the agreement they worked out with Edgar to keep everyone satisfied. Rubén Blades and Hank Williams coexist with Elvis Presley and El Gran Combo, the Mamas and the Papas take turns with La Sonora Matancera and Janis Joplin screams after Roberto Roena gets tired of beating the crap out of his bongó.

Marta tries to make eye contact with the scared john but she can see that he already has his eyes nailed on Karen, a 27-year-old Dominican with big brown eyes and soft mocha skin that she bathes daily in baby oil. Karen seems to have noticed and gets up to go to the bathroom in order to give the john a perfect view of her amazing gravity-defying derrière. The john shoots red laser beams her way. They fall right on her voluptuous ass. Marta can already see him promising Karen to get her out of here before giving her some money and going home to his wife and kids with the image of that caramel heart-shaped Caribbean booty burned in his mind for the rest of his sad, routine-plagued days. She hopes Karen gets to entertain the john for a few hours. The bar will be all hers if she does. When the hot kitty is away, the slightly older, less perky mice will play.

Karen comes out of the bathroom, sits back down on her stool and crosses her legs in slow motion. Marta thinks about how the number of clients she's able to get in one night is direct negative correlation to her age. Lately all the new clients, and even some of her regulars, go with Karen or Diane. Her hardcore regulars and a few random walk-ins when she's the only one left is all she gets. She understands that the johns prefer the supple and tight ignorance of the new girls instead of her saggy experience and motherly tenderness. She feels really sorry for the new generations. They all ignore that an ass chock-full of cellulite hides life's secrets while perky baby-smooth cheeks are the temple of attitude and uninformed immaturity. It doesn't make her sad, if there's one thing she has learned in her life is that, when it comes to beauty, the truth is often considered a turd on a stick.

The john finally summons up all his courage and moves to the stool next to Karen. She smiles coyly and Marta knows it's a done deal. She breathes out and relaxes her tummy. No need to keep up the uncomfortable posture just for the regulars.

A few minutes later the man gets up and follows Karen. She sends Marta a smile form the door that says, "Look on the bright side, the next one's all yours." The door closes behind them and doesn't open again for about fifteen minutes.

When the door opens again, David walks in. Marta recalls it's the 3rd of the month, the day David gets his retirement check. He walks to the bar and greets Jimmy. Then he walks up to her and kisses her on the cheek.

"How are you today, Anita?" He has been calling her Anita since she can remember.

"I'm doing well, David. How are you?"

"Well, I was sitting at home and there was nothing on the television so I thought I'd pay you a visit." The man has to be close to eighty and his smell reminds her of that constantly. He's one of the only three or four clients that she takes care of in the little apartment she has just above the bar. There's no way in hell he can afford a motel and she can imagine his living quarters all too well. She wants nothing to do with yellowed newspapers on every table, scant lightning, a television always on to drown out the terrible silence, a phone that never rings, a dirty toilette with a thick shit-ring all around it, a collection of dried moth and fly carcasses under every window, a dark couch that has served as the final resting place for his hair for the past three decades, a few scattered pictures of his dead wife and his military son, an empty fridge that hums way too loudly and a small plastic radio that keeps him alive when the electricity dies and the television that keeps him all alone.

"That's very nice of you, David. Would you like to go upstairs and have a drink with me?"

"Oh, sure, that would be very nice." He always gives the same reply.

They walk up the rickety wooden stairs that start near the bathroom on the left side of the bar and they don't speak at all until she has opened the door to her little studio apartment and they're both sitting down on her couch.

"What would you like to drink?"

"Do you have any grape juice?" He asks.

"I think I have some. I'll go check." That's her standard reply. They've been doing the same song and dance for close to a year. Marta walks to the fridge and opens it. The grape juice she keeps for David is toward the back, next to her eggs and a few yogurts. He always asks for the same.

They chat for a while and, as always, he finally cries, says he feels really lonely and only wants to be held. She turns on her TV. A video is playing. A young woman in a beautiful gown is singing. There's a helicopter. The young woman suddenly has a machine-gun. Her voice is beautiful. Marta wishes she looked like that and sounded like that. While looking at the beautiful songstress, she gets naked. He, as always, remains clothed. Then she takes him by the hand and they climb into bed. He buries his face between her breasts and is snoring loudly in no time. Marta looks at the watch on her bedside table: 11:24 p.m. She will wake him up around midnight, get dressed and head back downstairs to work for another couple of hours. Then the hunger starts, the deep thirst that is all she can think about.

Uncle Silvio died in a car accident before showing her how to keep the gods in her blood under control. Since then, this is her life: johns and moving around too much and cultivating relationships that end badly for someone. This time, David is the victim. She's been asking questions for close to a year, but by now she knows no one will be too surprised if he died in her bed. She places a pillow over the old man's face and presses down. He doesn't struggle much. She looks at the TV while he twitches a bit. The lady's name is Lana Del Rey, it says on the corner of the TV. She likes that name. She likes her face.

She wonders if she has gods in her blood, too.

Marta feeds on the old man's *emi* and decides to call the cops in the morning, after she gets a good night's rest. Out in the streets below her window, someone screams violently. It happens every night. She stares at the slow-turning ceiling fan over the bed and closes her eyes. Satisfied, the gods in her blood dictate the rhythm of her heartbeat with the drums, and soothe her with their ageless, eternal song.

THE LAND OF OTHER: FARAH ROSE SMITH

It began with a pull of the heart into lands unknown. After a period of unrest, when a flickering of muscles descended into a tiring ache, I awoke to find my higher self staring at me from across a distant plain. An imprint of an earlier life, reflected in form and function beyond the veil of some perilous Afterworld. I took in sights through sunken eyes, where senses scattered like so many pebbles on the breathing shore. There was no dignity in this, though it came with a sense of awareness, often reserved for newly fragmented minds. Delights descended into the cold illuminated waters. I succumbed to the peril of the gale overhead. The floating glory opened up to me in that moment and dissolved, like morning mist. One really can venture out too early before sunrise. In that way, I hold a never-ending regret. There are no sights free from the garnish of torment. Not anymore. No sweetness free from the grip of the ice, choking me with the burden of these remembrances.

The Doctor serves as an earthly foil in this labyrinth of mourning. I tell him to take my blood and he resists, like the other clever emissaries of his profession, so attuned to modernity that they forget the methods of their predecessors. When blood drips from my arm, I feel my son floating in the distance. Would they drain me of all, I may even see him breathe. He didn't understand that this room was not a place of healing. That there are no such places

—or fish, or men, or the worms beneath—or me. That there was little hope, in any fashion, of returning to that precious former life.

The aging doctor has flown from the tarnished pages of elder collections. He has that look of playful deceit in him. He isn't without humor, though I scarcely listen. If I dare to, I will surely turn to a deeper madness. When in an exile in the mind, essential learning often includes the muting of voices in that way. To avoid the onslaught of some sick and grinding anger, that others may live around me in a lesser horror. That blindness, shaken from me by the pitfalls of a dreadful life, does not go unmissed.

I tried to explain to them the meaning of it all, but only murmurs fell out. My nostrils flared, taking in the sweet but useless fragrance of Spring. "There," they said. "Her senses are in order." Not knowing how pronounced they had become. Not knowing the torment of their persistence. I hate the smells. The sounds. Everything that touches my eyes and mind in this oppression.

Something lit up the trees. I can see it from my place by the window. An electric pulse, flashing over the leaves, igniting them – flickering embers of ivory and grey spitting out over the road. These are the living things, neglected by my former mind. How I long for their absence.

I remember nothing of the slide. Nothing of screaming wheels, or broken glass. Nothing of the coldness in the water. There were no sirens, or seraph songs. Only blackness from the bitter corners of my mind. Some would be thankful for the absence of thought in such a place. It became only another pain for me. I am without him now, and without the memory of his loss. Not permitted to see his body, as he had been interred by the time of my waking. These are the misfortunes woven for me.

It had been an age since I'd last seen the horse. A crooked white stallion with wavering legs, long dead and buried on the island off of the coast. They'd shipped him off after retirement, as they did with all tiring beasts. My morning thoughts wandered to the old shore. Memories are rarely provoked without reason, and this was no different. The upstairs hallway was thick with the smell of him. Hay, hair, and dirt from the stable hit my nostrils as soon as the bedroom door opened.

The old beast was making his spirit rounds, I was sure of it. Images swam through my head, decorating the hall with the length and breadth of the great stallion. He would have been a snug fit in the narrow space, with hooves clopping on the tarnished wood and either eyelid grazing the golden walls. I thought it fair to yearn for the shore we found together. Perhaps it might have been a novelty for Oliver to see the waves from that place. The smell came as a comfort. One in a silent row of moments we sometimes long for. Those that arrive before or after some great upheaval, like a calling card from lands beyond logic. I never believed in such things. Not with my old mind.

Oliver despised beaches. His only memory had been the dreadful scurrying of bugs in the granules between his toes. They set off a creeping panic that he had not yet forgotten. It took a great deal of convincing for him to accompany me to the old shore that morning. Ice cream and the attendance of several toys strewn about the back seat. That, and the repetitive telling of his favorite rhymes, though I sensed he still couldn't understand them.

In retrospect, I could have examined the odorous hallucination. Logic is latent in the early hours for some, and I'd had a night devoid of rest. I might have noticed the window left open a crack and wondered if an unkempt vehicle had gone by. Or street sweepers—the most likely scenario—though I didn't hear the hammering of those engines at any hour. Did the damned horse matter so much that I had to wake him?

Few venture out to take in the sights of a winter ocean, though these were the times I found myself, in earlier years, galloping atop the old stallion from cove to cove. Oliver hesitated, watching winds blow sand off of the dunes. I picked him up and carried him onto the beach. Soft gray granules, unusually large when one thinks of sand. Like cane sugar, tinted by the reflection of the overcast sky. The water shared this hue, without the ebb and flow of waves to break the palette. This was decidedly not the way I'd remembered it.

What are oceans without waves, but canvases of defeat? I didn't see it in such a way then. Oliver looked out to the horizon. Discomfort surged through him. He held on tighter to my chest as I shifted. I thought of the old horse again as the expanse of the shore came into view. I'd imagined the beast roaming there, and of his life on the island several times over the years. The white coat of his youth faded into ivory, at home in the high grass and salty air.

I'd known a rider or two who paid visits to their steeds after retirement, but never felt compelled myself. Why? I figured the old horse was sick of me. I'd taken him by one to many hornets' nests and snake pits in my day. The old beast seemed relieved, the day they loaded him up into the truck and hauled him down the street to the ferry. I knew I'd miss him, but it wasn't as though they were shipping him down to the butcher for stew meat. He'd have a good life out there. In a place, deep down, I knew I'd never see.

The waters were so still. Unsettling to the point of birthing an uncanny rumbling in the gut. I held my son in my arms, taking in the smell of salt. It had the look of a storm's premeditation. Dark grey clouds loomed on high over the farthest reaches of the sea. Oliver turned his head stiffly, looking out to the horizon. His heart pumped heavily and I felt it through mine.

I'd had my tastes of floating shadows over harbors in that town. Those of the heart and the mind. Seeing was another thing entirely. My eyes were once watchers of sterile valleys and subtle cries. Not the twisted abhorrence of a primordial earth.

Oliver gripped my neck, not remembering the wound of worlds pulsating there. I dropped him in the sand. Sea foam flowed through his boots. Gloom churned inside of me. He wailed – more so than in any season of retribution that had come to him. He shuddered. I bent down to lift him up, cradling him close to my chest.

"Will you take me home now?" His eyes were wide, like one who has seen something untimely and rotten in an ill-fated distance. The nostalgia had been enough for me. I carried him away without glancing back at the sea, or the darkening skies above.

Mother, father, aunts and uncles hover over me like a vat of flies, always aching. A breathing pustule, living, without life. I struggle to sit up, to the dismay of seeing every hand held up against me. They don't want me to try. "There is no honor here," they are saying. "No dignity in this defeat."

I sit weakly, warring with my brain in a loathsome time-after-matter. My mind sits on an elevated platter, above the somber plain. This is the first stop towards the Land of Other. The gift of the senses to that unknown, endless realm.

It watches on, even now.

That gentle stirring of a familiar world lives on in me, but I am betrayed by these wistful images. I knew them once, though long has passed. Of water-bleeding skies and scarcely hidden rays. Of differences which made us all ashamed. I could sing a song of passing to the light, but there are no ghosts here. Only cruel shapes, draped in blackness, mingling at the edges of my eyes. They've been around since sanity's fall. Since the error that ripped me back into this detachment. I call out into my own oblivion, a vault of tired silences. Might these shadows make a meal of me and sweep my hands from ground to sky?

It'll never make sense to my mind. Not the way it sees now. Not the way it remembers. The pit of blackness remains, as dense and unyielding as it was the first time I tried to think back. But, there is something. A thick, penetrating whir—the sound of the raging deep.

The greater fear, living outside of the shame of this, is the idea that I will someday remember. That out like the flight of birds from some crippled birch, there will be everything, strewn out before my eyes. A canvas of horror, untimely in its arrival and altogether maddening. I can see myself there, consumed by the final breaking of the lucid plane. Words will come out in dribbles of spit, mopped up by whichever poor soul is tending to me at the time.

———

His father hadn't the stomach for insular burdens. He called me Asphodel, like Brönte, only for the pain of knowing. The child was mine in blood and in duty. In this, there was no regret. Only a silent sadness for a boy without a father to hold dear. This is not a world for such a loss. I would have thought the man better than all that. On the morning of the accident, my neck still bore the hollows of his hands. There are fears hidden in the hearts of aging men, more unstable in their dreams than the young. There were no vows, no declarations between us. Only careless passion in unconsecrated beds. There are shameful acts in this age of glass, but these acts leave only a faint imprint on my heart. They gave me the gift of eternity, and the strength of knowing when one must leave. In this, regret was an unnecessary expense.

I miss him in the thoughtless hours of aching, but it is the most subtle of my pains. He'd remembered the trinkets of my desire. Gentle potions of lemon and ice, blue roses, black orchids, timeless books, and gentle touches to those ugly places inside that birthed a long-sought stillness. I will only have the memory of that passion. Only one kind of love lasts on earth, and it doesn't manifest in brutal marks upon the body.

How does one describe a state of longing for the world in which they live, as though it were eons past the final desecration? When toes are jammed in sands of the present-day and the sun burns on overhead? The first sensation of the Afterworld was the onslaught of a side-swept gravity. Unable to stand or step by earthly measures, collapse took the place of wobbling.

I began to see the world as he had seen it. Senses gave way to a glitch-laden abhorrence in the eyes, ears, nose, and mouth. Light rays swooped down like falcons over a shadow of the deepest shade. The formless chaos, watching from the Land of Other. This world after death, after destruction of the mind. In these days of retirement, I hope to find the door above to other kinds of silence. A gateway. A place entirely different from the abhorrent wash of tragic life. The Afterworld is here, not there. This must be understood. These visions of torment rely on the burdens of earthly eyes. On the dreadful cadences of a ruined brain. The Land of Other is another world entire—exalted and eternal.

I remember hills of gray on the horizon. The call of tyrants young and old, descending. We think of a division of placement after the dark pull. Directions, held in polarity, as we think of good and evil. I think rather of a Captain's wheel, steering through a boundless sea. There is no direction in which there is no destination. No place bound by duality. A betrayal of omens shocks them, on the brittle earth. They know not the Land of Other. A land that is no land at all. A oneness that is a multitude.

In the dawning hours of my predicament, I looked for my son. In the shadows of the distant plain, I felt him wandering. How I fear these unknown worlds. In those times of watching and wondering, a creeping revilement caught inside of me. Shame has wings that fly out to the darkened skies, telling dwellers of our black and earthly gales. There is no love like love with doom above us. I would penetrate the sky with arrows, bleeding the guardians of the Afterworld. Lifting the veil from rock to rock, or cloud to cloud if only to know that he does not linger there alone.

I sat with him in circles, on the porch, bleeding yellow jackets from the rickety banister. Rocking him on my knee, singing songs of cheer in the dying season. This would be my strongest memory of him, had I not learned the unpleasantness of the addled mind. The post-apocalypse in bloom; my organs, shutting into a rotting phase of limitation. Something he had known all his life, but I had no idea of it. He had received the rejections inherent to such a being. The stares and taunts. The sickening judgments of man, given only to those unfit for lives of tradition and conformity. I protected him the best I could from all of that. There is no horror like hateful eyes upon that which is yours.

I look around my bedroom and all I see is rupture. Decay put on hold for me, waiting until I get out of bed to collapse in a pile of dust. My swollen feet stick out from beneath the lining of the comforter in yellow lace. The bureaus are a similar muted yellow, delicate and ornamental in their design. Not unlike the décor of affluent girls, chosen by their mothers in preparation for their inevitable arrival on society. We were no such family. Every piece was inherited from the street, though we made no note of it.

They've removed the photos of him from the bureau. The closet is shut, so I know nothing of the contents. If they remain, or were sold to afford my convalescence. My sore attempt at rising resulted in a comical stumbling. A humiliating feat for anyone at this age. I am not as I was in the womb—human, or altogether assimilated. My brain grips the eons of a strange, infirm ever after. I will not be without it now.

The perilous Afterworld becomes me. I am its fate and it is mine. The whistling whirs, the purity of time falls to ash. I am the bringer of such brokenness. I am the deceiver of such days, Godless in this sea of static. No enchantment leaves my lips without severity. I would fling insults at the skies, should I not fear the locking of the door. I would surrender myself, bodiless, to the wars of a thousand worlds. The gaping wound, my heart, enveloped in a gossamer glow. The pains began to leave me, and I knew I loved them. They were all I had of my son within my grasp.

Is there enough of him in me for them to let me through? If I am as he is, vulnerable, gentle, willing? Thrust before the door to be taken or left? Would I see him reeling in the distance? Would I see myself in his eyes ever again?

The first steps are the heaviest, and as ungainly as in youth. I wonder if the shadow watches as I pull myself up from the ground. I had the strength to hold a book today. To turn three pages without help. This is a new luxury.

With healing comes clearer memories of these bleak days. On the first day of my waking, I was carried into the house by two. Bodies shuffled around me, tending to my every need, though none had been asked. I was voiceless for a time. In those first hours in the protection of what had once been sanctuary, I cowered under a floating blackness, hovering over the window facing the road. When I dared to look at it directly, a blinding light flashed. With a shrill crackling, the shadow was absorbed by the world, as one might see a tissue slide off of a table. I am not without the feeling of these watchers now.

If flames were to ignite the distant sea, would this torment fall to the eternal blackness? Might I wander aimlessly in the horror between worlds? Permit me to the Land of Other, in pieces. The part of me beyond the veil lives on. I see it there, beside him, in the shadows.

There, where toothy blossoms grow, and blue trees bow to touch the earth in secret places. Where hearts grow as soft as flowers inside every breeze. Where spirits kiss to kill the wounds of earth. Heal his wretched ailment there, before myself. Cleanse the spray of poison from his veins.

A thousand visions fill my bones with aching. A thousand voices breathe into my mind. Here I stand petrified before the twisting gorge, torch in hand and held to spirits, without means to measure time or torment.

If it is guilt that brings us to the door, then what might open it, but the hope of absolution? We are such creatures, still. Warring in mind and body, thirsting for the drink of eternal forgiveness. There are those who would seek nonconformity, or abnormality, as a decorative veil. It is these I wholeheartedly wish to avoid. They don't know the grip of the Afterworld, or the manner in which the parallels sway. In the twilight hours of my ruin, shadows grew in rooms beyond living vision. The majesty of the ethereal footman. The mysteries of men without flesh. This new and abhorrent earth after loss. With arms outstretched to skies of red, out to the higher world. The place where these hands, these eyes, this mind may come to a living rest. This is the song I will sing as I fly out of the shadow place.

I find myself endlessly afflicted. Of domestic duties done and accounted, I am the failing mother. I could not digest toadstools like honey. I did not want to live in the shadow of his exit, but even in this, there is a frail rebirth at hand.

"You can throw a pearl ten fathoms deep," the Doctor said. "It will not return to the mouth of its mother. Down, down it will be cast, into the crevice, illuminated only by the angler's lamp."

I lean back in the agony of hearing, in the glow of the northern window. My deep red hair falls to my sides. Seemingly unnatural in shade, but the shade of my birth, nonetheless. Stray sands glow copper in the faint light bleeding through. This doesn't bother my eyes. It is subtle enough—a delicate glow, reminding me of the onslaught of days. In these cruel months, I found my only hope in the strange shapes of light dancing on the window sill. Doubts as to my healing melted there, like so many waves left behind lessening storms. The Doctor, satisfied with my progress, packs his bag for the final time. "You will heal completely, young lady. Whether you want to or not."

Today was made for walking, and the silent crawl. I can shuffle my way around now, and thusly, have led myself down the slope of the garden to the patch of tiger lilies. All have shriveled to nothing in the August heat, save for one in brilliant bloom. With eyes struggling to adjust and my scalp beating from the rays, I touch the petals as though they are the first of earth.

Fighting the urge to pull off each finger, planting them in the soil so that one, through flesh extended, may he grow back to live as he lived. The sun on my head is death. Death, unbridled, unhinged, beating. I stand tall in the onslaught of the rays. The dark pull to the endless night carries on. I return wearily to my confinement, without defeat. I have seen and I have felt the rays again without succumbing, and this was glory enough. Tonight I will sleep, and I will sleep in peace for the first time.

It's here now, gliding towards me in the gilded pre-dawn. The world at the stage of breaking—underwater, frigid, and real. That is the most gripping part. The authenticity, as though I had lived and breathed it all in full awareness, never having forgotten a detail. Logic plays with me in this, I know. There are regrets interwoven in this realization.

An aggravation that only I will ever truly understand.

My hands still gripped the steering wheel. The bones of my fingers jutted out like the metal armatures of those too-tall buildings that leave us without light. The fragments locked my hands in place. Scarlet waters mixed with the eternal blue, surging forward amid glass through the shattered windows. In part, from wherever my head had been torn open by the crumpled metal. The greater portion of blood—that of a body, entire—came from the back seat.

Survivors of great horror often speak of the angst, the apprehension, the instinct within that warned them of their impending experience. They wade into the story with descriptions about the sights and sounds, and with maddening optimism, spin it in some way so maybe even they can handle reliving it all. Am I guilty of this? Without question. But of this moment that was hidden from me for a time, of the progression of horror within seconds in a descending tomb, I have neither the will nor energy to describe. I will say only this: that in the twilight of your doom, when that apprehension kicks in and the tolling bells bear down upon your senses, I hope that you will be spared the remembrance. I will not speak of him as he was in that moment. I will not speak of that moment in time ever again.

I grip the white fence, flakes of aging paint crackling in my palms. The sun is bright; an oppression, still. Even in this, there is a seed of becoming.

The Land of Other beckons. I am not ready. I'll stand in the light until then, in wait of a distant shadow. It is all more bearable now. In a simple dream of quiet oceans in the sky, I will wash ashore. To each hand drawn upward in refusal of my way in, demanding I fall back, I will bury a laugh beneath my breast. There may be no honor here—but there will be.

SAD GIRL: MONIQUE QUINTANA

The story of the Sad Girl tattoo goes like this. When I was a kid, I was in love with a boy who lived down the street from me. It was 1997. His dad had a tattoo shop in the Tower District, and he was teaching his son at home in secret. His apprentice. The boy was a teenage prince with a buzzed head on the side and long black hair on top and khaki pants with his last name initial on his belt buckle.

On many summer nights, I floated my way down the street to their basement. My favorite nights to do this were Sunday nights, when the Art Laboe show was playing on the radio. His father had him tattooing on tiny fetal pigs. I asked him once where his father got the pigs from, but he didn't know. It took me a long time to get used to seeing the little pigs, but after awhile they began to look peaceful to me, like they were just sleeping.

One night, the boy tattooed a pig with a cluster of misshapen stars. I leaned over his shoulder as he did this. I moved in closer to smell the pomade in his hair, and I touched his shoulder, the tattoo pen still steady on the smooth pink skin of the piglet's stomach, and then I moved in even closer and wrapped my arms around his shoulder and lightly brushed my blood red acrylic nails on his neck. His hands remained steady on the animal. I kissed him all over his neck like a fevered butterfly.

The basement smelled like rust and gas and oil, but I could smell the lingering bits of his drugstore cologne. He smelled like bright blue soap. He put the tattoo gun down with the utmost precision and them grabbed me by the wrist, running his thumbs over the translucent skin there, the veins of my wrist going to nowhere but him.

Do you want me to give you a tattoo? he asked me.

He pulled my hair away from my shoulder and somewhere in the house, I could hear someone gathering ice from the icebox, the small chips of water making their clink in an empty glass, and I could feel the clink reverberate in my wrist.

But where would I put it? I asked him. I felt my voice quiver like little bird hiding in its' nest.

He cupped his hand over my left shoulder, at the very top, as if he could feel the bone beneath.

If you put it here, then you can hide it, when you don't want no one to see it.

I returned to his house the next day and by that time I knew exactly what kind of tattoo I wanted. It would be a simple thing. A cliché thing. I'd get Sad Girl in Old English because everyone always said that my face looked sad. It had been here and there like a floating balloon that some child had accidentally let go of. I knew it didn't make any sense, and that's why I wanted to do it. I thought that maybe I could talk him into putting an old-fashioned perfume bottle with lacy trim to go with it. I cut a picture that I had found in an old paper doll book, so I could show him exactly what I wanted. When the needle buzzed alive like a hatchling bird on my skin, it felt good.

I had felt a certain kind of pain like that. I had just started going to Planned Parenthood to get birth control shots and that particular place, that shoulder cap, had grown friendly with the pain, the pinch, the sting. But unlike those shots, which shot me with the antidote to life, this needle was filled with an even more friendly kind of venom. I felt honored to have him staining my skin like this, his slender fingers making it forever, not like the transient way when he put his fingers inside me, inside my body. This kind of ink would drum and then echo more that I would know. After a moment, I heard the fall of his father's presence.

His father's shadow bloomed before us, and all we could do was look back at him. He asked him what he was doing and he set down the tattoo gun, and it began to rattle on the dirty tabletop. His father asked again and again and then he grabbed his son and threw him against the wall, and he looked as if he was a bird pierced there amongst the rust and the tools, flesh amongst mechanical things. He was my bruised prince and then his head began to bleed, the tattoo gun still humming on the table.

The screeching of his father's tires were the last boom and echo in that house. I took Nicky by the hand and led him to the bathroom where I ran the water in the sink, the mirror fogging up with mist. There weren't any clean towels there, so he gave me his white tank top, and I ripped it to make a rag and held it under the water until it was warm and wet and felt good in my hands, and I wrapped it around my fingers like it was lace and touched it to the hurt in his head. The blood made a tiny pool in his black hair and then on the thin white cloth like a cloud or a flower with buds, growing haphazardly from its garden of cotton and bleach.

He turned around and touched my shoulder blade, and the memory of it, the sore ink shock of something only half-way done came back to me, and I shivered, despite the mist. The pale green tiles from the countertop felt cold at my fingertips, but I could feel the sweat on my neck shaking down the small of my back. It was still summer after all, and the heat still hung in the air like the blades and knives in the basement below, his father's possessions like bones without their body. Nicky was something else entirely. Nicky looked at me like my eyes were made of glass, the band of blood still adorned my knuckles like gloves with their fingers cut off. He kissed me, his mouth shaking and tugged my hair softly, like there was a bell somewhere inside of me that was about to ring.

He told me he would go to the clinic in the morning, but for now, all he had was me. He wanted to shave off his hair, and I told him that he didn't have to, but he insisted, quietly, but urgently, his mouth still a shaking, a murmur on mine, his shoulders thick and waiting in the frame of the mirror. I wanted to turn him small and push him inside the mirror and tell him to come back to me when it was safe to, but he needed to be there, a flower stem sprouting and shaking out of that bathroom floor.

He shut off the water and handed me the razor from behind his shoulder like a candle or a sheet of prayer. I pulled the machine buzz along the center of his head, watching his face in the mirror, his lids closed and slanted as if in sleep, but his mouth pulled tight, a dark brown color I had never seen on him before. I traced lines on his head with my eyes and the blade beneath the blood wrapped on my knuckles. He took my wrist and pointed to a phone book on the bathroom floor, its cover tattered from water like rain. He told me to stand on it, so that I could reach him. His hair fell to his shoulders and to the dark nook of his arms, and fell to his feet and the seams of the floor, the linoleum yellowed and speckled with dirt. I switched off the blade and set it at the sink like it was the moon. Nicky put his mouth on mine, particles of hair in between our tongues like stars.

I was trying to find us in the mist of the mirror that was falling away like smoke. No pomade at his ear, no black song at his temples. Instead there was the pull of his hand, the unwinding of the fabric on my hand, the doing away with it, its falling of boy stained ribbon. He unzipped my shorts and put his hand inside, trying to undo the small folds of me, like fingers in a paper fan, spinning away, my body crushed against the cold sink, and my shorts fell around my thighs in an orb, him inside me, shaking, his mouth on mine, shaking, my hand on his shoulder blade, my crush against his body, I touched my hand to my mouth, the blood dry and salty and warm with his sweat, sweet from the mist that had fallen from his head like a spray of flower buds, and he kept saying he wanted to leave, his voice in the rhythm of my skin and bones, and the blood running through my pinks and legs, the paper fan still beating against him. He wanted to run away and be with me, and I ran my hand along the buzz of his head.

I stole him way in his father's '64 Chevy Malibu. It was blue. We packed his clothes in a duffel bag and drove away from his house, into the soft lights of the street. I thought the sky was the same pink shade of an abalone shell turned out. It's insides exposed, patchy sky resisting the drop of night. We knew the night pulling its window shade could only be good for us. Nicky wanted to go to a drive-in movie theater, so that we could collect our thoughts, and we could figure out what we wanted to do. We had a stack of cash and his father's favorite tattoo gun asleep in his bag. It was retro movie night, and there were girls and guys walking around that concrete heaven with thick black swoops of ink around their eyes and pompadours sprayed stiff and shining.

We parked in the middle of the drive-in, so we could see the new racecar track in the distance. There were children laughing softly and throwing popcorn bits and ice in the air. Radios went in and out in billowy waves and static. The scraping of lawn chairs against gravel were a song to me.

The movie playing was called *Happy Girls*. Nicky told me he has seen most of Elvis's movies, but he hadn't seen this one. His favorite one had been *Fun in Acapulco* because there was a little Mexican boy who plays a phone trick on Elvis in the movie. He told me this as he leaned against me, his head on his shoulder, his breathing in syncopation with the moon and the breeze that touched the sweat on my neck. I kept one hand on the steering wheel and thought the wheel felt like the moon, too. I kept my hand there in case we needed to drive off in a hurry, in case a flash of light found us there. All his father had to do was report the car stolen, to lasso his boy, to tether his son back to him.

I looked at Elvis, and I thought Nicky used to have long black hair on top of his head like that too. I ran my hand along his ear lobe, and I wondered how long it would take for his hair to grow back, how long for it to swoop around his temples and how long it would take to touch the slant of his right eye, which twitched in a tiny way as he watched the happy girls and boys dance on the giant movie screen, snapping with little bubbles like air. The sky had grown dark, and dust began to come in from the windows, coating the tight leather seats of the car, and the dust was so light, I don't think Nicky even saw it there. There was a soft hum from the racetrack next door.

I could see the cars going around in circles, the track lit by a string of Christmas lights hung from poles and wires sprouting out from the track like trees. Elvis was dressed all in black and dancing with a woman in a white dress, her hair in a perfect flip, her hips spinning like the rings of Saturn, in the most perfect O. My hand shaking and shaking on the steering wheel, and I knew there was no breathing of Nicky, nothing to wake him, not even the sound of the screen or my throat bleeding in dust.

———

Nicky is a tomb, a needle wall injection, a brown boy turned pale skin, hair growing around his ears only because he's not living. There is a metal cup for flowers cut from fabric, bright blue with plastic drops, diamond shaped to look like dew. I pull the cup from its stem and hold it in my palms like it's lit and it's wax, the kick of my son a knock to my bones, he's clutching on my rib cage beneath this teenage dress of skin smudged and scrubbed away of blood and pomade and steady breathing.

Outside this burial place, there is a patch of pumpkin flowers that look like the pale passing hue of a bruise. I scrape and dig away dirt with my fist and my fingers and my nails, and I place the metal cup in the shallow ground. I want the cup to make a mechanical sound in the dirt, but it doesn't. I take the locks of black hair and wrap it in the ribbon of cloth turned brown-clouded like sky. It becomes a tiny ball in the palm of my hand. I hold it to my nose, so that my tiny son can smell it, so that it can enter through the holes and scars of me and the sting of shoulder blade and through the lungs of my son, who waits for me in shapes of crescent and tissue and bone. There is no taste of his father there.

It is only a negative, a hum, a burial, and a gun.

CORINNE: JC DRAKE

I never flip through my yearbooks from high school or google people that I used to know; I'm looking at the faces of ghosts. I grew up in teeth rot America, candy floss America, the giant hyperreal suburbs of Dallas in the 1980s, flush with cash from real estate and petro dollars. Acres of ugly brown houses packed with pink people burning and rotting under the Texas sun, all the trees cleared away to make room for just one more development. The primary exports from that place and time were boredom and cheap labor. Most of the kids would fall in behind their parents and do the same things; burn and rot.

There were always people who wanted to get away and I was one of them. The escapes: parties, drugs, booze, promiscuity, and the naughty mischief of an artificially imposed adolescence. At seventeen there was nothing more they could teach us and we stood around waiting for our own lives to begin, killing time and trying to get laid.

We just wanted to hang out and have fun; one of the best places was called Hell's Gate. Despite the sobriquet, the spot was beautiful, located on Possum Kingdom Lake just far enough away from our parents to get into trouble, but close enough to get out if we needed help. The Gate was a little out of the way inlet where the water was always calm. An island just off the shore which we all eventually tried to swim out to.

Every Saturday night was a party. Campfires, college kids, old men with their bass boats perving on young girls—there was always booze and plenty of weed and usually a handful of needle jockeys trying to escape the claustrophobia of their addiction. The last time I was ever there was on a Saturday night, sometime in early October. I rode out to the place with two other guys in back of an old pickup truck, open to the wind, my long hair lashing my face raw as we roared down the highway. My friends couldn't hold their beer and were passed out in the back of the truck by 10. I just wandered around, longneck in hand, sipping beer, taking a few tokes, and occasionally sitting down to listen to somebody's story or hear them pick a little guitar. By midnight I was tired and ready to crash.

I started back to the truck where I planned to bed down, weaving my way through the woods and parked cars. That's when I heard a noise. It was a girl's voice, a moan and a faint cry. I figured it was just some couple knocking boots in the back of a car, but something about the sound of her voice didn't seem right. I slipped through the field of parked cars, my eyes adjusted to the faint light of the stars. The sound was coming from a new white Mustang convertible with the top down.

I heard a male voice as I got close: "C'mon baby. C'mon. Open up. Yeah. Open up."

In the tiny back seat of the car a boy about my age had a girl pinned underneath him. He was holding her by the wrists, his pants down below his ass, trying to force her legs open. Suddenly I realized I knew the guy—he was from my school. He was nobody; a poor little rich kid. I took my last pull of beer, flipped the bottle upside down, and hit him across the back of the head with it.

It didn't knock him out; he let out a grunt and a moan, as he started trying to get off the girl. I grabbed him by his shirt collar and yanked him out of the car. "Deacon, you piece of shit. Get up. Get the hell up and put your damn pants on."

"Wha, wha? YOU? Get the fuck out!" Deacon fell on his hands and knees.

I helped the girl out of the car; she pulled up her panties and tried to fix her hair.

"Sleep it off Deacon," I whispered, "don't do anything you'll regret tomorrow."

She was in shock but was starting to get herself together. I held her by the shoulders, guiding her through the parked vehicles to my buddy's truck. hat's when I saw her face for the first time.

Corrine.

I knew her. Or at least she was in my English class. Corrine. Leather skirts, spiked frizzy hair, heels, red lipstick, and pale skin. Corrine. The girl who laughed too loud and smoked in gym glass and carried vodka in her Thermos. Corrine. The girl whose image I held in my mind at night when I touched myself and made a mess on the bed. Corrine. Everything I thought I wanted and wanted to be; freedom in human form. As I held myself next to her I began to shake.

My idiot friends were drunk and asleep in the truck. I reached into the space behind the seat and pulled out an unopened fifth of Seven Crown. I walked Corrine to a spot where a couple were sharing a campfire alone. I handed them the Seven and asked them if they could beat it. I sat Corrine down on a log and stoked up the fire. She stared into the flames for a long time before finally looking up.

"I know you. That guy from English class. Poetry Boy."

"What?"

"Sorry," she laughed a little. "I don't know your name. A few weeks ago you recited the most beautiful poem. It made me cry… I've been calling you Poetry Boy."

I grinned inwardly and recited some lines:

> *"I shut my eyes and all the world drops dead;*
> *I lift my lids and all is born again.*
> *(I think I made you up inside my head.)"*

"That's it! Did you write that?"

"Me? No. It's Sylvia Plath. My favorite poet. It's called 'Mad Girl's Love Song.'

"You must love it if you've memorized it. Who's your mad girl?"

"Oh. I, uh, don't have one. I mean I had a girlfriend. We broke up. She left.

Said I was too much trouble."

Corrine smiled. "Trouble? You don't look like trouble. You seem sweet. What you did back there with Deacon. That's nice. But I didn't need any help, ok. I can take care of myself."

"I guess."

"Oh. You jealous? Maybe you've seen me in class, Poetry Boy?"

"My name is Chris."

"Chris. Really? I'm sorry. I actually didn't want to fuck Deacon tonight."

I looked into the fire and picked up a stick, moving a few logs around. "Hell, why would you *ever* wanna fuck Deacon? He's trash."

"Trash, huh? I bet everyone is trash to a boy who memorizes big poems just so he can recite them to pretty girls in school." She laughed again. "Like I said, you're sweet. Deacon's not. But he's just a boy. This is the best life he's ever gonna live. Me, too, probably."

Corrine got up from her spot and came over to my side of the fire where she sat down next to me, pushing her body close to mine for warmth.

"It's cold, baby, let me just sit here."

I shivered, but not from the cold, my dick rock hard in my jeans. I put my arm around her and held her tight.

"Oh," she said, "you feel like a man. Someday you're gonna make a real woman happy."

I blurted it out: "I'd like to make you happy."

She was quiet again, her brows knitted. "I guess that's how it is. You saved me from Deacon, so it's your turn to take me. I suppose I wouldn't mind."

"Jesus, no. It's not like *that*. I don't want to do anything you don't want to do. I'm not *him*. Look, yeah, I've been watching you in class and…and there's nobody like you. You're beautiful and free and *alive*. This whole fucking city is dead and you're the most alive thing in it. I think I love that."

She laughed a bit and looked into my face. "You are sweet, Poetry Boy. Give me another line."

> "'I dreamed that you bewitched me into bed;
> and sung me moon-struck, kissed me quite insane.'"

"You sure you didn't write that?" She laughed again. "But look, baby, I'm not free. Ain't none of us free. I only fuck Deacon because he's got stuff I need. We all have things we need. Why are you out here? Bored. That's why I'm here, too. But look, you're gonna go on and do something else. But not me. Not Deacon. This is us. Forever." I pushed my lips to hers and kissed her. I didn't care if it was wrong. And she threw her arms around mine and held me, shivering together in that cold night, by the last of the fire. When our lips parted we sat quietly, the booze and weed from the night catching up to us. We fell asleep in front of the fire and I did not dream. I had no reason to.

The sound that awoke me at around dawn was Deacon's voice, calling out for Corrine. He finally found us and stumbled into our little stolen camp site.

"Corrine," he slurred, concussed and hung over, "get away from that piece of shit and let's go."

"No," I said, "she's staying with me."

Corrine was awake. "I'm afraid not, baby, I've got to go."

She stood up and pushed her hair up and her skirt down. I leapt to my feet. "What? You can't go—this trash tried to rape you! I...I..."

Deacon reached into the pocket of his letter jacket and pulled out a baggie, letting it unroll in his fingers. It was a quarter full of an ugly, jagged white powder. Corrine smiled weakly and kissed my cheek.

"Like I said, Deacon's got stuff I need. I'll see you in class, Poetry Boy."

She walked passed Deacon and disappeared into the woods, leaving me standing there alone, eyes wet. I did see her in class, but she avoided my attempts to talk to her. Sometimes I could see her smiling in my direction or laughing privately at something I said. Then, after Christmas break, Corrine was gone. She never came back to school and no one seemed to know why. Only that she'd gone.

I always wondered what happened to her. I imagined to myself that eventually she'd found a good man, settled down in one of those brown houses, and kicked out a few kids, all in imitation of happiness. Many years later, the night before I got married I found myself possessed by the imp of nostalgia and plugged her name into Google.

I never flip through my yearbooks anymore or try to find what happened to my old friends and lost loves; theirs are the faces of ghosts.

SPHINX TEARS: CARA DIGIROLAMO

Fireworks scattered, expanding galaxies of stars into the sky, clutched hands, spinning, turning, barefoot in the dry California grass. A red dress blurring into a white dress, the taste of lip gloss and sucrose-sweet Smirnoff Ice. That night, it felt like the summer would last forever.

Harlow didn't remember if the memory was real or sphinx tears anymore. At least she wished she didn't.

Her phone buzzed, chattering against the glass on her nightstand. Harlow untangled herself from the sheet and rolled away from the overheated body in her bed. She let it vibrate in her hand, the name, the time blinking on the screen. 3AM, Calvin. There was only one reason her brother would call so late.

She said nothing when she accepted the call, and neither did he.

"They found her?"

"Yeah."

Harlow slipped on jeans, a bra and a hoodie and stepped out onto the balcony, closing the door behind her and breathing in the warm summer night air.

"What was it?"

He sighed. "They don't know what she took yet. Heart failure."

A breeze carried the scent of eucalyptus and dry dust to her. It clotted her throat, choking her.

"I'm going to call Allie."

"What? Why the *fuck* would you—" Harlow's voice cracked.

"She should know."

The line went silent. Calvin was gone. Harlow opened her photos. Her sister Madison's face, painted like a harlequin, red for blood and black for crow and white for dust. Her face again, but clean, bright, and laughing, in her ugly high school graduation robes. Just a kid, dyed purple hair still dripping on her t-shirt, and two girls both with stained hands behind her. Harlow herself, and the other girl.

She shoved the phone into the hoodie pocket. Plastic packaging crackled under it. She took it out, and it glimmered in the balcony light.

One last packet of sphinx tears.

"I don't really do hallucinogens," Allie said, standing awkwardly on one foot, her stained hands stuffed in the pockets of her jeans.

Up on the rooftop of the resort hotel, where a very important conference of very important people was taking place, thirteen-year-old Madison Harris shook the packet in Allie's face, her purple hair brushing against her eyes. "It's not a hallucinogen. It shows you the *future*."

"It shows you *a* future," Calvin clarified. "A good one. It shows you being happy."

Harlow had learned to read the softness in Allie's face, the quirks of her lips, the liquid movement of her eyes. An only child, Allie had never learned to hide her feelings, not like the Harris kids had.

"I don't know," Harlow said. "You've never been happy. It might not work for you."

"That's so mean, Harlow." Madison protested. "Of course it will work. Come on." She shook a tiny bit from the packet into everyone's hand. There was barely a crystal for each, only a few moments, but it was enough, it had always been enough so far.

Harlow remembered the tastes she'd had before, flashbulbs going off as she strolled along a runway, wind in her hair as she drove a convertible down a cliffside highway, a glass of champagne and the glint of a proffered diamond. Nothing certain, nothing concrete. But Calvin said it changed as you got older, the visions grew closer in time, more detailed, more real, until maybe, *maybe*, you could figure out how to make them part of your life.

Harlow could do that. She was going to be happy. She was going to get what she wanted.

Allie, nervousness written across her face, settled in next to Harlow, the roughness of jeans pressing against Harlow's thigh, where it showed bare below the hem of her sundress. Crystals cupped in her palm, Allie lifted her hand and offered a bump against Harlow's. "Cheers?"

"Bottoms up."

The taste of sphinx shot off in fractals across Harlow's tongue, startling her nervous system into hyperdrive. The back of her head gooshed like a waterbed, and Harlow shut her eyes, the network of bursts, like the flaming jewels in Indra's Web, spreading from her tongue to the blackness behind her eyes.

White.

White sheets crumpling, sunlight caught in them. Harlow blinked her eyes open to meet brown ones, soft and familiar, a warm weight over her hips, and then a smile, murmured words and soft kisses up her throat and jaw before finding her mouth.

A weight landing on the bed beside them, fur, the yowl of a hungry cat. Harlow flailing out to push him off. Laughter vibrating against her neck. *Your turn. Your cat. Why is he only mine in the mornings?*

The gooshing came again and Harlow scrambled for balance, scraping her knuckles on the shingle of the flat rooftop. Her brother and sister and Allie were coming back, Calvin jerking his hat into his lap to cover his hard-on, Madison grinning like a thief, and Allie--Allie's eyes were wide and she was staring at Harlow like she'd seen a ghost.

"God, I can't wait to do that again," Madison moaned, leaning back against the planter. "It's so good. I'm totally going to be a model." She grinned at Calvin. "You just got laid, didn't you? Harlow, Allie, spill."

"Shut up," Harlow said, getting to her feet, hating how her knees wobbled. "Private."

"Allie?"

Allie's smile was weak. "I'm really not that into hallucinogens."

The resort's pool boy had biceps so big that Harlow couldn't even reach her fingers around to squeeze them. He smelled like sweat and Axe and he shaved his chest, smooth and tan and glossy under his v-neck.

He teased her and gave her his number and then smiled at Calvin over her head. Sphinx tears were only supposed to give you hallucinations of the good futures, but everything has side effects, and Harlow saw Calvin on one of the hotel beds, helping the pool boy shuck his pants, she saw her father yelling, empty rooms, and dead eyes, dead, dead, dead.

When she got caught kissing the pool boy and her father smacked her across the face and called her a whore, she stopped seeing the flashes. She swallowed the blood welling in her mouth and smiled.

Madison lay slumped on their shared bathroom floor, her head swelling where she'd hit it on the tub on the way down. Harlow shook her, unbuttoned the collar of her school uniform shirt, felt for a pulse, and shook her again. When her eyes opened, they were hazed, the blue almost purple, the white silvered.

"*Madison.*"

"I'm fine. 'm fine," she beat Harlow's hands away. "Just sphinx."

"You need to cut back." Over the summer, with friends, it was different. But they were home now, Allie back in Italy at school, and Madison couldn't get high and pass out in the bathroom on a Wednesday.

"I'm fine," Madison hissed. "I'm not the one so frightened of being happy that I chased it away." She rubbed her head. Then flinched.

"What is it?"

"Nothing," Madison scrunched into her shirt. "Just a badflash."

"Already?" They weren't supposed to come until a few hours after the sphinx had worn off.

"It's fine. I like them." Madison staggered to her feet and balanced herself with one hand on Harlow's shoulder. "Keep you on your toes. I know people say they're the worst things that could happen, but with Dad around, they're just warnings of what to avoid."

From the roof of the resort hotel, Harlow could see all the way to the horizon. Nothing but dead grass and low hills, studded with the occasional group of cows.

"I thought going to California meant going to the beach," Harlow grumbled.

"Not Sacramento."

Startled by the unexpected response, Harlow turned to see the girl she'd briefly met the night before, one of her dad's friends' kids, sitting in the shadow of a large metal vent. The girl stood, shoving her phone into her pocket, and came over to the edge, pointing. "There, that highway? You can take it all the way to the coast, to San Francisco, and then get on Highway 1. It's cliffs and ocean the whole way to LA."

"Want to go?"

The girl—Allie, she remembered—laughed. "What, you gonna steal a car or something?"

Hands on her hips, Harlow gave this new girl a once-over. Pretty, but she dressed like she didn't know it. She was crazy for wearing jeans and flannel on a day as hot as today. Still, if she pulled her hair back, people would notice her. And the tank-top under the flannel was fine. She'd do.

Harlow shrugged, then tipped her head and offered a smirk. "I've got prospects."

"Oh, good! You're here! You can hang with my roomie!"

Harlow let herself be dragged through the party. All models, skinny jeans and earth tones, and decadent, colorful designer drugs. Madison fit right in, her hair dyed professionally now, her slightly dilated pupils. She had one thing clearly going for her. It was always hard to tell if a Harris was high.

"Harlow, you know my roommate."

Of course, Allie, in a soft hipster sweater, looking uncomfortable and drinking water. She'd known Madison and Calvin still kept in touch with her, but Harlow tried to ignore it. Seeing her felt like a badflash, but it was just a memory, the memory of kissing her a long time ago, dizzy with sunstroke and alcohol.

"Hey," Allie's voice was soft, the vibrations more scattered than she remembered. "How's France?"

"It's good." Harlow shrugged, her hands in her pockets. "It's not living with my dad."

Madison shoved Harlow and she thumped onto the bench beside Allie. "You guys still like sphinx tears, right? It hasn't done shit for me in forever. My life right now is what it always showed me anyway." She grinned dropped a few packets and slid away.

Allie didn't speak. Harlow wondered what to say. She didn't know this girl anymore. Being kids, whispering generic teenage secrets for one summer didn't mean anything at all anymore.

Allie fiddled with one of the packets. Her hand turned and the scar on the inside of her wrist caught the light. Harlow didn't ask. It didn't have anything to do with her. Calvin had mentioned that a friend of hers had been sick, but Harlow always changed the subject when he tried to talk about Allie.

Harlow tore open a packet of sphinx tears. It was easier than talking. "Wanna go?"

I-don't-really-do-hallucinogens-Allie held out her hand.

The haze drew around, and Harlow found herself on a sofa, knees up, leaning on the edge. Madison sat crosslegged on the floor, setting up a game board. A guy Harlow didn't recognize, tall and handsome with an easy smile and well-applied eyeliner, bent over Madison, offering assistance. Harlow turned her head to find

Allie clambering onto the couch beside her. She hooked an arm around her neck, laughing at something the tall guy said, and leaning in to press her head against Harlow's cheek.

And then, like an avalanche, the dream slithered away, tumbling, disappearing, and Harlow spun back into the party, the small booth, with a girl she didn't know how to talk to, whose eyes glistened with unshed tears.

Allie sniffed. "Sorry. I just . . . I saw a friend I haven't seen in a while."

"Tall? Guyliner?"

The damp paper napkin tore between Allie's fingers. "Don't tell Madison about this. She thinks if people sphinx the same thing they're soulmates, or something."

"Or something." Harlow rubbed her temples. She grabbed Allie's water only to choke on pure gin. "Jesus!"

Allie smiled.

It was hard to tell when the Harrises were high, but Harlow could never tell when Allie was drunk.

———

Madison had been missing for three days before anyone noticed. Harlow's valley-tech investment consultant boyfriend had asked her to marry him and she'd spent the weekend riding him to show her appreciation.

Calvin called on Wednesday. "I texted her Monday, have you heard from her?"

Harlow had spent the next forty-two hours lowkey needing to vomit.

Madison—hair like stardust—wings on point—she'd gotten out, gotten away from their dad, gotten everything she'd wanted, grasped that happy ending the sphinx tears promised. Wasn't it supposed to last?

———

The dump of a tamale shop, hardly more than a counter and two tables kitted out with plastic lawn chairs, steamed. Allie sighed happily and shrugged off her jacket. Harlow, who'd been dying of heatstroke even outside, shook her head. The girl was always freezing and had terrible taste in restaurants. She eyed the dirty mop in the corner.

"Seriously? Here? We're going to die of salmonella."

Allie waved her hand. "It'll be fine. Can't you smell it?"

"Windex?"

"*Authenticity.*"

Harlow rolled her eyes, but let herself be dragged to the counter, while Allie ordered rapidly in Spanish. Allie had been to Spain. She'd been all over. The farthest Harlow had been away from home was this trip to fucking *Sacramento.*

They came away with a heap of sweet-smelling corn-husk packets and set up on the wobbly lawn chairs with four different kinds of spicy sauces and two more kinds of chopped relish. Allie waved her hands enthusiastically as she described the contents and how to pair them. Harlow mostly didn't listen, just watched, and ate what she was instructed to.

"Fine. You were right. It was good," Harlow admitted, as they stepped out of the sweltering little shop and into the beating dry heat of the road. "I wouldn't have minded you taking me to this kind of dump so much if we were like in Italy or somewhere. But I still don't believe you can smell authenticity."

"I'll have to prove it to you." Allie grinned. "We'll just keep doing it. I'll take you to dive restaurants all around the world."

"I'd still rather go shopping," Harlow complained, but when Allie took her hand, she didn't wriggle it away. The girl's fingers were like ice. Harlow was doing her a favor.

A glimpse of softness among the black—Harlow sought the texture of a knitted sweater, long hands closed around the cheaply bound hymnal. They disappeared again into the crowd. Calvin came over to hug her, saw her face, and refrained.

Madison, beautiful as ever, lay in a fucking box.

Harlow went to wash her hands. She washed them over and over again, staring in the mirror at the chilly lines of make-up that her shaky hand had applied. The last packet of sphinx crackled in her pocket.

The door moved. Allie's dress was red-lined, peeking out from the black, crimson and ultra-fashionable in a way that meant Madison had picked it out for her. She had a black sweater on over it, a loose openwork jacket, long enough to flutter on a level with the hem of the dress.

"Madison would hate you wearing that sweater with that dress."

Allie stood silent, their eyes only meeting in the mirror. "Madison has to suck it now." She breathed out, putting her hand to her face. The silvery line along her wrist flashed and then was turned away.

Slowly, Harlow drew the packet of sphinx out of her purse. It crackled as she held it up. "One more time?"

Allie's head tipped forward, her silky chestnut hair falling like a curtain around her face. She nodded.

Harlow poured the crystals into each of their palms. "Bottoms up."

They bumped their knuckles and drank the poison.

The same church shivered into view, but no black, instead, a rush of noise from a rowdy crowd outside, pouring out the doors after Madison and her new husband. Everything was drenched in flowers and models and laughter. There was Calvin with a boyfriend, guyliner from the last trip, and then Allie, bumping against her in front of the sink, backing her up into the counter. Terrible matching dresses, closed-mouthed playful kisses, lacing their fingers together—Allie's fingers were always cold. Harlow brought her hands up, rotating them out.

Allie's wrist was smooth, no scar.

The dream faded. Harlow found tears in her own eyes. Sphinx tears were supposed to show you the future, not a present you'd gotten lost on the way to. "It's too late."

Allie nodded. "I've known that since last time. The guy in that one . . . he'd already died."

"It could never have been like that."

Allie shook her head, but her fingers hovered near Harlow's cheek, and then rested on her face, rubbing across her lower lip.

"When we get to LA we can get on a boat, sail around the world. I'll carry your bags while you shop—"

"—and I'll let you take me to all your dirty hole-in-the-wall restaurants."

"But we won't get out at the first port."

"I'll keep you too busy in our bunk."

Harlow melted into her, sorry and broken. *You were my soulmate. You were. But not anymore.*

Allie pressed a kiss to the side of her head and held her wrapped in her arms.

Bruises were forming around Harlow's mouth as she sat up on the roof, still stinking of Axe and chlorine and boy-sweat. Allie held ice against Harlow's cheek and worried her lower lip between her teeth. "You could tell someone about this."

Harlow shook her head, wincing as the bruise jarred against the dripping bar towel full of ice. "Who'd believe me?"

"Maybe my mom—"

A snort. "They're friends." Harlow looked out toward the slowly setting sun. The rolling golden hills seemed to stretch forever, but the small dimple where the highway lay broke through them, disappearing off to somewhere—somewhere else. "I'm fine," Harlow said. "I did what I had to do."

Allie's lips tightened, her gaze flicking away. Which was worse for her, Harlow wondered, watching her get smacked or watching her make out with the pool boy? She'd do either again, to not ever see another badflash of Calvin lying dead in a heap. She'd do whatever she could to look after Madison too.

A crunch and clink, Allie's hand—even colder than usual from the ice—pressed something into hers. Keys, from Allie's mom's rental car. "We said San Francisco." Allie ducked her head, a curtain of hair falling over her eyes. She swallowed before she continued. "Take Highway 1 all the way to the port of LA. Find a ship. See the world?"

The keys slid into the lap of her flowered sundress, and Harlow found her fingers curling inside the fall of Allie's flannel, gripping onto the clinging tank-top underneath. Her other hand cupped Allie's cheek and drew her near to kiss her, just once, pressing hard enough that the bruise on her mouth ached. Allie's lips parted under her touch. Her sigh tasted of sadness and the heady glitter of sphinx tears.

Then Harlow let her go.

"I can't."

———

Paper cups and a stolen bottle of wine. Feet dangling over the edge of the rooftop. The sparkle of sphinx against the darkness of closed eyes. Wind whipping hastily tied scarves as the convertible raced down the cliffside highway.

Maybe this time they'd spin out and plunge down the cliff face into the ocean. Maybe this time Dad would hit her for real and she'd smash her head into the table. Maybe this time she'd be brave enough to take the turn off that the sphinx had seen, the one route to that world where they all could have been happy.

Maybe next time.

RITUALS OF GORGONS: LARISSA GLASSER

1

When the truck hits her it's like a jump-cut. No fade out, no stars, no waxing wave to bridge her ride now. She only had to blink her eyes once to make it happen—the impact, the bending of metal, the shattering of triumphant bones.

Now it is just her on the sidewalk. She sees a lot of feet not going anywhere. They're all keeping their distance, giving her space.

She looks down at herself. Her body is curved the wrong way, a rag doll thrown in anger. The street noise is muffled as through a thick, warm scarf. She's trying to look past the tarmac and see faces and eyes but she can't move that part of her.

The sunlight is an auburn fog.

When the nausea hits, it crushes her sternum, her reality kicks in and she begins the pilgrimage. She is an accident, she knew that from the very beginning. Of course, she can't remember what she was before that. Or is she willingly blind to avoid some truth hiding from her there?

It's really cold. Some bloke with a thick upturned collar brightens as he recognizes her face from the news and steps closer. He pulls out his phone and as he begins filming her, she floats out of herself and watches everything unravel from above.

2

She is worried she's going to be late. It's the first true thaw of the year and she decides her bike will be quicker. She doesn't want X to think that this reunion meant nothing, after all.

She'd thought she'd never see X again. The abandonment still haunts her, she's gotten used to that. She was powerless to find her. It was as if the forest had just swallowed her up.

But the returned voice was true enough as it came over her speakers, her Dante Rossetti-inspired banana jawline was real enough, her eyes wide enough as they gazed at her through the monitor.

But this still took convincing. She'd never said why she'd vanished to begin with. X had said she wanted to explain it to her in person. X was worried she wouldn't believe her. So much can be misinterpreted online, as we all know well enough.

She wants to sit next to her again like before.

But she wants X to come back more than anything, even though they'd never finished the ritual.

3

There is unfinished business. These are things left unresolved, unaddressed. As she hovers above her own body, she looks down at the street at her jagged features. Her jaw looks wrong. Her eyes look milky and coin-shaped. It's better to focus on her clothes, as blood and urine pool beneath her. It's a mild day for not-quite-spring so she wanted to wear the black dress with the white roses because she wore it on the day she'd first met X quite by blind chance in the park.

She also remembers finding this black cardigan in the middle of a busy intersection. It was pristine, with nary a loose thread. No one had run over it so it might have only just been shrugged off by someone, or it flew out of a car. It was something without origin. No one had come back to claim it so she put it in her bag and hurried to the other end of the street before the light changed.

When she put it on at home not only did it fit her perfectly, it made her arms look thinner and her neck smaller. She'd been beside herself sometime later when she'd thought she'd lost it in the laundry but she later found it rumpled in the folds of her black sheets. Her bed swallowed a lot of things, but she'd been glad it had given the sweater back. It was lucky. She felt grateful for that much.

Not so lucky today.

The crowd continues to grow around her. Her breathing is shallow and quick. Her bike looks destroyed, an inverted pretzel. The truck that hit her remains idling at the alley junction, bellowing grey exhaust until people in the crowd finally admonish the driver to cut the engine. He goes back in the cab to do just that and as their eyes wander away from him she watches the driver cut a line of coke. He is going to be off-schedule for deliveries.

Someone zips up on a scooter and almost plows into the onlookers. The semicircle shatters a moment as people step back and away from the new arrival.

4

The shower is her most vulnerable place. It's worse than the mirror because she is there with her body, her flesh hostage to her folds and the scales. Here is the incomplete ritual made real.

The hot water feels good against her back, and makes her want to stay despite her dysphoric relationship with her nakedness. This is better than looking in the mirror, more intimate. The mirror vexes her, because she cannot avoid staring into her own, accusing eyes.

She has dealt with this for so long, she thinks she should be used to it by now but she isn't and never will be.

The memory of X asking her to tea comes back to her in a crushing wave, and the natural process by which this occurred, another girl accepting and liking her for who she is and not what she can give them, temporarily relieves her self-loathing. X made her feel like a person, instead of a product. She'd gladly have traded her celebrity for obscurity.

Each glimpse of X's face cuts her heart, the mass of her wavy black mane reflected against the tabletop where they put their saucers at the far corners. She never fully appreciated the beauty of Mediterranean women until X flailed into her life. X's olive skin brings her brown eyes in full brightness before her, and the dark floral pattern of her dress dances from neckline to hem. It is very much like her own dress, but she cannot help but stare. She thinks X does this all so much better, and she wonders if this girl is the key to helping her find a sense of balance in her own life.

She snaps out of it as the girl from the counter brings their tea, gives them both a weird look. She is more worried about being recognized as who she is than of being clocked. X doesn't seem to notice or care about the tea server's distaste.

She likes X's confidence. It's growing on her. X can be someone good, she thinks. She hasn't been lucky at all and she'd not wanted to go out or do anything other than shopping or work, and even then, only behind layers of scarves. The paparazzi have been aggravating. Just when she thinks they've gotten tired of hounding her, they pop out from behind another corner and speed off before she even has the chance to tell them to go fuck themselves. She doesn't like to shout at them anymore because she's still self-conscious about her voice. Heads turn. She hates it still. She wants to get back at them somehow. Freeze them in their tracks.

She is still absorbing X's voice, a full-depth resonance, baritone yes, but as a saxophone might sound in a soft 1980s ballad. There is also a breathiness in X's voice, and this magnetizes her along with X's dark eyes. Usually she tends to look away, but she wants to maintain eye contact with X during this tea, because X is being kind to her.

X asks her if it's okay if she moves her chair closer to the middle of the table, the glare of the sunlight is getting on her nerves. She instinctively moves her own chair to stay at a polite distance from X, but then she changes her mind. She likes the idea of X sitting closer to her.

She blows at her cup and sips at the edge. English breakfast with orange and skim, she always finds good energy from the taste, or at least it distracts her from feeling so much doubt. This is the awkward early phase of transition for her, and she wants to ask X discreetly as possible when or if things will get better. X carries herself so well, and she wants to know how she got to that place, or if she will even be welcome.

Instead she asks X what she got, nodding towards her cup. The steam floats into the sunlight, looks pretty. X says she got a jasmine-green hybrid. Sometimes it's best to experiment with tea especially in Britain. You can pick something at random and usually end up with something decent. She tells X the truth that she's usually been afraid to try new things, especially since the huge blow-up in the media over the holidays. She hadn't wanted anything to be public, she just wanted to take care of herself and go back to work.

X tells her she obviously isn't completely afraid to try new things. If something sucks in your life, X tells her, you can change it, and she knows that well enough. X edges her own cup towards her and invites her to have a taste.

5

The scooter rider dismounts and shoves past the onlookers.

Even from above, she hears the rising screech of his camera flash gathering power to itself. The sunlight is still relentless and unforgiving, but she knows how these people work. The crowd begins to murmur a little as he snaps a few test shots of her body splayed out on the sidewalk. She sees her own eyes register him and then they quiver toward the others, imploring for help. She doesn't know if anyone has called for an ambulance. She saw many of them filming her with their phones and a few were speaking, but she couldn't make any words string together. She tries to shut her eyes tight but then her view from above gets obscured so she tries to blink as much as possible instead.

She remembers what had happened to the Princess in the tunnel. As the paparazzi pursued her car on their bikes and caught up to the wreckage, the trapped Princess wept and cried out as their flashbulbs went off. She remembers thinking that seemed like such an indignity. She never wanted to imagine what the Princess was thinking while that was happening. Perhaps she thought of her lover, dead beside her, and that had to be a horrible feeling as the rest of her body cruelly hung onto life and the mental and physical pain must have been soul-crushing. Although she had only ever seen the Princess through a media lens, she'd always thought the Princess put others before herself, and when she finally dared to venture into her own dreams or desires, it set in motion some monstrous countdown to tragedy. Her fate seemed inevitable.

Now, broken in the street and hurting to breathe, she wonders what she's done wrong to bring this on herself.

She knows she has failed X somehow, their ritual still incomplete.

Did her body just shift down there? Had she moved one of her hands? Her breathing is coming faster as the photographer actually stands over her and continues to ingest rapid fire shots. Someone breaks from the crowd and yells at him to stop, and turns to the others and asks if anyone called an ambulance for her. The questioner is met with vacant stares.

Some of them haven't completely processed who she is, and has been once before.

It's salacious, indeed it's so marvelous and farcical.

She feels cold. She hovers closer down to herself to try and see past the photographer who obscured her view from above. When she sees her own face again she sees herself crying, her face twitching and struggling to regain its muscular range of motion and expression. She doesn't want to shut her eyes, despite the blinding flashes which are crueler than sunlight.

She tries to draw her own gaze back. She doesn't like to see herself all helpless like this. She knows it's getting bad because she is beginning to hate and blame herself again. Only seeing X could ever stop those sneering voices from re-entering her head.

6

X stands naked in front of her as the snowstorm rages outside the flat. Neither one of them know if they'll be asked to stay home from work tomorrow, as the streets of London cease only for alien tripods. Still, they're up very late smoking weed and drinking X's tea. X likes the orangey kind now, she turned her onto it. But something about it also tastes different to her—she fancies this may a side effect from X's weed.

She has the shades drawn so the only light in the bedroom is coming from the television. X turned her onto Buffy the Vampire Slayer, but right now they have the sound turned down. She tries to not keep looking at the bluish-green birthmark on X's inner thigh. But the skin there looks chapped, flaking. X seems to put a lot of moisturizer on it but she doesn't want to bother X by asking about it.

Besides, there is other shit going on—

X wants to know what happened to her today to make her cry so bad.

They came to her work, she tells X. Right to her own office where she was unable to get away. She'd been debugging someone's coding mistake at her workstation and was so in her zone she hadn't heard the cameras going off until a few minutes in.

When they saw that she saw, the cameras shifted a little to let the reporter in. She recognized him from WorldNet, the ones who had been front paging her in print all winter, and even doxxed her on their newsfeed. She'd had to start using burners due to the harassing calls. Social media for her was right out unless she could use a public terminal at a library or cafe or something.

She shouted at them to get out and her voice went wrong.

She was answered with derisive laughter and more questions about her junk.

When her coworkers finally managed to get a security guard to muscle them out of the building she was sobbing onto her keyboard. She looked back up at the screen only once to see the damaged code, and past that, own reflection in the windowpane. These were the toughest months and she didn't know if she was going to make it through. She didn't regret trying.

In the bedroom, she asks X how she could possibly go back to the way she had been. X tells her yeah, this early part of transition sucks ass and it all makes her unhappy but not nearly as unhappy as she'd obviously been before and she shouldn't let those fuckers win, that defiance would be the better option. She asks X but what if they never stop, they know where she works and she doesn't want to leave that job she's good at it and they were good about letting her stay through the entire process of lining her shit up. Should she try to pay them off or something.

X lights a fresh joint and hands it to her. X says that would just invite disaster, that they'd make things so much worse for her if they thought they could blackmail her for their silence every second of her days. She tells X she doesn't know what her options are anymore. X tells her to hurry up and smoke.

She obeys.

I don't like things that hurt you, X tells her.

The weed tastes even more amazing.

X then says she knows of a way to get them to stop. And they can have fun while doing it. She likes the sound of this.

The storm clears up, and they fuck towards the first morning light.

7

The ambulance arrives. One of the paramedics shoves the photographer away from her body, but many other paparazzi have come during the interval and keep up the footage at all angles. Some people have begun shouting for them to stop, that they have enough, but their pleas are ignored by the lot. This is their job, one of them mutters. Another one of them says that the public has a right to know what happened.

Her eyes dart from side to side. One of the meds extracts a stretcher from the back to the vehicle. She begins to panic.

She knows what's coming.

And as the truck driver cuts a fresh line of coke inside his cab, he glances over at the medics as they begin to examine her and determine the best way to move her onto the stretcher according to their training. Her body is bent at a sideways angle so they try to begin.

It works.

Her mouth.

She SCREAMS.

Her voice.

It burns.

Seeing the blood pooled underneath her one of the medics starts cutting away at her clothing. He thinks the wound is at her pelvis. Before she can say anything, her penis is out and they also see the verdigris scaled consistency of the skin along her abdomen. They step back from her.

What the fuck is this, they ask.

Her eyes brighten and transform.

8

X has brought her to the forest, just as she'd promised.

They both stand naked at opposite ends of the drawn circle. The night air is cold but X taught her long ago how to adjust to it through sheer focus and strength of will. These instructions had appealed to her meticulous nature.

She has also fallen in love with X.

X had mentioned once that she'd studied Thelema but that its supposed adherents were just undisciplined, bratty patriarchs who didn't even care about even the most basic principles. X cared very much about Magick, and she'd told her that there was no power in something you didn't actually feel passion for. The world was already brimming with falsehoods and charlatans so why play along with that?

She doesn't know. Her own belief system had once been materialist and her only academic interests reside exclusively in coding and gaming. But X fascinates her with this new prospect of stopping the harassment by any means necessary, even with whatever [M]agic[k] is supposed to be.

We can make our own reality. X tells her this a lot. She wants to believe it, to make that principle its own reality instead of this other bullshit.

X asked her if she'd ever heard of apotropaic magic, a universal principle of averting misfortune and in her case—the evil eye that peers at her from behind the seeming safety of a camera lens. Some people mistake this magic for superstition, the whole knocking on wood thing, but X said the media coverage had been her own evil eye, and that this ritual, The Ritual of the Gorgon would indeed work through the power of its own sight, and would protect them both from not only the gutter press but from the rest of the fuck-world who would try to hurt them.

When she asked X how long the ritual had existed and where it had originated from, X only told her she'd inherited it from many sources. That was all X would tell her about it. X asked her if she trusted her and she said she did.

The Gorgon had long been a protective symbol but the principle of her monstrosity also appealed to her. She had been made to feel an outcast, wholly undesirable, an object herself of aversion and dread. And yet The Monster is powerful as all fuck and by that same token their utility, their outlet, their non-stop sick entertainment. It had made her transition unbearable until X had come along. But they'd kept after her for the last several days and she was getting really pissed off.

She had taken X at her word, but then she had also asked X to promise she wouldn't leave her after all of whatever was supposed to happen.

X promised her with a hug.

The woods are quiet this night, but she is constantly looking over both shoulders, expecting paparazzi to emerge from behind any one of the given oak trees. They'd capture one fucking hell of a moment, she muses. Two naked trans women standing by some ungodly chalk symbol set with metal braziers at each of its seven points. Her dick looks shriveled by the cold night air but X really seems to be getting her blood up as she lights the fires and it gets warmer. X instructs her to keep her stance within the circle.

She obeys.

She keeps watching X very closely. She looks at X's thigh birthmark again. The hectic firelight makes it look bigger than she remembered.

The coals alight and X blesses each fire in a strange dialect, she steps along points of the symbol carefully and with a learned rhythm. X reaches into her messenger bag and pulls out a small pouch which she shakes a little and continues her mantra. She extracts a tiny vial, and begins the circuit again but in the opposite direction. X pauses at each of the seven braziers, dashes a small spray of oils from the vial onto the glowing coals. Each time a huge steady column of silver smoke rises high into the night. They watch as the smoke trails bend into each other, intertwine as one, and continue up towards the sky.

Across the circle, she asks X how many times she's done this. X silences her with a short, cold, hiss and she obeys. Her eyes once again focus on the still-gathering smoke, but something seems not right as if this is overkill, too much too soon, getting loose from X's control.

She watches X's dark hair rise up and come alive, it dances all around her head as if blown about by industrial fans in a music video.

The smoke follows X. It spreads in all directions, becoming so thick and pervasive and then the heat escalates. The smoke then reaches her, and quickly blocks X from view.

The chanting stops abruptly.

She cries out to X. She doesn't care how baritone she sounds, this is beginning to get scary for her in a different way. Something is definitely off.

The heat escalates further. She has to wipe the sweat from her forehead. Where the fuck is X.

The cloud is all around her now. She can't even see the trees anymore. She looks down at herself. Her involuntary erection is unpleasant, considering the circumstances. Maybe she doesn't want the magic to work anymore.

Fear grows in her and begins gnawing at her self-hatred.

Stop this X, just will you please just stop it.

She feels a sour, coppery dryness inside her navel. Her hand strays there and something inside of her feels like a bad wound. As the skin begins to shift around her belly she cries out, her entire system burns with terrible defeat. Then a single wave passes through her from her scalp to her toes and everything starts to get fucked up when the scales begin to spread from her belly up towards her nascent breasts. The color is darker, the bluish-green glimmers in sharp contrast to the engulfing smoke. It has the same basic characteristics as X's birthmark.

Then the wind finds her and cools the pressure. The scales slow down and cease their journey just shy of her heart. The partial transformation is an unfulfilled promise, just like everything else in the universe.

Whatever the [M]agic[k] was supposed to be, she only knows that it decided it didn't want to finish with her.

The wind gathers momentum and another wave passes

through her, beginning at her toes this time and crashing into her head. She falls backwards into the soil.

When she opens her eyes again there is only the cold night of the forest.

The smoke, the circle, the braziers, the fires are gone.

X is also gone.

The dark scales remain at her midsection, a cold new reality that should not astonish her but it does. She watches her breath contract and expand there and she touches the new skin. It's not as painful but it feels grimy and resinous. Her penis is asleep again. The tension in her being is epic.

She calls out to X one more time but her voice dies in the air.

9

The paramedics are laughing at her.

It's the same coldness and helplessness of the forest where she lost X during the winter. She hovers closer to her face and recognizes only the fear there. She wants to be able to move her hands to her ears and block out the noise of the laughter which is augmented by a growing murmur of the still-gathering throng along the sidewalk. Some of them are shouting at the medics, telling them to help her and get her to the hospital, that she's a human being and what is bloody wrong with them. One of the medics turns to them all and points to her, you call that human are you right pissed or something.

Defeated, she descends back down into her own headspace and waits to die.

The heat grows inside her again like a thick blanket, soothing the humiliation somewhat. But she still wants to be able to move. She wants to get on her bike and get to the cafe to see X where they first hung out and ask her what happened and why did she break her promise. She wants to cry in front of X and not in front of these shit-heels.

I will not cry in front of them.

She repeats it to herself. She is gathering herself. Something is happening. She can move her toes.

I will not cry in front of them.

I will not cry in front of them.

Can she move her head? She would like to see better. Is that X biking up the street. As her neck moves it cracks and hurts but it obeys the edicts of her starved brain. She can see her fingers quivering, clawing at nothing. Are her nails growing longer now? That can't be X.

I will not cry in front of them.

I will not cry in front of them.

I will not cry in front of them.

It is X. She shoves one of the medics out of the way and is immediately at her side. It can't be real because nothing else was ever real.

X says something to her but she cannot quite make it out. The medics' backs are turned to them both as the crowd edges closer. She will cry in front of X only.

Why did you leave me there.

You promised.

I'm so scared.

Why did you do that.

X leans in closer and whispers to her. There is a way to complete the ritual, even now with the workings strewn astray. The Power of the Gorgon has transferred to her and only she can complete the cycle. She is the one being targeted, wanted, used up by the media. But her initial refusal of the counteractive power, whether it had been her fear or incredulity, had opened the gateway only partially. Only she can finish the ritual.

X lifts the hem of her dress, revealing her inner thigh where her birthmark-scales shine beneath the true sunlight. The scales along her own belly illuminate in kind as ancient energy of the monstrous, of truth, and of thirst for belonging in a shite world that hunts monsters rise between them in a mist of glitter. A storm rises between them, all stars and wind and heat. Two solid streams of glowing, writhing serpents meet and join between them, causing their erections to balloon and reach for each other. Their yearning for each other had never waned. Just as with the ritual in the woods that night, their two streams finally meet, embrace, and wrap around each other. These lines intersect, constrict, and entwine into a single column that shoots into the sky, far above the heads of the onlookers. She and X rain serpentine ecstasy upon each other, undulating with hope and rekindled love.

X's eyes lock onto hers, brighten, and as her body and mind both heal from their trauma, she rises from the street. Their scales spread all along their skin as lightning. Their hair writhes with ageless magic, and finally, she elongates into opaque, viscid form. X leads her into full being.

They turn to the crowd, the paramedics, the paparazzi.

10

The Ritual of Gorgon is complete.

The truck driver who had hit her on her bike missed everything. He was coming down from his high when X arrived on the scene and he was cutting a fresh line on a small mirror he put on top of his passenger seat. By the time he sat back up he saw the people frozen white, and right past them, two beasts towering above them. The giant serpent women had gazed past their quarry into their own reflections in the shop window and turned to stone.

Passersby in a double decker bus who had happened to be glancing out the windows at the scene were similarly petrified where they sat. The lorry driver saw the Gorgon's eyes reflected from the shop window into his own rearview mirror and after he turned to stone he crashed the bus into oncoming traffic, and the chain reaction killed six adults and a baby.

The monument still stands today, all of the bodies, Gorgon and human alike, occasionally frosted with the grime of the eternal city. The municipals clean them off every spring and autumn. The truck, left abandoned there by its owners. The driver goes on WorldNet, telling his side of the story many times and he's made a good living for himself. He contemplates this as he drops dead in the summer garden that hosts his daughter's roses.

Every lunar month when the sky is clear, the full moon hits The Gorgons, illuminating their frozen-grotesque features, and they both fall in love again.

And every time it feels new.

THE WIFE: VICTORIA DALPE

She pressed her forehead against the glass, savoring the coolness, enjoying the way her eyelashes brushed against the window. Beyond it she could see the street—gray concrete, wrought iron, the vibrant greens of new growth. It was a rainy spring day. Although she could not smell it, if she squeezed her eyes shut she could imagine it. She adored the smell of rain.

"What are you doing, Vivian?" His voice startled her, broke her reverie, sent her head darting toward the doorway. The sudden movement caused the bandage at her throat to throb, her hand fluttered to it absently. She knew there would be a face print on the glass, advertising her guilt.

He stood only a step or two into the room, his height and girth filling the space, stealing the air, redefining the geometry to accommodate his mass. Even ten feet away, even standing, she felt small. He did not move further, just crossed his arms over his massive barrel chest and waited.

Obediently, she stepped away from the window. As soon as she did, she missed it, missed the freedom of the window. Every face that passed had a story. Every closed door she saw out there held mystery. Every shuttered window encapsulated another life.

"You can't just spend all afternoon daydreaming out that damn window. Now come fix lunch. I have work to get back to." His voice boomed in the small space. She hurriedly stepped away from the window. He blocked the doorway and when he did not step away, she tried to brush past him out the door. His arm shot out and stopped her. His massive hand could encircle her entire bicep. She was aware of his strength, without him having to squeeze. Even now, when he was trying to be gentle, his hand was a vice. He simply wasn't built for gentleness, his every movement was a threat, purposeful or not.

"No kiss?"

She shuddered, avoided his eyes, and looked past him back out the window. He waited, his fingers tensing on her arm. Finally she nodded. Turning her head she stared at his bulbous nose, ruddy and pitted, and his fleshy lips. Those lips would be womanish if they were on a softer face. She puckered and pecked, trying to be as efficient as possible. But he pulled her in, pinned her with his arms. His mouth opened, tongue darting out past his lips and into hers. His stubble scraped her cheeks raw, his mouth tasted sour.

When he released her and she nearly fell back. He mistook it for a swoon and smiled wolfishly.

Moments later, he stood in the doorway to the kitchen, arms folded, and stared at her as she set out the bread. Leered at her as she stacked meat and cheese. Grinned at her as she ladled soup into a small bowl and placed it on the table for him. He settled in, smacking his lips, and tucked a napkin into the collar of his dress shirt. She stood in the furthest corner of the kitchen, her back nearly touching the blisteringly hot radiator.

He ate, un-quietly, and grumbled when he realized she had not provided him a drink. Two large glasses of milk later, he was up, burping and patting his stomach, then rubbing his entire face with the napkin like a towel.

"That was lovely. Never thought I'd like having a wife at all. But I am so glad I found you, Viv." She dropped her gaze and nodded. He kissed her on the head and strode out, the pots and pans jangling as his great weight passed by. When she heard the front door close, and his footfalls on the sidewalk, she released the breath she had been holding in.

That night she tossed and turned. Nights were always the hardest for her.

Every night, he forced her to go to bed with him early. She was a night owl though and spent most nights laying there, staring at the ceiling. She knew he feared her alone and awake in the house while he slept. He did not trust her. He would not admit it, but she could tell. If she so much as wanted a glass of water, he would grumble, suspiciously and come along. Something in her knew he shouldn't trust her, but the thoughts skittered away like shadows meeting light. She tugged at her bandage and tried to find a comfortable spot. A small persistent thought circled her head: he knew enough stories to be wary.

She tossed and turned. Too hot, too cold, entangled in bed sheets, and always his great weight—like a fallen log—pressing her into the mattress. She could hear the night sounds outside the window: fire trucks tearing through the silence, lone footsteps of predator and prey, cats in heat yowling. She longed to be out in it, she longed to feel the soft caress of moonlight on her skin, the wind in her hair, the vastness of the sky. She had forgotten how long it had been since she had been outside at all.

Her dreams were always filled with flying. She'd soar through indigo skies, streaking above the sea. Her reflection always raced her below in the dark water. She'd dip down close enough to run her fingertips through the waves, and feel it's inky spray. She'd luxuriate in the wildness and the freedom. She was weightless and unfettered.

Then she would wake with tears on her cheeks, an ache in her heart, the phantom salt air dissipating in her nostrils as the dreams faded.

It wasn't always this way, she remembered only fragments, but there had been a life before this one. A life where she was free and laughed. She had faint creases at her eyes, laugh lines, so surely there must have been a time when she was filled with laughter. There must have been laughter enough to etch it into her face. But her memories were fireflies, blinking in and out, eluding her capture. The more she tried to remember the more the pain at her throat forced her to forget.

And the pain at her throat kept her from sleeping. On this night the pain was more intense, she knew it was because she tried to remember. The dressings were irritating and her skin had a rash where the bandages wouldn't allow it to breath. She wanted to scratch at it, but that only made it worse. Often she would wake at night, her hands frantically tugging at the wound, nighttime fingers operating without her mind's consent. He would be cross with her, if he noticed the bandages loose. He hated the look of the wound, he found it repulsive, and always forced her to keep it tightly covered.

She was uncomfortable: hot, in pain, frustrated. His snoring body half over her, sweaty arms and hairy legs pressing her down. Instead of feeling endless despair, as she often did staring up at the ceiling, she felt anger. What had he said earlier that day? *I'm so glad I found you.* Found. Something was missing from her life and while she could not remember it, she knew it was gone. It angered her— this absence. And she knew he was to blame, the big lout: a gross, cruel, man who somehow entrapped her.

Trapped. Not Found. Trapped. Once the word tickled her mind she could not let go of it. She did not know other wives, forbidden as she was to leave the house, but from what she could glean, they went outside, they were allowed to. They had jobs, same as her husband, and they would leave their homes each day to go to work, or to the store, or to the park. They were not trapped like animals that took the bait and fell into a trap. They were not prisoners, locked into their homes. Oh, he says they are. He assures her that everyone has a secret wife at home —that stays home— that no one knows about. He promises her that. Behind every door there is a wife, bandaged up and hidden away. And when she asks about the women she can sometimes see on the street in front of their home? Prostitutes, is his answer. They're tragic, unmarried woman who must have sex for money to survive.

But what was the difference between those women and her? She was forced to pleasure this porcine mountain of a man, willing or not, and cook for him, and care for him so that she would have a place to live. She had no job, nothing besides him and taking care of his home. Wasn't she a prostitute as well? He beat her savagely whenever she attempted to go outside. Once he loosened a tooth, another time blackened an eye, and two of her delicate ribs were snapped beneath his boot. He thought she was escaping, but she just wanted to smell the air, to feel it on her skin. So she sat at her window day in and out.

She envied those women on the streets, those 'prostitutes,' some with small children in strollers even. Walking so freely outside. They may have to lay with many men, but perhaps some of those men were attractive? Or kind? At least there was a variety. She glared at her husband in the darkness, trying to remember why she married him.

Her neck throbbed.

But that was the rub. She could not remember specifics, but she knew she never married him. She couldn't even remember how she got inside his house. Found, he said. She knew she would have never chosen him, over all others. His small eyes were cruel, and he smelled, even after a bath. No, she would never have been duped into agreeing to marry him. Would a parent have allowed it? Did she have parents? How did she get here?

She scratched absently beneath the bandage and it burned.

And yet, somehow, here she was.

He cleared his throat, deep in sleep, his lips smacking together, and finally he rolled off of her. His weight lifted, allowing a breeze of cool air to dry her damp sweaty skin.

You must remember, Vivian.

Vivian? Was that even her name really? He called her that. But she felt very little tie to the name, she could not remember anyone besides him even calling her by it. She snorted, she could not remember anyone else ever speaking to her.

Her entire body was suddenly covered with gooseflesh and she *knew*. Vivian was not her name. She could not recall her name, but she knew, at her core, that Vivian was only a name he *called* her. She was tugging at her neck, desperate for more air.

The anger was fighting with panic. What had he done? How had he done it? Erased her memory. Renamed her. Trapped her in this house where she cooked and spread her legs and cleaned. Were all the women outside prostitutes after all? Or was she a fool? He was not a smart man, she knew that, so how had he imprisoned her here? Complacently believing all he told her.

She found it hard to think, the burning, itching at her neck distracting her. Clawing at the red raw skin beneath the bandage relieved some of the discomfort. But what she really wanted to do was pull off all the damn dressing and let the wound get some air.

Why not? He was deep asleep beside her. And it had been months with little improvement.

Carefully with wet eyes and shaking fingers, she pulled the damp wrappings, inch by inch, her breath short, and finally it was off. The yellowed gauze was a pale bundle on the floor.

She breathed a sigh of relief, her delicate throat filled with joy at the feel of fresh air running over it. The wound ached, it's sickly sweet odor tickling her nose, turning her stomach. Oh, how it throbbed in tune with her pulse. With careful fingers she explored the injury. She could not recall how she got it, just that it had always been. Trembling she felt the puffy damaged skin, and the feverish heat it threw off. The cavity in her throat was large, the skin so tender she could not turn her neck too far in any direction. Her fingertips an inch above could feel it pulsating and hot, the hole.

Just feeling it in the darkness was not enough, not tonight, when her blood was boiling, and her mind was so close to discovering something. The indignation and pain forced her up and out of bed, creeping on silent feet, cautiously listening for his steady breathing. It went unchanged.

She closed the bathroom door, as slowly as possible, and only once sealed, with a towel along the floor, did she turn on the light. And all though she looked in the mirror daily, on this night it felt illicit.

And there she was before the mirror. Her eyes large, almond shaped, golden. Her face pale as milk, sickly, shiny with sweat. Around the bandages, her skin was rashed. Yellows and purples orbited the hideous wound. And out from the gaping hole, bigger than her fist, sprouted feet and feet of her dark hair, shiny as a wet seal, as if it grew from her throat. She leaned nose to nose with her reflection studying that hair, a thick rope, thicker than an anaconda, coiled up and buried deep in her ruined neck.

Ugly. Horrible.

Surely she had not put all her hair-- *longer than she was tall*-- a ghost memory whispered-- into a hollow in her neck? Did her husband? Obviously the skin was infected. It stank of gangrenous rot, and showed myriad colors never seen on healthy flesh. She whimpered as she fingered the mouth of the wound, coming away damp with the yellow leakings and watery reds. Even the gentlest touch caused shocks of electric pain up and down her spine. Her eyes streamed and she bit the inside of her mouth to prevent making a peep.

Staring at the strange and grievous injury, the anger blossomed into something darker, reds fading to blacks. This had all been done to her. Of that she was sure.

And with a strange epiphany, almost whispered in her ear, she remembered something.

This wound kept her complacent, weak, full of infection and corruption, waiting on that man like a servant. A servant he could splay wide and pump full of his seed whenever he wanted. His servant, who was forbidden to go outside or even to speak with another person. She had no memory, but what she had now was the knowledge that there was something missing. There was a void inside of her that had not existed even a day before. Something was stolen from her, her name, her identity, her life. And this gray-faced imposter in the mirror had been traded in her place. And there was little doubt *he* had orchestrated it all.

With a will of steel she wrapped her hands around her hair where it met the flesh of her throat. It was crusted with the wet and dried blood of months. She breathed deep, meeting her eyes in the mirror and wishing support. *You are brave. You are taking yourself back. Do it.* And with a resolve she had never felt before, she gripped the hair in two fists and pulled.

It hurt like she was being flayed alive, every nerve on every inch of her body lit up in small searing flames. Her blood ignited like gasoline rivers. Her heart tripped, her bladder released, and her lungs squeezed and seized. She fell, consciousness ghosting her away, her head striking the sink on the descent. The trauma going unfelt when added to the cacophony of sensations exploding within her. Finally darkness swallowed her up, formless, mindless, and peaceful.

When she gasped awake her senses flooded in noisily, fighting for dominance. The overhead light blinded her, the sound of her heart chugging and blood rushing her veins deafening her. Every inch of her skin tingled, each hair follicle waving frantically for her attention. And her hair was free: long, longer than her memory, longer than she was tall. It was wet and heavy, streaking the floor with a stinking slug's trail of her fluids. She could barely lift her head the weight of it was so great.

So she rested, squeezing her eyes shut to block it all out. And only then, in the quiet of her own head, did she realize what was no longer missing.

Her memories. Her.

Em. Her name was Em.

It was like a deluge pushing and vying for her focus. Rushing in from all sides: her life, her sisters, her... freedom. She could hear laughter, and feel the caress of familiar hands, a thousand days of sunshine and rain, of moonlit nights.

She shot up gasping, ignoring the pain and the weight of her hair, even the throbbing hole in her neck was barely felt for once. She pressed her hands to her eyes, overwhelmed. She stared at the bathroom door, envisioning that sleeping hunk of meat on the other side.

She rose, her anger blinding her. She remembered it *all*.

It had been night, a beautiful clear night, the sky, a soft plum lit up by thousands and thousands of stars. And Em had been dozing on a long, strong tree branch, enjoying the night.

Alone.

Although her sister's warned that it was not safe to venture into this forest, she had gone anyway. She was the youngest and had a tendency to defy her older, bossier, siblings.

And then He came, he and others. With their snares and traps. And she tried to flee, but they were prepared, too prepared, she realized too late. They were hunting *her*. And it was as if they knew everything about her. She tried to flee, to fight. But they shot her with a dart, tangled her in a net, and when she tumbled from the tree, before she lost consciousness, they trussed her up and bound her mouth. She moaned, fighting wildly even as the drugs swarmed her system and pulled her under.

"She's a strong one," he chuckled. "A fighter. Guess she'll be mine eh?" And they laughed, all the men, standing above her in a circle, too dark to see their faces. Her heart raced, and she looked for her sisters, hoping they would sense she was missing—that they would know she was in distress. But no one came to her aid. Consciousness fled like a candle blown out.

And now she was back.

Em rubbed at her eyes, tears streaking her face and her bloody hands. She reached for the doorknob, feeling more alive than she had in months, movement caught her eye and she turned to her reflection. She looked back and no longer saw Vivian, the scared thing all wrapped up in bandages.

She looked down at the frilly nightgown, soaked in her juices and clinging indiscreetly. This was the last item of *Vivian's* she would rid herself of. And she did, pulling the thin fabric, shredding it with her claws. It fell away in tatters and she breathed out in relief.

Free. Her hair fell to the floor, dragging and wet, but slowly untangling itself as if sentient. Her golden eyes wide, aware. Em walked close to the mirror, nearly pressing her naked body against her reflection. She had missed herself so much. And the two of them smiled now, revealing two rows of dainty needle sharp teeth.

She opened the door, letting the light fall onto the bed. He snorted, rolled over, and then sat straight up, his sweat shining face paling as he looked upon her.

She was on him in two long strides, moving faster than he could see, gliding through the space like a blade. She bowled him back with her weight, her hair rising around her, writhing like a thousand snakes.

He whimpered.

And she laughed.

This mountain of a man was afraid and his fear nourished her. She breathed in the stink, and let her tongue rake along his pock marked cheek. She savored the sour taste of his primal animal fear.

She let her clawed hands dig into the flesh of his shoulders, her toenails digging into his thighs. He screamed out, his mouth wide, and she took the opportunity to press her mouth to his, pulling his tongue out between her sharp teeth, severing it. He wailed and they were both soaked in the fount of blood that erupted from his mouth. She bathed in it, luxuriated in its warmth. He choked and gurgled, eyes wide, reduced to a sheep at the slaughter, eyes rolling mindlessly.

She pressed her nails into him deeper, digging through muscle and sinew, the pain forcing his mind to clear and focus on her. She wanted him to understand that she was strong and powerful and dangerous. She wanted him to fear her and marvel at her. She spat the hunk of tongue to the floor and pulled one hand from his shoulder to wipe at her mouth. She could do this for hours and while tempted, the night beckoned and she could feel the moon pulsing past the gossamer curtains.

She let her bloodied hand run across the coarse hair of his chest. He shook and shuddered, vainly trying to rock her off, but she rode him like a cowboy, squeezing his fat gut between her thighs . She gnashed her teeth at him, and he blubbered, the blood spilling out the sides of his mouth, a wine glass overfilled.

Her palm ran over his ribs to the soft space just beneath, she could feel his heart chugging—at a rodent's breakneck speed—and she wanted it. She pulled her arm back, flexing, and with a roar she punched down, through the soft belly skin and the insulating layers of fluffy fat, past the strong abdominal muscles and then inside, wriggling through ropes of intestines, and soft organs. Hot gasses belched out as she pushed her arm further. His eyes were wide, all white, rolled back in his skull, and he wheezed trying to get his breath. She found her prize. Searing hot, and moving like a lizard in a sack. She squeezed, enjoying the force needed to get her hand around it, and the teeth gritting strength it took to pull it out. He screamed, more an animal keen, before his head dropped, eyes wide, mouth wide, dead.

She pulled the heart out. Big as a cows. And Em looked at it in the darkness. It beat once, twice, the last of the blood pumping out onto her arms and body through the torn ventricles. She turned it side to side, admiring the thick muscles, and strength that such an organ would need to animate a body as big as his.

And with a laugh that shook the heavens, she bit down into it, gnawing like a dog. And she ate it all. It sat heavy and hot in her stomach and she savored the closure it gave her.

She was finally free. Stepping off him daintily, she stretched, luxuriating in the feel of air on her skin and neck. The hole had calmed to a gentle occasional pang of discomfort, the skin finally healing. Her hair hung over her like a great cloak. Its weight was no longer a burden, but a comfort.

Barefoot, claws clicking on the floor, she went to the window. Pulling back the curtains she saw acres and acres of rooftops clustered together. And further still, the glint of the ocean. And the moon was above it all, welcoming as a mother.

She pulled up the window and balanced on the sill. Glancing back she stared at him. Her captor. Her husband. Em snorted. Now he was little more than a hunk of rotting meat. He lay spread eagle on the bed, a perfectly round, fist sized hole punched into his chest. She absently ran her hand along her own gaping hole, at her throat. It almost felt good.

A breeze passed by her, on it the smells of the city, of the sea, of a thousand lives lived out in each window she could see. And the yearning for the night pulled her out the window. She was airborne, dropping the two stories fast, heavy as a stone. But she was not a stone, and the air was her mistress as much as the night sky was. Her hair unfurled, catching the errant breeze, and pulling her along it. She lifted, weightless, and flew up above the rooftops and spindly chimneys, streaking across the sky, gaining speed, higher and higher. She could no longer tell her rooftop from any other and she was glad for it.

The city grew smaller and smaller. She spun, corkscrewing through the sky and clouds, luxuriating in her hair, longer than her by twice now, wrapped around her, hugging her in its warmth. She looked ahead, to the ocean. She wanted to feel the surf on her skin, to clean the life of Vivian off her body once and for all.

She was nearly to the shore and the briny air was intoxicating.

The moon was bright enough to see her shadow, a blot of ink on the glowing sand.

She called out, in joy, in exhilaration. Her call was piercing, causing windows to rattle, and dogs to howl for miles. And there in the distance, Em heard a response, then another. Her sisters. Her heart doubled in size picturing each of their faces, hungering for their embraces.

And she became a trick of the moon, a shadow, a mystery thing, once more.

DAYGLO REFLECTION: MANUEL CHAVARRIA

When Aimee Kim stepped out of the shower that morning and wiped the fog from the mirror, she saw something different. Her cheeks were full and pink, her teeth whiter, and her hair—usually a mousy nest of split ends and dry strands—shone under the lights, a rich chestnut that became a deep green at the ends. The Aimee in the mirror smiled and tilted her head, and the Aimee outside followed suit. This earth-toned goddess was her best self, and, having glimpsed her destiny, Aimee vowed to beckon her vision from its hiding place beyond the clouds of condensation and into the proper world.

In her room, she let her towel drop, and she stared down at her body. Her feet were too wide, and her ankles were thick. Her breasts were large, but lopsided. The mirror in her room told her different things than the mirror in the bathroom did—that transcendence was not a foregone conclusion, and that she could not simply assume that her flaws would be burned away under the harsh light that greeted her while she toweled herself off—that her dreams were not everything.

Aimee finished dressing, and pulled her hair back into a long ponytail. The morning air was cold. Her ride to work was typical, and drab, the road littered with rusting, frost-colored cars that absorbed what little sunlight there was rather than reflecting it back at the gray and desperate sky. Behind the clouds, the sun appeared indistinct and hazy, its glow dull, as if it had moved on, leaving only a slow and receding shadow in its wake. Aimee stopped at a drive-thru for coffee, and as she waited her turn, while the man in front of her piled special request after special request upon his fucking coffee order, for god's sake, she pulled down the visor and flipped open the mirror to see if she was still beautiful.

She wasn't. The dull grey outdoors had drained her of color, and what stared back at her was a dark-eyed wraith, hair like thin tentacles, and she half-expected to turn to stone.

The car behind her sounded its horn, breaking her reverie. The car in front of her had gone while she was distracted. She glanced in the rear view, and the woman in the car behind her glared holes through her. Aimee was embarrassed, but out of spite she waited before pulling forward, and she didn't even raise her hand in a *mea culpa*. It was the small rebellions that kept her sane.

She was the first one to arrive to work, which was not exactly out of the ordinary, but it happened infrequently enough that she always forgot to label her keys. She tried—and failed—to open the door with key after key, getting to the last one—had to be that one —just as one of her colleagues got there, pushing her aside with a little giggle and a nod "hello," the right key in the proper hole without a thought.

Aimee seethed, but she pushed it down and walked in behind her: Lauren, the blonde, who walked with a little hop in her step everywhere—

Up the stairs to work: HOP

On her way to her car: HOP

To the pseudo-Mexican place across the street to get a burrito: HOP

Along piss-soaked sidewalks from which tent cities sprouted like fungus, as the city's economic pole snapped in half, each piece falling away from the other without even a "fuck you" shouted over a shoulder: HOP

Lauren went straight for the Nespresso machine and popped in a pod. Her brow was smooth, her eyes light, and her smile never faltered.

"Aimeeee, what did you do this weekend?" Lauren squealed, her voice still the voice of a young girl.

Aimee exhaled slowly to avoid a sigh. "I was at home. I spent time in my patio, with my cat."

"Oh my god, do you have pictures? Can I see?" Lauren was taller than Aimee, and she leaned into the space above Aimee's head. Aimee took a step back.

"Uh...sure." Aimee pulled out her phone, pulled up a photo, and then turned the phone to show Lauren. "Her name is Beatrice."

"BEATRICE! SHE'S SO CUTE!" Lauren screamed as she grabbed the phone and began swiping through Aimee's photos.

"Just..." Aimee whispered. "Be careful. Please." Her voice was sandpaper and her eyes went wide, but Lauren didn't notice—she just kept smiling, and her cheeks grew rosier. Aimee looked away, and caught a glimpse of her reflection in the breakroom window. She could see a hazy outline of the vision she'd had earlier that morning, but as she approached the window, the outline was over-taken by a dreadful reality. Her hair seemed tattered and worn and cracked like dry mud. Her lips were chapped. She was pale and drawn. She could see dark circles developing under her eyes in real time.

Her phone was suddenly thrust back in front of her face. "Who is *that?*" Lauren demanded to know. It took a moment before Aimee could focus on the image floating in front of her, but when she did, she blanched.

"...I don't know his name..." she said in her smallest voice, and she could feel tears welling up, but she refused to release them—not in front of this blonde monster, never. "He's just this guy. It's just a picture."

"Well, he's *cute* and you definitely should talk to people instead of sneaking photos, you *sneak!*" Lauren said, cheerfully, as she play-slapped Aimee's arm. "You can also use that thing to make calls, you know!" She strode out of the breakroom and into her office, its off-white walls luminous beneath the spray of sunlight from the windows that surrounded her desk.

Aimee stood with a coffee cup in her hand. Her bathroom

mirror was clear and bright in her mind. Upon its gleaming surface, she danced in a floral print dress, the skirt twirling out from her tan legs, her hair blowing in the breeze, strong and colorful. She closed her eyes tight so that she could hold onto the image. She carried it with her as she sat at her desk.

After work, Aimee took the long way home, following her usual detour—the one that placed her at the park bench across the street from the bookstore where the guy in the picture worked. She'd liked sitting at that bench anyway, had read there once or twice, but she'd only begun regularly parking herself on it after she'd seen him the first time.

It was his walk that attracted her at first—slow but straight, sort of an amble, but with a sense of purpose that could be gathered if you looked hard enough. Aimee liked that, and she liked that he was quiet; she never once saw him speaking more than a sentence to anyone. She saw in his behavior his own series of small rebellions, the kind that had carried her through so many days. She watched him move, his body lean and hard—she was sure—beneath a Black Sabbath t-shirt and a pair of blue jeans. She didn't believe in concepts like destiny—she was far too intelligent for that—but she knew—it had to be instinct—that he was a kindred spirit, another swimmer in the deep tide seeking a friend in a world that had outlived human connection.

She hadn't yet been into the store; it was better to study his habits first to be sure, wasn't it? This was not a world that rewarded uneducated guesses. She wasn't some dead-end idealist; she allowed for the possibility that he wasn't everything that her stupid heart had made him out to be.

He stopped short, and looked back, not at her but in her direction. She froze, her lips peeled back in a grin that she could feel grow desperate under the risk of his stare. He scratched the back of his head and scanned the horizon. Once she felt sure that she was out of his direct field of vision, Aimee lifted her phone into position and quickly snapped a photo.

Soon he was out of sight, and she allowed herself to breathe.

She gazed at the image onscreen. She ran her two middle fingers along his strong jaw line and across his thick, dark eyebrows. He saw her now, she thought.

———

Emboldened, Aimee stopped at a salon before heading home for the night. The morning's vision still danced behind her eyes, and rather than risk letting it escape while she slept, she felt compelled to pay homage. She gave her name to the front desk, and she sat and she waited patiently for her name to be called. She did not read. She barely moved. To watch her was to wonder if she even breathed. Instead she drew herself inward and focused on her memory: she ran in circles with the wind in her hair... it billowed behind her like a silk sheet, and it changed color under the rays of a warm and friendly sun, now brown, now green, now something else entirely... an animal unto itself, crossing oceans of time.

Aimee described what was in her head to the stylist, who, in response, regarded her quietly and at a distance, as though she were watching some strange, iridescent insect crawl along her forearm.

———

When Aimee got home, she went to her bathroom immediately. At first she stood in darkness; the morning was distant, and she was convinced that whatever she had seen had been an extension of her dreams—dreams which comforted her when she was frightened, when her bed felt cold and it was all she could do to cling to her pillows and ride out the night.

She flipped the light switch; the scene in the mirror was bright —brighter than it had been in the morning. She didn't just see a vision of herself this time. She also saw a lush and expansive field full of flowers at the far edge of their bloom. Through the tall grass she ran, bathed in sunlight, lips red and hungry. Behind her a number of peaceful woodland creatures milled, grazing. In the distance, above a line of swaying trees, Aimee saw the sun, its corona a dizzying mix of pinks and greens against an unnatural sky that shimmered blue, then faded to ochre before settling into a deep umber.

As the color settled, Aimee's doppelgänger looked at her, and the grazing animals lifted their heads from grass and followed suit. Their eyes glowed, and they all leered at her, lust written on their faces. Even the sun seemed to burn hotter, the bit of sky surrounding it flashing a deep orange.

Aimee flailed for the light switch and hit it just as the animals began to advance on her. The bathroom went dark, and the scene disappeared. Aimee sat along the edge of her bathtub until her heart stopped pounding. When she felt like she could stand again, she walked to the mirror and laid a palm against it. It was cold, and flat, and solid.

Aimee avoided her bathroom the next morning; she had taken what she thought she'd need the night before—what she could identify, anyway, feeling around her cabinets in the dark.

She made herself up in her bedroom. She was unshowered, but she hadn't really exerted herself the day before, and she didn't think it made much of a difference; it wasn't as though she was known for showing up to work having put in a great deal of effort; finally, her relaxed approach would work to her advantage. And, in fact, in light of her fear of the bathroom and her lack of sleep, it was almost as though she had just stepped out of the salon—no shower to wash away the stylist's efforts, no tossing and turning during the night to flatten and distort her new look. She smiled, and rubbed a bit of lipstick from her teeth.

In the back of her closet, Aimee kept a dress not unlike the one from her visions. Its flowers were not as red as they once were, and the deep blue field on which they'd stood had gone a musty grey, but it wasn't clothes that made the woman, she'd read once, but quite the opposite—it was, in fact, a matter of confidence and a dedication to style, and now Aimee had both in spades. She laid the dress against her body; her breasts were perky and even, because she decided they were, and her ankles were slim, and she just knew that her feet would fit perfectly into the red heels she'd purchased two years before, shoes that had been too narrow but didn't seem nearly as daunting now. Aimee felt warmth spread through her chest. Today was a new day.

She stepped into the dress. The way the dress hugged her curves made her feel sexy. She pulled on the heels; perhaps they were still a bit snug, but she was sure that her legs looked amazing, and besides, a little pain was helpful to the spirit; it built character. For once, Aimee couldn't wait to get to work. She even hoped Lauren would corner her in the breakroom again; it was Lauren's turn to be left speechless.

Aimee arrived at work a little later than usual; she had taken some time to bask in admiring stares while she walked to her car, and again as she made her way toward the office. She threw open the door to the office and walked in triumphant, catwalk style: one foot in front of the other, hips weaponized... she winked at the receptionist and blew a kiss at Lauren as soon as she saw her rounding the corner.

Lauren stopped. Her jaw went slack. "Are you *okay?*" she asked. Then she got close to Aimee and whispered, "Are you drunk?"

Aimee backed up as though she were avoiding a slap. "Absolutely not!" she said, and put a hand on her hip.

"Aimee, babe, you look like a wreck. You look like you haven't slept at all. Did you sleep?"

Aimee looked around for a window—any sort of glass—but there was nothing in the hallway.

"Ohmygoodness!" Lauren squeaked, her eyebrows high, her hands held up near her face as though preparing to prevent her head from launching into outer space. "Were you with a *boy?* Were you with that *guy?*"

Aimee's face went blank. She didn't see the hallway any longer, or the receptionist, or even the office. But she did see Lauren, alone, standing in that field, a simpering cow blind to the crueler aspects of the natural world. Aimee's lips drew back in a sneer. She raised her arm, her hand thick and hard like a bear's paw, then she brought it down swift and clubbed Lauren along the side of her head. Lauren crumpled.

Aimee leaned over Lauren's writhing, confused form, and she shouted: "IT'S JUST A PICTURE! HE'S JUST THIS GUY!"

She saw the receptionist again then. The woman was standing, hand at her mouth, eyes alert with fear. Aimee looked back down toward Lauren, who had pulled herself into a fetal position and was taking shallow breaths. The receptionist reached for the phone. Aimee backed away, then turned and ran for the door.

Aimee wasn't certain that she was headed for the bookstore until she got there. She had no plan, just hope that the guy from her pictures was there, because she needed someone to understand. She didn't see him through the windows. She would have to go inside.

The store was quiet. Jazz played softly over the speakers, and the woman at the front counter was absorbed in a book. She could hear movement toward the back of the store, so she crept that way, peering around shelves, haunting the stacks while she searched for him, the one person in her shrinking circle that could offer her some solace. She thought about the set of his jaw, and about his eyebrows, and about those thin, wiry arms gathering her up in an embrace. "Everything is going to be okay," he'd say, and he'd run his hands through her soft hair.

Aimee still didn't see him. She would have to ask. This was a moment for bravery. She straightened up and stepped to the information counter. The woman there was turned away from her, and she said, "I'll be with you in just a second." Aimee ran her fingers along the countertop. It was scuffed and stained. When the woman finally turned toward Aimee, she went stiff; her attempt at a smile failed, and she stood wincing.

"How can I help you?" she asked. She did not step closer to the counter.

Aimee barely noticed. She leaned forward, conspiratorially. "There's...this *guy*." She held her hand up to her mouth. "He works here," she whispered. Then she stood straight and pushed her hair back over her shoulder. Her fingers got tangled in a knot, which she ripped free. "I need to find him," Aimee continued.

The woman stammered. "Um." Her eyes narrowed. "Which...guy?" she asked.

Aimee's eyes widened, and she looked down and smoothed a wrinkle on her dress. "I don't know his name," she said. "But he works here. I've seen him. Leaving."

The woman behind the counter crossed her arms over her chest. "I'm sorry," she said, "but if you don't know him, I can't just give out information about him. Maybe next time you see him, you could try introducing yourself. But I can't help you." The woman took another step back from the counter.

Aimee wanted to club her, too. Her eyes narrowed. She sighed. Then she turned and walked away. She could feel the tears coming. Embarrassed, she slipped into the restroom.

The light was harsh in the restroom, and it didn't offer Aimee any place to hide. She turned to the mirror, and the tears rushed out as she saw her reflection. Her hair was ragged. The ends were green, as she'd asked, but it looked as though the stylist has rushed through the job—as though she was simply trying to get Aimee out of the chair quickly; the color was all wrong, faded mud flecked with blades of sun-bleached grass instead of the deep forest color she'd requested. Her hair was a little wavier than usual, but the waves were twisted and matted. Her skin had begun to redden; the back of her closet had been awfully dusty, and she could see the irritation creeping out from beneath her dress. Her throat felt scratchy. The dress was moth-eaten; a line of holes ran along the hemline and up the side.

Her shoes were a wreck. They were cheap to begin with, and languishing for years unused and uncared for had left them brittle. The stitching had not been a match for the pressure from her wide feet, nor had the heels been up to the task of supporting her weight; one had snapped off at some point, and she didn't notice where, or when. Her ankles ached.

Aimee kicked off what remained of her shoes and left them in the bathroom. She walked out of the bookstore barefoot, her face smeared with tears and shame. As she walked along the sidewalk, away from the bookstore and toward her apartment, she tripped and fell face-first into the concrete. She pushed herself up and away from the sidewalk, blood pouring from a wound that opened along her hairline. She flipped over onto her back and stared at the sky, as dull and grey as ever, shot through with threatening clouds. She sat up, and faced the street, just as her kindred spirit—wearing the same Black Sabbath shirt and the same blue jeans—walked by, toward the store. He stopped in front of her, looked her up and down, said "Jesus, clean yourself up and get a job!" and snorted. In front of the store, a customer on the way out offered a cheerful "Excuse me!" as she stepped around him. He flipped her off and went inside.

All Aimee wanted to do was take a bath, but she hadn't so much as looked at her bathroom door since she'd stumbled away from the mirror the night before. She stood in front of the door now, pushing thoughts of those ravenous eyes out of her mind with memories of the smiling, dancing double she'd seen before that nightmarish flash.

She gave the door a little shove. It opened slowly. She stepped inside, closed the door, and disrobed.

She did not turn the light on immediately. She looked at herself in shadow; the gloom from outside had crept in, and her appearance in the mirror was drained of color. The dried blood that ran from her forehead and down her face in streaks was less a rusty brown than a dim grey, offering no indication that it had ever been alive.

Aimee's fingertips danced around the light switch. Her chest was tight, and her eyes were raw. But the mirror had never ignored her. It hadn't scorned her or insulted her. Even at its most terrifying, it had offered her more than the detritus of her life. Her fingers stopped their drumming. She breathed deeply, and her heartbeat slowed. She flipped the switch.

She saw herself, bathed in light—light that emanated not from a fixture or a bulb, but from her—from her body, transformed. The blood on her head was no longer a dim grey, but it wasn't a dry, rusty brown, either. It was a dazzling red that glistened. Free from the constraints of her dress and shoes, baubles that she'd purchased to impress other people, her body glowed: her breasts were lopsided, but they were full and beautiful and alive, aided by the asymmetry, which eclipsed the sterile aesthetic of some statuesque ideal. Her feet were wide, but they were strong.

The room grew brighter. She was aware, finally, that the world of the mirror was not some mystical other place; it was her world, the world as it existed beneath dresses and concrete, a world that had lain in wait, uncommonly patient, ready to move at the first sign of a crack in mankind's eternal guard.

Aimee in this moment was no bleeding heart; she was a tyrant, focused on a climax that would burn away pretenders and leave her basking, surrounded by those pools of light, greens, oranges, pinks, light under the growing sun, light that left her nude and reformed and ready to grab the mantle of her dead mother earth, to smile wide and fuck beneath all risen stars.

The light reached its brightest point. Aimee saw the sun high over the tall grass, fiery and defiant, no longer simply one color or another, but all of them. She took no notice of the animals that looked at her. The wind embraced her. The grass was soft beneath her feet. In the distance, she saw trees. The sound of their rustling leaves was soothing. She strode toward them, and sat beneath one, cool in the shade. Her pain ran out of her in waves. It all seemed so far away. A low branch stroked her hair. She sighed, lowered herself to the ground, and went to sleep.

CATMAN'S HEART: LAURA LEE BAHR

The most beautiful woman I have ever seen in this world is in the bathtub, thawing, eyes open. Me, I am ugly, lying here, waiting for her to wake, my eyes closed. But I know there is some evil magic spell, about to be broken.

Life is about to truly begin.

Catman sits on my belly, telling me that it's not quite time to move. It's time to stay, feeling the quiet weight of him, the soft heat. I open my eyes to stare at his handsome face. He is black as night, soft as whispers, voice a deep growl of a purr as I bury my hand into his fur. Tears dry in my eye. My face still burnt from the snow, my heart still hot and pounding. There are bad boys out there but the ice princess will vindicate my family.

"Catman," I whisper. "It's going to be okay, now."

"Would you rather lay (x, y, z) or Annie Dulvaney?" This, the running joke at school. The variables were ugly boys, ugly teachers, or sometimes, farm animals. Tripped walking home, I fell face first into the snow. I was grabbed with a grunt and turned over. Three boys stared down at me with some joke about me or a squealing goat. The moment stuck like the final words cast in a curse. In a fairy tale, a handsome prince would have showed up just then to save me. Or at least my brother, Sean. But no one appeared.

Luckily, Catman has my heart, and I have his, and when one

moved at me again, I jumped at him with Catman's courage, like he would if he were cornered by three stupid dogs. I scared them with my hands out like claws at their eyes, my mouth spitting screams and hisses of nasty words they didn't know I knew.

They said things about me and mother, but they ran.

Skin beneath my fingers. A sense of something like pride: I made them bleed. And run.

But I want to make them something else. Changed. Sorry to be who they are. Sorry like they would before a vision of an angel. Sorry. Sad. Shamed. Like me. I want her to change them, the way she changed me. Beauty can do that.

The body had arrived in a block of ice. It floated, the water delivering a crystal coffin, straight toward me like an answer to a question I'd never known to ask.

Used to be, I'd go and walk out on the rocks and go to the edge where I could watch the water. I went there that one day, I'm not sure what I was thinking about. Maybe mom. Maybe I was there crying because Sean barked at me, he was always so busy and tired now. Anyway, I saw it float toward me. A floating block of ice, but there was a color there.

Think of an ice cube, with a tiny, frozen, plastic fairy inside, the ice cube—cracked and blurred. I wasn't sure what I was seeing. I scaled down the rocks to the edge of the water. I couldn't quite discern what was inside the ice. Here, a red flare of coat. Here, a brown of hair. I had to run home to get what I needed to bring her back. I got a sled and a large burlap sack to cover the block of ice. I didn't want anyone seeing her—I didn't want anyone taking her.

She had floated to me, and she was mine.

I walked into the water to pull her out, getting my jeans soaking wet with the freezing water. It wasn't hard to move the block of ice, though. I pulled her onto the sled, then I pulled the sled back to my home. It was dark by the time I got there, but there was a moon and everything shone. I grew hot as I pulled, my heart thump thump thumped. I had a treasure. It had come to me, something magical, at last, something for my fidelity.

"Never believe in Fairy Tales," mom had said, sometimes weary, sometimes angry. Once on a gurney. "Never believe, Annie. There is nothing to believe in."

But I did. I do.

I pulled the block into the garage. The garage is as cold as an ice house, holding husks of broken machinery. There, Sean's motorcycle, missing a few pieces. He planned to work on it when it got warm. If that ever happened again. It seemed like it had been too cold for years. There, mom's old car, the battery pulled out of it. Something else Sean was trying to fix, until he got stuck or too tired. And here, the jewel that'd been delivered to me from the water.

I pulled the light and only then did I truly inspect what I'd brought home. I pulled off the burlap and stared down at the beautiful woman encased in ice. No, not just a woman.

A princess.

Long brown hair spread out around her face like a giant halo.

Her porcelain, flash-frozen perfect skin.

Blue lips.

Her coat was red and was held open around her like wings.

She wore a long brown dress, still tied at the bodice. Black stockings. Little boots. I thought at once that she might be one of the lost ladies of the Titanic. She had been frozen when it went down, or become one with iceberg itself.

Somehow she had slept through the last century and into this one. What beauty and grace she could bring, like a miracle. So, I named her after heaven and the character in movie Titanic: Celeste Rose.

Her eyes were frozen open, serene, just awaiting true love's kiss. And I know at once this is what Celeste Rose must have to wake up.

A proper prince.

Sean worked too hard. Since mom was stuck in the state hospital, with all sharp objects hidden and a steady dose of neurotransmitter inhibitors to keep her brain cool and not on fire, it seemed like all he did was work.

He didn't go to school anymore, because who knew how long mom would be in the hospital and someone had to pay the bills and take care of Annie.

Annie, who used to have pink chubby cheeks and bright lights in her eyes, now had pinches around her face, chapped lips and snot running down her nose. Always sick. She and that old cat, a pair. That cat was so old it was hard for it to walk, its eyes were half-milky with blindness. If it were just him he'd leave it outside, let it figure its way to the next thing, like everything in nature. But Annie doted on it, talked to it more than to anything. It may have been her only friend.

She was fifteen, now, could be her own person. Had she started to bleed yet? That's not a question he wanted to ask her. She didn't seem womanly. She seemed more stringy and pulled, walking with a stoop in her shoulders and her head down, almost as if she'd turned into an old crone and a younger girl at the same time with her little girl voice and constant fantasy life. And always talking to the cat.

Weird and getting weirder. He worried he'd find her one day like mom, with blood spurting out of her arms.

He tried to tell her, always, "Gotta keep positive, Annie. We got each other, at least."

When he came home, late as usual one night, his shoulders sagging and his muscles aching, she was standing near the door to greet him, like she'd been watching him in the window, waiting.

She pounced, all excitement.

"You have to see what I found, Sean!" she said, nearly dancing. "You have to see what I dragged in from the water!"

At first, he almost called her crazy. Couldn't believe she had pulled and dragged a body in here. But he held the word in, like it was the family curse they should never utter (said enough about them all, anyway). But of course, if they called the cops or whatever, whoever they would call about this discovery, wouldn't they somehow be implicated? Wouldn't this taint their family name even more? They needed to just put the body back where Annie had found it. That was that.

But as he looked closer he could see certain things about the frozen girl. Things that made it more than just a dead body. There was something about her that seemed still quick, still vital, and even dead she was stunningly beautiful.

"Celeste Rose," Annie said her name like a prayer. She was so beautiful that she made an ache in him so intense he never wanted to give her up, never.

But he couldn't admit something like that. He could only figure out how to reason it, to rationalize it, to make it something he could solve. The frozen girl was the first time he realized what those stupid fucking songs were all about, and all those stupid fucking poems. Because he would die to be able to make her live. He would die for her.

Annie's stories started to work on him. About how he could wake her. About how he was her prince. About how she went down with the Titanic and was stuck in an ice floe that with climate change was now melting, bringing her here. Stories about her life in a beautiful world, now gone.

Sean had his own theories. He thought perhaps she was out at a party, or in a play, or just the kind of self-possessed creature who would wear clothes that looked to be from a previous century, and she fell into the water. Or was perhaps pushed. He can't think that she was murdered, she seems to have been preserved alive—at night, he could almost swear he could hear her heart beating through the ice.

Sean had always been something of a scientist, an inventor, a fixer. He could pull anything mechanical apart and put it back together. Before he had to leave school to work, he was always top in his science classes. He loved to experiment, and so he began research and development of how we could bring Celeste Rose back to life.

―――――――

It was all about a coagulant and anti-freeze. He spent hours on the internet, taking notes, trying to figure out what he needs to mix and try. Sometimes Annie puttered into the room at two or three in the morning, as he was still at it with the blue glow of the computer on his face. Then he would tell *her* stories for a change, a stream about experiments people had tried bringing creatures back from a frozen state, temperatures, chemicals.

"It's possible," he conceded, that just maybe they could bring back Celeste Rose. "It's not just a fairy tale," he told her. "It's science." Did she know Walt Disney himself had his head frozen? Waiting for science to catch up and bring him back to tell more fairy tales?

"Look at this, Annie," he said. He had a goldfish in a plastic bag. He put it in the freezer, just until the water became ice, and the fish stationary in it.

That he thawed, and lo and behold it started to swim again. He worried a little when it butted its head against the bowl, worried it got stupid in the freezing process, and what that might mean for the mind of Celeste Rose. But then the goldfish soon swam as all goldfish do, and hope beat hard in his head and chest.

He tried it with a bird. A little yellow feeder chick. The bird didn't wake up, and the injection did nothing.

"I don't think you should keep testing your potions on animals," Annie said, sad at the sight of the dead bird. "All she needs is true love's kiss."

"And an injection to the heart," he said. But he said it with a wink. For the truth was he dreamt of the cold of her blue lips against the warm of his pink, and the blink of those eyes. He must wake her. She must live again. She must.

I didn't realize I was sleeping until I hear the door.

Sean is home. I am scared for a moment. Maybe I should have consulted him, asked him before I put her to thaw in the bathtub. But I can't wait anymore for his experiments. Now, she should be thawed enough from the ice that he can kiss her.

I hear the bathroom door open, and then a cry:

"Jesus, God! Jesus Christ! Jesus!" yelling and screaming names of gods I know he doesn't believe in.

"Goddamn it, Annie!" he shouts as I enter the bathroom. "What the fuck are you thinking?"

And I see her body. She has thawed, yes. But I guess I did it wrong. Poor beautiful Celeste, her face looks expanded, misshapen, fat. Her eyes still open and her big, bloated face floats like an accusation. He races out of the room and back with the latest potion he created while I turn off the faucet. Water is all over the floor and we are trying to not slip.

Sean is back with a syringe and he gets in the full tub on top of her, never mind that he is fully clothed, water splashing everywhere.

He rips open her dress, her bra, and inserts the needle right into her heart, a liquid pushing hard into her. A plunger of blue down deep down into her as he gulps huge breaths. And then holds them.

We wait.

Awaiting what? A gasp? A yell? A curse for fucking this whole thing up, for making her fat, for all the water everywhere? For Sean with his face red and his sopping wet pants desecrating her, ripping her dress so her poor breasts are exposed and he is on top of her, watching her face for some signs of life?

No, nothing happens. Nothing happens at all.

"Goddammit Annie!" Sean says at last, wiping what seems like snot from his nose. I guess he is crying? I haven't seen him cry since I was a little kid.

I just stand there.

"Why the fuck did you just go and do it? Why the fuck, after all this time did you?"

I don't answer.

"Are you so fucking stupid or crazy or both?" And he knocks my head against the wall.

Just a second of pixie dust vision that comes back quickly, but I can tell from his face that he is feeling so glad and so sad to have hit me like that, like a kiss, like a fuck, like a punch in the jaw, so wrong and he knows it but it felt good somewhere.

I hit him back.

Don't care that he's older. Don't care that he's tougher. Don't care that it might be easy for us to die with too hard a hit on the tub or the floor and slip with the water, or is anything plugged in? Good thing I'm not the type to dry or curl my hair. Good thing we are too poor and ugly to make ourselves beautiful or we could be electrocuted and then there would be three dead bodies, all of them ugly now, all of them so, so, so ugly.

We fight hard. Like we used to fight when we were kids, biting, kicking, pulling hair:

"You let go."

"No, you let go first!" and neither of us ever let go.

He's not fighting back; he's just holding my arms, now. I have his ear in my mouth and I am biting down, tasting blood and he is pulling my face off of him. Not hitting back. I want him too, though. I want him to *hit back, hit back, hit.*

No. He won't. Now he is on top of me holding me down.

He does not rip open my shirt.

He injects nothing into me.

He looks down at me with nothing but pity and shame.

"Stop, Annie," he says. I suppose pity and shame are what I am due.

I give up.

He gets off of me. We go back to the bathtub. We stare at her. Whatever potion he injected into her has only made it worse. She is breaking apart. Her skin is like gum chewed with a handful of peanuts, sticking to everything but itself.

"What do we do now, Annie?" he whispers.

I leave the room. I go to the kitchen, open the drawer beneath the sink and take out four black plastic garbage bags.

When I come back to the bathroom, he is still just staring at her, watching her disintegrate. I pull Celeste Rose's stocking legs, which give like they are made of dough, into a garbage bag. And then her top I pull into another bag, and the bags meet in middle, which I wrap with another bag. One bag left, in which I scoop all floating bits.

I go and get the sled. I need Sean's help to move her because she is so much heavier now. We slop and flop her onto the sled.

He helps me to get the sled out onto the snow.

"I got it from here," I say. He nods, turns and walks back into the house.

I pull Celeste Rose's water logged, skin-shedding body within plastic bags back to where she first floated up.

I slip a couple of heavy rocks into the bags. A piece of something that feels like snot sticks to my hand. I realize it is actually probably part of her skin, but I can't bear to look. I tie up the plastic bags good and tight with those rocks as her gravestones, to weight her down.

I should rip through the plastic and kiss what is left of her lips. I should say,

"I love you, still." Or something about how I will always remember her beauty, even now, but I can't.

I push the sled out onto the water. I watch as the sled tilts and dumps her out and down. It is black out. No moon.

I wonder how I saw to do it.

But I did.

Once Upon A Time, I wished I was an ice princess. Beauty held timeless. That by some magic my lips would turn that shade of blue from the freezing water. My skin held in perfect static and ecstatic loveliness. But then, it can all just slide off you, that skin. And people who love you betray you with their neediness and stupidity. When you are so beautiful, people want to make you their own, and that wish destroys you and makes you nothing but more garbage.

I wanted the boys at school to cry. I wanted to love her, to find her a prince, to be her. But never to break my brother. But this, I have done.

He sobs in the other room, long gasping sobs.

His heart is broken. And I broke it.

But I cannot be sorry, because if I am sorry, it will be too much. I will get too hot and I will start to bleed and if I bleed, then I will bleed out. And then there will be no one left for Sean to take care of, and everyone needs someone to take care of, to stick around here for.

Me, I have to stay here so I can take care of Catman.

He is sleeping on me, now, for I am still warm for him. My heart frozen for all, but him. We try to sleep, me and my cat, the sound of my brother crying, a constant, like waves of the ocean.

And we live, but I will never wish to be happy or beautiful, ever after.

PANIC BIRD: SELENE MACLEOD

A crow swirls on air eddies, enjoying itself in the warm autumn sun, the last before winter's freeze. This morning I could feel a cold tongue creep against skin still thirsty for summer's kiss. Frost will settle in soon. The crow flaps its wings, spreads them again to catch air and coast, unmindful of my watch from the second floor window. It lights on the neighbor's roof, and pecks at something tasty it finds in the gutter.

For the moment, my own panic bird sits calm in its cage of bone. Imagine it asleep, head under one wing, breast rising and falling as it dreams. I wish it would stay in slumber, but as soon as Adam's key turns in the lock, the panic bird will flap its frightened tattoo against my chest. Wait for the sounds, the swish and click. The sound of street traffic reminds me this world is more than just me and the crow that doesn't even know I'm here. I wish it could stay like this, in stasis, some semblance of peace before Adam gets home and there's another fight. My doctor gave me some pills, but I don't like taking them. They give me a head full of cotton batting.

He's late. Shadows are longer and it's going to rain soon. The baby—she's no baby anymore, almost three, but I still think of her that way—is staying with my mother.

"He didn't even let the body cool before he moved you in," my mother said once, while in her cups. Sober, she just clucks and recleans, re-ties, re-diapers. When I found out I was pregnant, she told me I'd never be any good as a mother. Too unstable. Too many wounds, the scars a remnant of my war against my own skin. It's been at least a decade, but I still think of the bite of the blade, the thin lip of a new scratch, opening. And the heat, when it starts to heal under a black scab of infection.

The first drops splash against the window and I look to the crow, just in time to see it take wing, with a purpose. Rain gathers and runs against the glass. A flock of smaller birds takes off over the neighbor's yard, frantic and all moving in tandem. The most peaceful sound, which you can only hear if you're alone on a quiet street, is the sound of birds in flight, a dusty rustle, the sound of exertion.

I reach beside me and turn on the lamp. When I see my ghost-face reflection, doubled in the panes, I turn it off again. All this is a distraction. I keep going over in my head what I want to say to him, how to confront him when he gets home. That is, if he decides to come home tonight.

As if summoned, Adam opens the front door, real and solid. Normally, I would stand up, meet him at the door with a kiss, tell him about my day and listen while he tells his. We would feed the baby and get her ready for bed, then have our late dinner and read together. Poetry, sometimes novels, but always the words we love so much, that brought us together. The words we have in common, despite his being so much better than mine.

"June, are you home?" Adam calls. At the sound of his voice, the panic bird pokes up its head. I take a deep breath before I reply, "In here."

"What are you doing, sitting in the dark?" Adam comes into the living room and fumbles for the light switch. No matter what else happens in our relationship, the sight of him makes me catch my breath. He's tall and lanky, with a deep warm-whiskey baritone voice and a commanding presence. When he reads, I surrender to him, an audience of one. Not just me, either. I've watched him read to a group and they all stop, as enraptured as I am with his words.

"It's not that dark yet." I hold my hand up. "As long as I can see my hand in front of my face I'm good." Normal. I still sound normal, even cheerful, despite anxiety's peck peck pecking in my chest.

"Where's my good girl?" He means the baby. He looks around as if she might be hiding.

I smile at the mention, the thought of her. "She's at Grandma's tonight. I thought we could..."

A roguish grin from him, and I'm melting again. "Say no more. I've been wanting some time for us too, just the two of us. Mind if I shower first?"

I wave a hand in agreement, permission, acquiescence. Exhale away all the things I wanted to say. Maybe later, maybe another time. I'm kicking myself for being too wishy-washy to confront him about his cheating, or to leave him once and for all. If I stick my head in the sand and pretend it's not happening, it will go away. Maybe I can convince myself I made it up. Fidelity is only a promise anyway, one we never got around to discussing. I scratch at my leg, where scars live under my clothes. If the fabric is thin enough, I can feel them.

He emerges from steam and soap smell, a towel around his hips, and I follow him to the bedroom. Raise my arms for him to pull off my shirt, then I remove my bra while he slides off my pants and underwear. I kick them off, lie down on the bed on my back. He's a generous lover, who usually takes care of me first. Another reason to love him, to overlook his wandering eye. Maybe he's doing penance.

My hips move in time with rhythmic sensation, heat, slow circles. Oh love, dark and sweet. I close my eyes and give in to heat. Touch a match to paper and it will lick eagerly, creep along its morsel until it's consumed, and flame and paper are one.

Heat. Hotter and hotter, flames rising, smoke in front of me. I'm wearing a white dress and the desk is covered in papers, his life's work curls to black ash as I watch and laugh.

My body jolts as I snap awake and sit up. The blanket he drew over me falls back.

His back is to me, feet on the floor at the side of the bed. He laughs, to my relief. "I didn't think I was that bad at it." I can't tell if he's hurt or amused.

"No, honey. I guess I'm just tired. I feel like I never sleep anymore." I move toward him on my knees, to massage his shoulders and back. Kiss the nape of his neck and he arches his back. I nuzzle against him. His skin is warm under my hands.

"I had this weird dream. I dreamed I set fire to all your papers."

Tension across his shoulders and he draws away. "That's weird," is all he says.

I don't ask, and I don't pursue it.

———

"June, where's the envelope I left on my desk?"

After lovemaking, we had a late supper and talked about books. It felt like a ruse, like everything I wanted to say was on hold until a better time. It's morning now, the sun brightening the kitchen, the remains of breakfast on the table. Maybe it was all just a bad dream.

"What envelope is that?" I'm still toweling my hair as I walk into the study to help him look.

"A pretty important one, with my grant application."

"I haven't seen it or touched it." I take a look around, as if my fresh sight might reveal something his search hadn't.

"Well, it's just you and me here, and it was here when I left for work yesterday."

"Maybe the ghost hid it," I joke, with a shrug. Whether or not there's a ghost here depends on who's asking. The ghost may be the landlady's mother, or it may be Sheila. Sometimes, things aren't where we left them, and they turn up a week later in a completely different spot.

"There's no such thing as ghosts." He snaps his briefcase shut and pulls his jacket around himself. Brushes my cheek with a distracted kiss. "If you see it, could you please put it in the mail?"

"Will do. Love you."

He's already out the door and I can hear his steps on the stairs. He didn't say he loved me back, but I won't obsess over that.

After I finish dressing, I steel myself and pick up the phone to call my mother. So far, the bird in my chest is quiet, except a flutter to remind me it's not going anywhere.

"Hello, June, hon. Hang on a second." Mum's voice sounds happy enough. In the background I can hear the TV, and the baby giggling. Mum's dog, an irritable poodle, yips. I'm wondering if I should call back when she comes back to the phone, out of breath.

"Sorry about that. Whew. I got a delivery from Amazon." Sound of ripping paper.

"How's the baby?" One thumb nail isn't quite chewed to the quick, and I work on it. Wipe the damp edge on my jeans.

"Good. Great. She's playing with Blondie right now."

"I can hear. Make sure Blondie doesn't nip her." Get to work on the other thumb nail, as if my hands weren't enough of a mess.

"Oh, they're fine. You worry too much."

Purse my lips around the next comment that wants to rise to the surface. Everything is my fault.

"I guess." Trace the scar on the inside of my wrist, from my first attempt when I was sixteen.

"Now, Grandma would like it if she stayed forever, but what's your plan today?"

"I'm not sure, actually. I was thinking of stopping by the university to pick up a course calendar."

"Are you really going back to school? Can you afford that?"

The second time I tried to kill myself, I was twenty-one and I'd just dropped out of school after my lowest GPA ever. I took most of a bottle of acetaminophen and taped a bag on my head, but the tape came off. My roommate called an ambulance. I can still taste the charcoal drink, like inky chalk, black as a crow's wing.

"I'm just looking. Adam gets a tuition waiver, and he's not going to use it, so I might."

"That will be nice." Neutral tone. The one she uses instead of "You're an idiot, and that will never work." She's matured, too.

"And how's Adam?" she asks out of obligation. She never liked him.

I want to tell her about the mysterious calls and texts, the smell of the other woman's pussy on him, clear as spilled varnish. "He's fine. Working a lot." "You're sure about that?"

"What's that supposed to mean?"

She hesitates, and I hear a thump in the background, and more laughter from the baby.

"Well, once a cheater, always a cheater. A tiger doesn't change his stripes, you know."

"Look, I don't want to start this now. I'll be there to pick her up in half an hour." I hang up on her protests, sit for a moment to try and calm down. I haven't lived at home in fifteen years, yet the sound of her voice can still set me off like that experiment I barely remember from Psych class. Then again, the random response seemed to catch hold the hardest. When the pigeon pecked, there was no pattern to its treats. It would go on pecking, just to see.

Bev, the landlady, is smoking on her stoop as I make my way down the stairs. When she asks me about the late rent, I mumble an apology and she waves a hand. I'm lucky to have a nice landlady, and we're only a couple of weeks behind.

"I think you're right about the ghosts," I tell her. "Whenever something goes missing, Adam won't believe me when I tell him a ghost took it."

Bev nods. "My mum was a real joker. She liked to play pranks."

"Heh. A ghost that plays practical jokes. Go figure. Last time, I couldn't find my glasses for a week. They came back when I threatened to banish her."

"Yeah, that sounds like dear old Mum."

"Bev, do you know what happened to Sheila?" Adam would never say anything, just that she passed away.

Bev takes a drag on her cigarette and lets the smoke trickle out the side of her mouth. "She was pretty depressed, I guess. Ran her car off the road, but she survived the first try. A few weeks later, she went up into the attic and set fire to Adam's papers, then lit herself up. Died of smoke inhalation. Poor thing. That's why the attic is closed off—it's all charred from the fire."

I nod. Razor sharp beak in my stomach, my guts, my heart. Peck peck peck. "That's sad."

"Adam didn't take it too well. He was off for a while, from the university. He seemed better, when you came around."

"Uh huh. Well, I have to get going. Thanks for that." I wave goodbye and walk down our driveway to the car. Adam's car, but he leaves it most days and walks to work.

Sheila left her things behind, including a hairbrush that still smells of her shampoo and natural scent. The order of her things, the way she arranged her cupboards and linen closets. After I moved in, I rearranged everything, so I wouldn't be reminded of her. If there is such a thing as a ghost, hers isn't happy. Sometimes, I'll hear a crash from the kitchen when no one is in there. Or the oven door will be open. It's heavy enough, I don't think the baby can open it by herself. When she was small and I'd listen on the monitor for troubled breathing or other signs of distress, instead I'd sometimes hear her giggling and burbling. It's normal for a baby, I told myself, not wanting to go in there, afraid of what I might see.

Once in a while, usually when I'm near sleep, I'll catch a flicker out the corner of my eye, as if someone in a white dress just walked by. When I turn my head to look, nothing's there. Many times, I've been writing in the study while the baby naps, and the hairs rise on the back of my neck. I almost caught her once peeking at me from around the door frame. When I looked, she was gone. I don't know if my image of her is something I'm seeing, or if I've imagined the details. The white dress, long hair, even her expression. Adam didn't keep any photos of her, and I've never asked.

The strangest was the time I was dozing off, and Adam was away. With the baby curled up beside me in the big bed, smelling of baby shampoo and powder, I was almost asleep when I heard the distinct sound of a zipper, opening and closing. Close, as if right beside my ear. I snapped awake and popped my head up to look around, but of course there was nothing.

It's something I rarely admit to myself, but that's around the time I began to have suspicions that Adam was cheating. Maybe Sheila was trying to tell me something, or maybe I've made a tenuous link in my mind. If I knew, I'd be able to figure out the puzzle and put it down, instead of turning it over and over looking for the crack in a seamless egg. Peck peck peck.

When I pull into Mum's driveway, the baby is already running toward me on sturdy legs. I pick her up, swing her around, cover her face with kisses. Mum stands back, and the look on her face is sad enough to make me reconsider. This is how she guilts me into doing whatever she wants.

"Can't you stay for coffee or something?" Mum asks. "I don't get enough time with my granddaughter as it is."

"Not today. We have to buy some shoes, then pick up Daddy." The second half is a lie and I think Mum knows it, but she just raises an eyebrow.

"Well, give Grandma a kiss, then."

I hand the baby back to her, and step back while they say good-bye. Jealous, Blondie is barking from inside the house.

When I arrive home, Adam is crouched at the end of the driveway. I park in the neighbor's spot, roll down the window and tell the baby to wait a minute for me, then rush to Adam's side. A crow, maybe my crow, flutters on the pavement, one wing and its ribcage crushed. Adam is wearing gloves. He reaches toward the crow's head and its beak opens, lined upright like a thick black needle, still on the defensive in its dying.

"Wait, don't hurt it. Can't we take it to the vet or something?" I step closer.

"I don't think so, hon. Even if they can do anything for it, we can't afford vet care." Adam clicks his tongue at the bird, tries to stroke its head to calm it. It bites his finger and inwardly, I cheer. Adam takes a breath and before I can stop him, twists the bird's neck. It snaps easily, nothing to the bird but feathers and fine, hollow bones.

"You bastard." I turn around, go to the car and hurry the baby out of her seat and toward the stairs, leaving all her things. She protests. I pull her closer, not wanting to hurt her, not wanting her to see what Adam will do with the crow.

"Carry me, Mommy." She reaches up, supplicant, and I have to tell her she's getting too big for me to carry her up the stairs. I hold her hands and climb behind her, as she takes the steps by herself. The apartment door is unlocked, good, I can't see through blurry tears, and I grab a tissue from the bathroom. She turns on cartoons and settles down without me asking while I go to the office to finish my cry. The panic bird is free of its bone cage, flapping in my chest.

Adam's envelope, with the grant application that was so important yesterday, sits neatly on top of a stack of papers in the study. His cell sits on top of it, and the temptation is too great. I press the code, which hasn't changed because we're all about trusting each other, and I find text. Text and sex, sexy texts, little black letters on a white screen. A girl's breasts. Scroll through, there's no way to tell how long it's been going on, or even if it's all the same girl. I pitch the phone as hard as I can against the wall and it bounces, landing on the floor with its screen cracked. Stomp on it on my way to the kitchen, Adam's grant package and all the papers I can grab in one hand. I dig through the junk drawer, find lighter fluid and matches for the barbecue we put away in September. Smell of butane, blue and yellow flames lick the edge of the envelope, taste it, consume it eagerly, the butane smell replaced with charred paper. I drop his papers in the sink, pull a fork out of the drawer and turn them over until they're all burning, the edges curled and twisted into a mess. Hold my wrist as close to the heat as I can bear, until a mark forms.

"What the hell are you doing?" Adam's voice behind me. He's spattered with dirt from burying my crow. "What is wrong with you?" Red-faced, he slams the tap open, trying to put the fire out, but it's too late.

"Make something up. You're good at lying, asshole." Frantic fluttering, bash bash, peck peck.

His hand on my shoulder and I pull it off, shove him away from me. "I'm going to my mother's."

He follows me into the living room, where I scoop the baby up and grab her jacket. "Come back here! I want to talk this over with you. Why did you do that?" He reaches for me again and I duck away from his grasp.

"What's to talk about? Go talk to your piece of ass!" With the baby's arms in an iron grip around my neck, I seek my footing, hunting for each stair and nearly stumbling before my foot finds it. He's trying to block my way and the baby's wailing. I shush her.

"Get out of my way, Adam. I mean it." We're close enough to the bottom that I push past him, take the baby to the car and strap her in.

"It's not what you think. She's a student, she just has a crush on me."

"Stop lying!" Before I can control myself, I slap him, my flat hand hard on his cheek. He steps back in surprise. I look at my tingling hand for a second, as if it's taken a life of its own. Rub it against my leg and slide into the car, pulling the door shut despite Adam's attempts to grab it. I nearly catch his fingers in the door before he lets go.

I jam my key into the ignition, tears and snot running freely down my face, put the car in reverse and stomp on the gas. I nearly zoom into rush hour traffic before I catch myself and pause, waiting for an opening. Adam stands in the driveway, cheek reddening, shoulders slumped. Good. I can never hurt him enough. I am Strength, white dress, infinity symbol over my head. He's the wild tiger I tried to tame and failed. I should have known better.

It takes several minutes for traffic to break and let me into the flow of cars. I pull into the stream, try to ignore the baby's cries for Daddy after he's turned and gone upstairs, not looking back.

"He'll be fine, baby, we're just going to Grandma's for a little while. Mommy's mad at him but he'll be okay." Shrill note in my voice, feel my throat stuffed as if with dry feathers. I reach a hand into my purse, kept between the seats, my eyes still on driving. I touch my wallet, tissues, phone, until I find the smooth plastic bottle of pills from the doctor. Stick it in my pocket. My eyes burn, blur, and I take the tissue and blow my nose.

We drive for a while, long enough for the baby to fall asleep to the hum of the wheels. I'm reminded of the last car trip Adam and I took, just the two of us, after I found out I was pregnant. We went to the Kawarthas, where the cabin's caretaker tried to tell us the Lady of the Lake lived beside Lake Sturgeon. Adam recognized her as a version of La Llorona. A woman cries over her lost children, and forever walks the earth. This ghost, this ha'ant, looking for her dead children and stealing the ones she finds instead. Something else I never told Adam: I went for a walk by the lake one night, to watch the sunset. Dark came more quickly than I thought and I saw a woman in a white dress, a long way off. She started walking toward me, then I shut my eyes and when I opened them, she was gone. Like smoke curls from flame, an idea creeps into the edges of my brain and fogs everything else. Now it's there and I can't shake it. I can't go on with this life, nor leave her to it. I can't leave her with him, or with my mother. She can't grow up in this cruel world.

Auto-pilot. I shut my thoughts down to a single blank mission. No more memories. I drive to the store, buy a pack of chocolate pudding and a spoon while the baby is asleep in the passenger seat. I take the spoon and crush the pills the best I can, use the pudding to moisten them to powdery mush. I take a few myself, to take the edge off, then wake her.

"Here, baby. Here, my darling."

She takes the spoon and the pudding cup.

"Eat it all now, hurry."

Her eyes wide, as she spoons the treat into her mouth. Tears roll again, and I sniffle as I tuck my jacket around her. Start the car, and watch her as she drifts into a deep sleep. I turn onto a winding path that leads down to the Grand River. In the summer, the water below the bridge is shallow and full of ducks and geese, gradually deepening as you cross to the other side of the bridge. This late in the year, it will only be the rocks to keep us company. The temperature is supposed to dip below freezing tonight. A hill hides this area from the main road, and while it's wide enough to drive on, this path is meant for hikers.

Motion at the corner of my vision. I slam the brakes as the lean haunch of a deer narrowly misses the hood of my car. I spin the wheel and come to a stop at the water's edge. The deer, dapple-tan and antler-less, muscular legs working, leaps away, running along the shore. Panic bird thumps in my chest, irregular as if with broken wings. I kill the engine, my breath ragged. Softer, underneath my own, the sound of her quiet breaths, the sound of birds in flight, all dusty movement. Quiet, so quiet for so many of them.

A woman in a white dress, her shoulders dressed in black feathers, stands at the edge of the car. I blink. This time she doesn't disappear. It's too dark to see her face clearly, smoke-charred and featureless. She turns and calmly walks into the water. I gather the baby in my arms, her forehead cool against my neck, her breaths little fits and spurts. She's so limp. Take the first tentative steps toward the shallow water. Then another. Then more, until cold seeps into my shoes and swirls up my pant legs. All this weight on each step. I'm slow. I'm slowing, one rubbery step after another until I fall forward.

Water in my eyes, my nose, my ears, and I hear a crow's cry.

BECAUSE OF THEIR DIFFERENT
DEATHS: STEPHANIE WYTOVICH

Astrid's hands trembled. The ebony stone in her palm burned cold and a licked swatch of frostbite formed underneath as it rested against her mother's ring, a soft diamond with a dull shine, but one ornate enough to still be considered conventionally beautiful. Her sister, Camilla, smoothed out the corners of the tapestry on the floor while her other sister, Margaret, fed the fire with freshly-chopped wood.

"Do you think tonight will be different?" Camilla asked as she placed the black candle in the blanket's center. Her white-blonde hair burned bright against the color of dripping wax, and her dress, now torn and tattered from weeks of running, dragged on the floor, a dirty rag of egg shell white.

Outside, the brittle limbs of a dead tree shook its branches in the light of the moon, a haunting invitation that Astrid longed to accept. Memories of her mother's screams, of the black and blue bruises she put on her cheeks made her wince. Inside, Astrid tightened her fists around her talismans. *We didn't deserve this. None of us did.* She shivered inside a heavy sigh. "No, I very much doubt it. But if it is, I suspect it will be worse. Much worse."

The house the girls had been living in was more of a makeshift shack than a real home. It had been a hideaway of their father's—their foster-father, that is—and when the wind screamed, the hovel shook, whimpering against the cold. Inside there wasn't much: a wooden kitchen table, some mismatched chairs, a dusty sofa the girls took turns sleeping on. The cupboards held stale bread and some root vegetables that were freshly picked by Margaret, but the herbs and berries that Astrid and Camilla had collected and dried out for their tea were running dangerously low.

"You're probably right," said Camilla as she moved into the kitchen. "But I can't help hoping that you're wrong."

"Well, I hope it doesn't hurt," said Margaret, the youngest of the triplets. She warmed her freckled hands against the fire and then massaged the rope marks around her neck. "Death was especially cruel to me my last time, and now I have to deal with this for the rest of my life." She lifted her head to model her murder scars. "I don't even like chokers."

Camilla chortled. "You're so dramatic, Maggie."

After years spent dying, the last time the Margaret met Death, he stole her from the garden while she was gathering rosemary and hung her right from the rafters of the barn. The girls had barely even begun to prepare for their dying ritual when Camilla found Margaret's body swaying, cold as the stones leading up to their house, her blue dress the color of her face.

"That's easy for you to say," said Margaret. "Death favored you."

"Right, because nothing screams favorite like being drowned in the well."

Astrid stared at the window, her anger bubbling. "Is this all some game to you two?" Tears welled in her eyes as she gestured to the knife. "Well? Is it? Come then, tell me, sisters. Who does Death love best? Because let me assure you, it certainly isn't any of us." Silence hung heavy in the room as a pregnant pause painted Camilla and Margaret's lips. "If we don't succeed tonight, none of our suffering will have been worth it."

Tonight, Astrid would die, but after what happened last time, even her sisters dared not challenge her now. The memory of her last bloodletting still gave them all pause, and last night, Astrid's nightmares woke her just as blood and dirt gushed out her nose and mouth, Death's half-hearted attempt at choking her in her sleep, a wake-up call for the elemental agony that awaited her at sunset.

Astrid slid her mother's ring on, her breaths now shaky and sporadic. As the eldest, she would never admit her fear, but tonight's ritual would change the course of the coven, and if things didn't go as planned…

"Maggie, where have you put father?" Camilla asked.

Margaret picked up the fire poker and set it in the flames. The tip of the iron shone a fierce yellow-orange as it glowed against the backdrop of the night. She stood there, tongue-tied and frustrated until she could speak.

"He recognizes me, you know. I saw it in his eyes the other night as I was feeding him."

"That's crazy," Camilla said. "You know the spell doesn't work that way. Father himself said so. We're nothing but strangers to him now."

Margaret nodded, but Astrid could see the doubt on her sister's false smile. Margaret's inability to lie was something that she admired about her, an innocence of sorts.

"Now sister," Camilla said, her hand on Margaret's shoulder. "Let us fetch our father so we can find our wretched mother. This was, after all, his idea."

The two sisters headed for the barn, the sound of the bare feet a faint pitter-patter against the ground.

———

Back in the house, Astrid's thoughts locked in memory of the first time she and her sisters had died and claimed their elements.

Helena—their mother—overwhelmed from the synchronous birth of three daughters and shamed from the village for a pregnancy out of wedlock, developed a deep-seated hatred for her girls. Camilla chose water at the age of three when she survived her mother's attempt at drowning her in the bathtub after supper. Margaret was beaten to death at the age of five, her lungs collapsed after Helena left her for dead in the town square at half-past nine in the morning for dropping a basket of eggs, and Astrid was cut up and buried alive at the age of nine, her blood mixing with the soil as she bled out and became one with the earth six miles from where she slept earlier that night.

But just as the sun rose each morning, the girls kept coming back, their deaths, a farce, a mockery to their mother's postpartum madness.

Rumors of Helena's torture spread throughout the town, but with the girl's always alive and healthy, there was no proof of negligence, let alone murder. These failed attempts left her desperate, filled her with a manic rage, and with each attempt proving unsuccessful, Helena began to believe that the devil had cursed her womb with demons and that fire would be the only way to cleanse her soul and rid these monsters from this earth.

One night, after everyone was asleep, she set fire to the house, burning alive next to her girls in hope of silencing the witchcraft in their veins. Little did she know that she, too, was touched by magic. With her death, she had accepted her element, making her the fourth in the family, thus completing the circle and therefore, the Samuel coven.

When Helena woke the next day, her house a mixed pile of rubble and ash, she screamed, screamed herself hoarse as she collapsed, her fists two small boulders banging against the ground.

Her girls where nowhere to be found.

In the barn, Arthur moaned, as a line of blood dripped from the gash in his temple. Strapped to a chair and gagged with his black handkerchief, his weary eyes were too tired to stay open, and the fear he felt—if he felt any at all—no longer wore on his face as it had in the past, but none of that, as was evidenced by his head wound, stopped him from trying to escape. The girls were forced to learn long ago how to restrain him, and better still, on how to knock him out. The shovel seemed to work best. Practice and all that.

Margaret crouched down beside him and collected his blood in a silver chalice as she smoothed his thinning, gray hair, wiped the sweat off his brow. *I'm so sorry, father.* He moaned and a drop of spittle slid down his chin. *I drooled when I died the first time, too.* A mixture of guilt and panic blushed against her rosy cheeks and she wandered around the mostly-empty barn wringing her hands as she gathered up the courage to add her own blood to the mixture.

"Margaret? What's taking you so long?" Camilla asked.

The wind blew against the wooden frame of the chipped red door, causing it to howl as it rattled against the night's breath.

"It's—well—I don't know. Do we have to do this? It just seems so permanent and we've all died so many times already. Hasn't there been enough death in our house?"

"There has," said Camilla. "But that's why he has to die. Mother has to be stopped and this is the only way to siphon her magic and prevent her from hurting us, or anyone else, again."

"Can't we just wait a little longer to see if—"

Camilla turned rigid in the doorway, stiff as if she'd been turned to stone. "No. We've been through this, Margaret. The locator spell ends its cycle today. If Astrid doesn't die with the blood of father's death running through her, she won't be able to draw mother's magic out. And if she can't draw mother's magic out—"

"Then we die," Margaret said.

"Exactly. And thanks to father, this time, we won't come back."

Tonight was their one chance at redemption, and Astrid was the chosen daughter to finish what the four of them had started. Death by death, the girls reenacted their first brush with Hell, and soon, when Astrid's body was severed, mutilated by her two sisters, she would have the chance to kill their mother and save them all.

Margaret nodded in tangent with a tear that ran down her face as she slid the blade against her palm. "For you and Astrid," she said, bleeding into the cup.

"For those poor girls, too," said Camilla. "For all of us."

The echo of the decaying rafters hung thick in the air, the sound of Margaret's first body hitting the wall still an ever-present lingering in the draft-infested room. Their father, hunched over and sagging in the chair, looked resigned, ready to let go of all this torment, to give in and give up. He'd told them this day would come, gave the girls careful instructions, made them resilient, made them strong.

If the girls closed their eyes hard enough, they could still hear his voice, soft and masculine, the sound of a father before he betrayed them: *On the night leading up to your final deaths, I won't remember you. I won't fight you. But I will die for you and I will protect you. Take my blood and follow the spell. Don't let me die in vain.*

Over the past few years, their father had been watching his daughters die, time and time again, once every six months leading up to their eighteenth birthday. The stone Astrid carried hid them from Helena's sight, but the anger in their mother's heart continued to plague them nonetheless. The girls suffered night terrors and anxiety, a tortuous paranoia that turned them into daylight zombies consumed with fear as all across neighboring villages, girls were being snatched from their families and savagely murdered, their bodies left in the woods to the scavengers of the night.

As more children disappeared and more girls showed up dead, Arthur became desperate. The triplet's magic wasn't strong enough to protect them—not without the synchrony of their fourth—and the charms he'd picked up in the forest were no match for the torture that awaited them all, so with nowhere to turn where Helena couldn't find them, he left his girls, headed south for the crossroads, and once again, hoped that, somehow, he could make a deal.

For five days, Arthur walked, battling severe bouts of thirst and hunger as the summer heat raged on and the drought kept his throat dry. When he reached the clearing about 50 miles away from the village, he dropped to his knees, took out his knife and screamed as he cut the inside of his hand, pushed his bleeding palm into the dirt.

The Devil was all too eager to answer.

When he appeared, he wore the face of an old man, one who was weary around the eyes, smoked a pipe barefoot, and smelled of ash.

"Arthur, my boy" the Devil said. "I've been waiting for you to call! How long has it been? Eight-nine years now, yes?"

Hesitant, Arthur held his tongue, suddenly very afraid of the man—if you could call him that—who stood in front of him.

"Oh, come now. We're old friends!" said the Devil. "No need to be quiet after all we've been through, eh?"

Arthur picked himself up off the ground, wiped the dirt off his knees and thighs. He tilted his neck hard to the right, heard it crack up near the top of his spine.

"Something like that," he said. "How are you, Lucifer?"

"Better than you, I'm willing to guess if I'm standing here," said the Devil. "What can I do for you, this time?"

"I'd like to propose a trade."

"You for the girl's safety, I'd wager."

"No. The girl's safety in exchange for the soul of Helena Samuels," Arthur said.

The Devil put out his pipe as the shine of growing interest reflected in his eyes. "Helena Samuels? Ain't she the one they're calling the Woodwork Witch these days?" Lucifer laughed. "You're telling me *you're* going to kill *her*? Didn't work out so well last time for you now did it?"

"No, I suppose it didn't. But this time the girls are well into their resurrection age, and I'll..."

The Devil smiled. "You'll, what, Arthur?"

"I'll die for them so they have the sacrifice they need to counteract her magic."

Lucifer smiled a toothy-grin, his teeth stained yellow from nicotine. "But you know what happens if you die."

"I do but— "

"But the girls don't," said the Devil. "That's evil, Arthur, even for you. I suppose those don't know why you're so interested in them, either, do they?"

Arthur hung his head, the presence of guilt heavy on his shoulders. When the rumors of Helena's pregnancy spread through the village, the townspeople grew angry, disgusted that she had lusted into their village and spread her legs like a whore, tainting the loins of one of their men. One night, drunk on the fruits of a plentiful harvest, they left to find her, to teach her a lesson about what it means to be pure, respected. They raided her home, pulled her from her house by her hair, dragged her ragged into the woods. Together, they stripped her naked, spat curses in her name. Torches were lit against the sounds of her wails, but the men and women drank more booze and ignored her pleads for them the stop. The entire charade made Arthur sick just thinking about it, and while he hadn't thrown the first stone himself that evening, he certainly didn't do anything to stop the hands of the others.

Her face swelled like a too ripe, sour apple.

Her bones snapped under the pressure of hate.

Seconds had passed like hours, and after piles of rocks crowded her bloody face, sheltered her bruised body, the men and women left her and her unborn children, cold and alone, praying for death.

But what resurrected from the rubble that night, was something far, far worse.

Something they all had to deal with now, and something that all their daughters were paying for with their lives.

Arthur wiped a tear from his cheek, his heart in his throat. He deserved to die for what he did to Helena, but more importantly, he needed to make things right by protecting the girls. They, after all, were innocent in all of this. "Do we have a deal?"

The Devil took a hit off his pipe and the sweet smell of tobacco swirled around them both. "No."

"No?"

"That's right," said the Devil. "I said no. Not interested. I already have your soul, in case you forgot." He kicked the dirt and twirled around on his right heel. "Wouldn't mind the souls of those girls, though."

"That's insane," said Arthur. "Why would I give them to you?"

"Because you'll never catch Helena, and when you fail, I'll get three witchy souls instead of one, and since you're a good customer and all, trying to kill all these poor women, I'll even let you live. You know, as a consolation prize and all."

Arthur hated himself for what he was about to do, but he knew it was his only chance at freedom for his girls. He stuck out his bleeding hand. "You have my word."

"Always do," said the Devil, a hint of laughter in his voice. "See you soon, old friend. Oh, and good luck. You'll need it."

With that, Lucifer walked into the night leaving nothing behind except an unturned stone.

———————

Astrid rubbed the wounds on her wrist and thought about their plan.

For a little over two years now, the girls had been dying every six months at the cost of their magic, and while their spirits had gotten stronger, the curse had taken a toll on their bodies. This would be Astrid's ninth death, a final matching to the age of her first dance with demise, and her scars still wore prominently on her face, chest, and stomach. Camilla and Margaret had reached their numbers months ago—years even— and the constant spectator sport that her demise had become was getting harder on all of them, especially since the marks stopped fading after her last death.

According to their father's instructions, each time the girls died, they were reborn without a part of their soul.

Locked in the fires and condemned to suffering, there was but one caveat. If the girls could resurrect themselves and give Lucifer Helena in their place, he would consider it a fair trade and give them back their lives, and their souls, freshly clean from the stains of eternal damnation. But if they failed, they would forever burn in the wake of their mother's malevolence as she continued to spill blood, sparing no one, in the name of her three daughters.

Camilla and Margaret walked into the house, their dresses stained red, the chalice filled to the brim with blood. On the eve of their 18th birthday, none of them wore anything on their faces but fear.

"Is father dead?" Astrid asked.

The girls hung their heads and their silence was all the answer that Astrid needed.

"Good. Now hand me the chalice, and let's gather ourselves," said Astrid. "It's going to take me weeks to heal if I make it out of this at all, so we'd best start sooner rather than later." Astrid cut her hand, adding her blood to the chalice, the final component to the recipe: water, air, sacrifice, and earth. She rubbed her stone, her thoughts a constant maelstrom of anxiety. After years of meditation, her thumb had worn down the center and turned the token into a kind of worry stone. She hoped this would work, that their father's sacrifice would be enough to override the missing element.

She walked over to the blanket and laid down, her naked, pale body spread out like the Vitruvian man. The black candle was almost burned out, the wax spread out and sticking to the blanket in thin, black rivers. Arthur had told her that his blood would help ease the pain of dismemberment by numbing her body and temporarily blinding her so she couldn't go into shock. Plus, with her physical sight taken away, her psychic receptors would be sharper, leading her to find her mother faster.

"Astrid, are you sure you're ready for this?" asked Camilla.

"I don't have much of a choice," Astrid said. "We can't keep running from her, and this locator spell is our only shot."

She gripped the worry stone harder and remembered the first time that Arthur gave it to her. Three days after the fire, the girls were lost, wandering the woods surviving on berries, roots, and rain water. Arthur found them two towns over while he was out collecting firewood, and desperate for warmth and nourishment, the girls took sanctuary with him. At nine years old, the girls huddled together, sleeping in the same bed, their arms wrapped around each other, protecting each other the best and only way that they knew how. They were small, yes, but neither of them knew how strong they were until Arthur sat down with them one night and told them of the danger they were in.

Come here, children, come here. Yes, good, good. We need to have a chat now. You see, my girls, you three are the children of Helena Samuels, the one they call the Woodwork Witch. Do you know what a witch is?

The girls shook their heads.

Well, there are good witches and bad witches, and your mother, Helena? She's a very bad witch. The townspeople have been talking about her, about how she emerged from the fire in the woods looking for you three. She's hurt a lot of people since then and can't be trusted, so we must protect you at all costs. Astrid, this here is a meditation stone. I want you to hold on to it for me. Should you girls ever feel threatened, you need only rub it and think of this spot and the stone will hide you, keep you safe.

Since that night, Astrid has carried the stone with her day and night, through every death and rebirth. It's kept them safe all these years as they hid in the woods, traveling from town to town with Arthur, always hiding, always running. But not tonight. Tonight, she prayed that the stone would comfort her one last time as she came out of hiding. She would complete the last cycle of deaths for her sisters, and together, they would kill their mother and close the Samuel circle once and for all.

All they needed was her magic.

Her magic and her blood.

Camilla took Margaret's hand in hers, and together, they bowed their heads.

"Let us pray," they said in unison.

Astrid trembled, her one hand still gripping the rock and her mother's ring as the floorboards beneath her creaked.

"Lucifer, we beseech you to hear us. Our souls, with the ready stain of your hand, pray to you in this hour to help us locate, our mother, Helena Samuels.

Outside, the world grew darker, darker than either sister had ever seen the night dressed. The broken living room window let in a cold draft that mixed with the copper scent of their blood along with the smoke from the fire. If wolves dared to think of howling at the moon, they certainly swallowed their urges, cowering in fear from the thick fog the girl's words brought in along the forest floor from such hallowed prayers whispered in sin.

The girls knelt next to Astrid, kissed her once of the forehead, and then they all drank from the chalice, the taste of their family's blood ripe on their tongues as Camilla took out the knives. "We'll be right here next to you when you come back," Camilla said. "Be well, sister. You can do this."

Margaret nodded her head in agreement as Camilla continued, her voice soft but strong.

"With our sister's blood, we give you her last death, the ninth piece of her soul, and as such, the lives of the ones inside us all. Should we be successful in our pursuit, we ask that you take Helena's soul in good faith, and have mercy on our own. Blessed sin, we thank you and praise you, and in your name, we sign our sincerity with Astrid Samuels's blood."

Astrid could hardly breathe as her chest tightened in preparation for the blade.

Margaret made the first incision, a deep cut to Astrid's wrist, while Camilla, not far behind, sawed away at her eldest sister's thin, porcelain neck. Streams of red-black blood fell out of Astrid's veins, her arteries pumping her life into the candle wax that already stained the tapestry. Blind to the mutilation and numbed from her father's blood, Astrid laid still and tried to wait patiently for Death.

The early morning sun peeked through the windows, illuminating small flecks of dust that floated in the air like zero gravity confetti. Outside, the world was quiet, still opening its weary eyes, but the unmistakable squawk of a crow ruffled Astrid from her death, startling her awake.

"How long have I been out?" she asked to no one as the paled-gray bodies of her sisters desiccated next to her. She ran her hands over her body—her chest, her throat, her arms—and felt the gashes and cuts to her flesh, saw the gleam of freshly-exposed bone. Astrid knelt next to her sisters, and put her hand over Margaret's mouth. Nothing. She tried to lift Camilla's arm next, and while rigor fought her tooth and nail, at the end, she was able to bend her at the elbow.

"Okay, so not too terribly long. Probably around seven hours, give or take," she said.

Astrid searched the room, her eyes adjusting to her resurrected surroundings. Everything was the same but somehow not, like a tilted picture frame, a naked rose. The house had taken on a blurred effect as if a thick fog had wafted through and left behind a haze, dulling the color of life, almost muting it out.

The floor should have been covered in blood, but instead it

remained a blank canvas much like the stares of her sisters whose eyes were locked in hopeful evanescence, their gazes averted to the ceiling. She picked up her mother's ring and slid it onto her finger.

Alright, deep breaths.

All around her, the world fast-forwarded, moving in visions of quick pictures and fragmented still-frames. She heard screaming, the voices of little girls begging and pleading for their parents. She heard the cackle of a hag, saw the knives and the fire that burned in the rundown hovel Helena lived in deep in the woods.

Wind chimes made of bones hung off her front porch.

A blood-stained axe sat imbedded in a tree stump outside.

Astrid watched in horror as her mother laughed at the children's tears and ripped the flesh from their throats with her bare hands. Her nails were like fish hooks and her eyes were black, dead like a shark's. Killing Helena would be a mercy to the woman's soul, a kindness against the years she would spend burning in Hell, and the more the old woman laughed, the more the dirt started to pour out of Astrid's mouth, the taste of earth now ever-present on her tongue.

Images of her first death surrounded Astrid as the memory of suffocation and bloodletting returned. She saw her body, dismembered, lying in a hole, as her mother shoveled dirt over her face and body. All throughout her chest, she felt a tightening, a wet disenchantment with her limbs and torso as it was pinched and separated, then drowned in red.

This ground was her birthplace, her womb. She'd recognize it anywhere, its subtle sounds of claustrophobia as unforgettable as the woman who stole her last breath. Its taste was a reunion with Death.

Helena now lived where Astrid first died.

And now that she had the location, it was time to kill her mother.

———

It was nightfall by the time Astrid saw Helen's house, and by that point, the disarming had begun.

True, the stone had protected her for years, and Arthur's blood had brought her back from her final death, but she was far from immortal now, and her time was almost up. The ache in her flesh and bones was proof of that, and if she didn't siphon her mother's magic within the day's cycle, she, along with her sisters, would sleep forever, her body breaking open and dissecting itself piece by piece.

Before her, smoke billowed from the witch's chimney, and a faint glow illuminated the windows in a subtle yellow, a dying fire struggling to survive. Adjacent to the house, a dead garden prickled the earth, its vines shriveled and dry, clawing at the soil, climbing up the skeleton of the house.

Nothing can grow here.

All around the perimeter were warnings. Triangles all of sizes fastened with sticks and hair hung from the trees, archaic symbols of fire that shook in the wind like rustic contortionists. Astrid took one down and placed it in her dress pocket. She walked towards the house as if stepping on glass.

The surrounding area was a graveyard of lost innocence.

A girl's shoe.

A pink ribbon.

Remnants of Death surrounded her, their presence a constant reminder that she, too, died her once long ago, and that if she wasn't careful, could easily die here again.

Where's my marker?

Astrid remembered being nine and afraid when she woke up underground, her hands her only weapon. She dug through thick, but loose, dirt, clawing her way out of the earth until light reached her face. Shaking, she emerged from the ground, the blood and scars on her body still fresh. *Something* had sewn her back together again, and while she didn't know what, she wanted to be sure to remember the space where it happened. To honor the miracle, as it were.

She didn't know it was curse.

"There we go," she said, her voice the only sound in the quiet dark around her.

A small stone stood before her, her blood faded, but still undeniably there. She drew an upside triangle so she'd remember that she was once buried beneath its warmth, and then she drew a straight line at the type to signal that her heart had stopped.

Silly girl.

Astrid smiled a heartbroken grin. What she'd really done that day was accept her element in her blood, even if she thought then that she was just writing childish stories on rocks. She'd been innocent, pure, much like the other girls whose clothes now littered the space before her. Astrid ran her hand over the head-stone and closed her eyes. She wanted to say a prayer for the childhood that Helena had stolen from them all, but the anger that rose in her chest made her hateful, full of spite.

She knelt and kissed the earth, her hand on the stone.

"Thank you for saving me when I couldn't save myself," she said, tears wetting her face.

An owl screeched in the distance.

As she got closer, Astrid removed her shoes. Stones and bark dug into the soles of her feet, but she hardly felt it. Years of running had kept her calloused, made her numb.

Crouched down, she crept towards the house in a quiet slither as she evoked the smooth nature of a serpent. She slid up against the front door, a creeping vine trespassing on grounds meant for Death.

Inside, everything was quiet.

On tiptoes, she inched along the siding, splinters nestling themselves in her back. She peered through a dusty shard of glass, an acting window, crackled and waiting to shatter. Candles lit the nearly-bare room before her. A mixture of size and shape, they stood like soldiers littered throughout the space, their wax dripping and collecting on tables and shelves. In the corner was a chair. Threadbare blankets hung off its arm while an unconscious Helena slept, one hand draped over the side, her hand clenched in a fist.

Astrid took in her surroundings, but it didn't look like there was a way in that didn't calculate any risk. She'd have to further break a window if she leaned towards that option, and that would most certainly wake Helena up, and if she walked through the front door, there was no saying that the creak or click of the lock or door knob wouldn't wake her up.

Her eyes drifted back towards the axe.

Can I do it? Can I really lure her out here and kill her? My mother?

Memories of her burial flashed through her head: the suffocation, the fear, the dismemberment. For a moment, she swore that she could see Helen's face as the dirt piled over her torso and neck. Her eyes wicked, maniacal. She was laughing, laughing as she buried the corpse of her eldest daughter.

Yeah. I can do it.

Astrid crept towards the tree stump and wrapped her hands around the wooden handle. The wood was smooth and that gave her pause. She envisioned all the times her mother had placed her hands around it, all the times she'd swung and used it against the bodies of children she'd hallucinated were her own. The blade was dull, but it would do the trick.

If I can just get one good swing in. Take her by surprise. Maybe knock her unconscious...

A twig snapped in the woods.

Leaves crunched in the distance.

What? No!

Two girls—maybe 10, 11 years old? —were coming towards the house, their hair dressed up in ribbons, their clothes freshly washed. The one, a blonde with gray eyes, held a pouch in one hand, a rock in the other. The other girl, another blonde, this one with ice blue eyes, simply held a rock. She looked scared, unsure, almost like she didn't want to be here.

Astrid ducked down beside the stump as the girls made their way to the front door, slowly, carefully, as if they were playing a game.

The grey-eyed girl stuck her hand her pouch, and when she pulled it out, it was red, red like blood. She smiled at her friend and smeared a pentagram on the front door. Foolish girl. All she was doing was reiterating the elemental bonds between mother and child. Astrid hated seeing it there. A mockery. A reminder that she was blood to the thing that slept behind those walls.

The blue-eyed girl started to back away, but before she turned her back completely, she chucked the rock through the witch's window, the two girls now laughing and screaming:

"Woodwork, Woodwork, Satan's little witch.
Fetch me a girl, now, fetch me a bitch.
Momma says you're evil, Daddy said your dead.
Woodwork, Woodwork, soon we'll have your head."

No, no, no, no, no.

Inside, Helena woke, her screams the rival of every blood song and murder ballad. She tore of out the house in a rage, her hooked claws scraping against the woods of the front door and porch. Astrid was waiting for her, a silent sentinel in the shadows.

She swung once and landed the axe in the center of her back, the sound of crunched bone splitting through the air. Helena howled, her body crashing against the ground. She reached behind her and tried to grab at whatever—whoever—attacked her, but there was no time for rebuttal. Astrid has lost everything and everyone, including her life, to this woman. There were no second chances.

With her elbow, she bashed the window, shattering the already-cracked glass. She picked up the shard and dove at her mother, plunging it into her neck. Blood gushed out in crimson fireworks as the Helena choked and spat out blood. Astrid wanted to dismember her, to choke her, to drown her. She wanted to take her life nine times over and make her relive the pain and fear that her and her sisters carried for all these years. No death would be good enough for this woman, but she would settle for what she could have: a new life with her sisters, a free life, a quiet life...

Astrid bent down, and stared into her mother's eyes, allowing the witch to finally see her face.

"We didn't deserve any of this," Astrid said. "But you? You do. You deserve all of this."

Helena smiled as she saw the face of her eldest, her body convulsing, dying as it struggled to hang on. Her elongated stomach bulged as she shook, her limbs weak twigs held together by nothing but bones and flesh. Her eyes were dark, soulless. Her teeth razors masking behind chapped lips.

Astrid thought about touching her face, but decided against it. The idea of this woman's flesh on her hand was unbearable. She didn't want any more of her connected to Helena, not even in a final kindness. She turned to walk away, but once her back was turned, she heard it. It was a quiet sound muffled in an impending death, but nevertheless, it was unmistakable. Behind her, Helena laughed, laughed until a high-pitched cackle died on her lips.

Too afraid to look back, Astrid kept moving forward, away from her mother, away from this nightmare.

She'd wondered if her sister's hearts had started beating again.

And then like a fool, she dropped to the ground.

It was morning when Astrid awoke, her body bruised and aflame with ache. Everything hurt and her vision was blurred, the forest around her, an expressionist painting in brown and green. She pushed herself up, the drumming in her head loud and constant. *What? What happened?* She ran her fingers through her hair, and they came back red. Blood. *How hard did I hit my head?* She reached and grabbed a large stick, used it to prop herself up so she could stand. Slowly, the word came into focus.

Behind her, Helena dead on her porch, the axe still planted firmly in her back.

In the distance, she heard a familiar voice. The voice of the gray-eyed girl with blood-soaked hands, no doubt coming back to play another prank.

Astrid inched towards the house on a sprained ankle, her stomach full of knots. A hollowing growled inside her, an insatiable hunger mixing with the intense nausea that threatened her gullet. She smelled iron, craved meat. Her fingers twitched, her jaw locked.

She rested against a tree, trying to catch her breath, but panic coursed through her body as her chest filled with fire. Around her, the world started to burn. Flames licked the land, engulfed the canopy in a haze of smoke and ash. The smell of dying was everywhere, and inside her, Astrid could feel the fire and the earth mixing together.

An earthquake.

A wildfire.

Burning limbs fell from the sky and the girls screamed. Astrid could hear the desperation in their voices. Such urgency. They were so delicate, so frail.

She moved towards them, her pace quickening from a limp to a sprint, her hunger growing, rising within her. She emerged from the embers a fraction of who she used to be, her nails now sharp, curved, knife-like and begging.

Their throats were so soft, their flesh, so supple.

It took no time at all to kill them, and she ate with a fervor as if she'd been starved her entire life. The pit in her stomach calmed as she pulled their ribbons from her mouth.

"What's happening to me?" she asked, her voice lost somewhere in the echoes of the flames. She wiped the blood from her mouth, her skin now leathery, chapped.

The choir of dead children sang to her.

> "Woodwork, Woodwork, Satan's little witch.
> Fetch me a girl, now, fetch me a bitch.
> Momma says you're evil, Daddy said your dead.
> Woodwork, Woodwork, soon we'll have your head."

In this distance, she heard laughing.

Lucifer's hand grabbed her shoulder, his voice both as smooth as velvet and as harsh as stone. Maggots wrapped around his eyes. His smile, a stitching of human hair and pieced-together flesh.

"Welcome home, witch," he said. "I hope you're half the woman your mother was."

Astrid swallowed hard, the bones of the girls surrounding her.

The Devil paced as he rubbed his hands together in a playful jest. "They'll be here soon. The townspeople. I'd run if I were you," he said.

"But I... I didn't mean to. This is a mistake," Astrid said, her eyes begging.

"It's always a mistake, isn't it? Even Helena blamed her sins on me at first," he said. "But see, I don't make people do anything. I'm just here to watch you all go to Hell."

A rot spread through Astrid's body.

Clumps of hair fell out in her fists.

"Oh, and before you ask, your father and sisters are fine, just like I promised. I am a man of my word after all."

"And I? I don't remember this—whatever this is—being part of the deal," Astrid said, her voice cracked, anxious.

Lucifer smiled, his teeth a string of black pearls.

"Funny thing about making deals with the Devil," he said. "No one ever reads the fine print. You didn't think I'd take Helena's soul and leave her work here unfinished, did you?"

The weight of his words sank in.

That's why she laughed when she saw it was me. She knew I'd become her, the very thing I hated most. She died knowing she ended up killing me after all.

Fearful for her life and the sentence she'd been served, Astrid fled the woods, her mother's curse riding her back, Death, still on her tail.

"Run, Woodwork. Run," Lucifer said.

And run she did.

Never once looking back.

EDITOR

Leza Cantoral is a writer & an editor.
She was born in Mexico & she lives on the internet.
She is the Editor in Chief of CLASH Books.
yesclash.com
clashbooks.com
lezacantoral.com

MEET THE TRAGEDY QUEENS

Laura Diaz de Arce is a writer and general malcontent from South Florida. She mostly writes for Smoking Mirror Press in between angry letters to her congressmen. You can find her complaining in ALL CAPS on twitter @QuetaAuthor

I keep telling myself I am **Laura Lee Bahr**: part clown, part mystic, all about it. I work with twice-exceptional kids, I write, I act, I direct, I sing songs, I try to remember that life is just a waking dream/nightmare that I get to play/fight in. I hope I am Rebel Scum.

I'm **Lisa Marie Basile**, living in New York City. I'm an editor by day. I write poetry and essays and I make magic. I am working on a nonfiction book, a no-bullshit grimoire, LIGHT MAGIC FOR DARK TIMES (Quarto, 2018) and a novella for Clash Books. I'm a dreamer, a chronic Scorpio, a swimmer, and a witch. I am also the founding editor of Luna Luna Magazine, which is a digital coven of light and dark. I'm the most put-together fucking mess you'll ever meet.

Max Booth III: Raised in Northern Indiana, I hopped on a bus at age 18 to Texas, and I've been here ever since (I'll be 25 in July). I raised the bus fare by ghost-writing Wikipedia articles for indie writers. I've worked as an overnight stocker at Walmart and various other less-famous retail stores. Currently I am a hotel night auditor. I'm also the co-founder and Editor-in-Chief of the small press, Perpetual Motion Machine, the Managing Editor of Dark Moon Digest, the co-host of Castle Rock Radio: A Stephen King Podcast, a columnist for LitReactor, and the author of several novels, the latest being The Nightly Disease. I don't know if I have any weird quirks. I suppose, for it to be a legitimate weird quirk, I wouldn't even be aware that it was a weird quirk. It would just seem like a normal thing to me, right?

I'm **Manuel Chavarria**. In addition to writing, and hustling for freelance editorial work here and there, I work for TASCHEN at their offices in Hollywood, located in an outdoor space designed to look like a ship at sea and called Crossroads of the World (I have not taken the time yet to verify if that is accurate). I've also been working toward starting a small press here in Los Angeles. When I can pull myself away from the publishing industry and all its attendant arms, I enjoy cooking (I'm not bad), playing the saxophone (I could be... better), and trying my hand at other assorted arts. I am a restless soul.

Victoria Dalpe is an artist and writer. She lives with her husband, filmmaker Philip Gelatt Jr. and their young son in Providence, RI. From their attic window they can see H.P. Lovecraft's ancestral home, which is now a Starbucks. Victoria Dalpe loves horror, folklore monsters, and painting skulls all day. Her first novel, Parasite Life, came out January 2018 by ChiZine Publications.

Cara DiGirolamo is currently in recovery from graduate school, where she studied Linguistics, wrote a dissertation incomprehensible to normal humans, and learned to skate.

JC Drake: I admit, as a male writer I am proud to have a piece in this anthology. I think our voice is over heard (or over shouted), but in this case I feel like I had something new to say. I'm not a writer by profession, I work for the government and try to help decision makers make understand a world full of information. Writing is my hobby...it's the thing that keeps me sane and grounded. I'm also fascinated by mysteries and spend my free time exploring them, I travel a lot, and my wife and I own a haunted house with a grave in the back yard.

Larissa Glasser: I work as an academic librarian at a large university. It's a really wonderful day job because I have so much access to research. My workplace is actually adjacent to Prince Street in Boston, where Sylvia was born in 1932. I played in punk and metal bands for a couple of decades, but I've shifted my priorities to writing over the past five years. After a recent health scare, I became even more determined to get my work out there.

Devora Gray wasn't born a Las Vegas native, but growing up in Sin City with conservative God-loving parents from the Bible Belt and the high deserts of New Mexico did some wacky things to both her outlook and sense of humor. She is the author of Human Furniture. You can follow her on Twitter @MsScarlettD

Patricia Grisafi. I live in the East Village with my husband and our two rescue pitbulls, and we're expecting our first kiddo in June! I taught college English for eight years while working on my PhD, and now I work as an Associate Editor at Ravishly as well as freelance. I also volunteer at an animal shelter and enjoy hiking and horseback riding. I love horror movies, true crime, and dark tourism — like visiting places where murders or tragedies have taken place.

Gabino Iglesias: I'm a hustler who writes, reads, and reviews. Last months poet Isaac Kirkman called me a leviathan, so I'm using that as my new bio. I live for books, music, and the magical weirdness of life, death, and the spiritual places between and beyond those two. In the age of the bruja, I'm a Caribbean brujo with too many strong opinions.

Ashley Inguanta is a writer and artist who learned how to time travel this year, but she can only go from years 1400-2018. She lives in Florida most of the time, and recently she became friends with a librarian herbalist who is teaching her how to appreciate the swamplands. She is the author of The Way Home (Dancing Girl Press 2013), For the Woman Alone (Ampersand Books 2014), and Bomb (Ampersand Books, 2016). She is currently showing and working on several Poetry Room installations.

Kathryn Louise: I'm a writer and photographer from Olympia, WA, an MFA candidate at Pacific University, an Evergreen graduate, occasional model and filmmaker and former aspiring forensic anthropologist.

Selene MacLeod: holds a BA in Communications from Wilfrid Laurier University, and lives in Kitchener. She works nights, daydreams too much, and writes too little. Her work has appeared in several anthologies and a few ezines, mostly of the crime and horror persuasion, so writing "literary" stuff is a real treat.

Tiffany Morris: I'm a writer, tarot reader, and witch from Nova Scotia. When not chanting or buying crystals, I can be found looking for UFOS and window shopping overpriced makeup.

Monique Quintana: I'm a Pocha/Xicana who hails from the Central Valley, "the other California." I live that adjunct English teacher life and have an affinity for the Muppets, Ramón Novarro, red lipstick, Ray Bans and the band, Prayers. My real last name is Gonzalez and I'm an Aries. Moon in Virgo.

My name is **Tiffany Scandal**. I'm an author, editor, podcaster, photographer, and former nude model over at Suicide Girls. I enjoy drinking coffee and playing with pussy (cats) all day long. My hair color changes as often as my mood does. I live in Portland, Oregon.

Lorraine Schein: I am a poet and sf writer, read Tarot for a hobby, and try not to take myself as seriously as her (though I've been institutionalized too). I was intrigued by reading about Ted Hughes' other woman, who died the same way, and his somewhat anti-Semitic comments about her. My poetry book, The Futurist's Mistress, is available from mayapplepress.com.

Farah Rose Smith: I am a writer, editor, lapsed short film director, musician, and artist. I have a passion for Latin American and Middle European lit (especially German fantasists), blues music, Symbolist/Surrealist art, and got my start writing Weird fiction. In my spare time I am studying to become an art historian and dancer.

Christine Stoddard: I'm a writer, artist, and the most Type A free spirit you will ever meet. When I'm not writing copy for The Man, I'm writing books, staging photo shoots, making small films, and getting my hands messy dabbling in various visual art forms. Taking risks is what allowed me to start Quail Bell Magazine. It's what got my first full-length poetry and photo book—Water for the Cactus Woman—accepted by Spuyten Duyvil Publishing in New York. It's the very reason I got to be the artist-in-residence at Annmarie Sculpture Garden, a Smithsonian affiliate, in Maryland last summer and why I will be a visiting artist at Laberinto Projects in El Salvador this summer. It's the reason my work has appeared in the New York Transit Museum, the Queens Museum, the Poe Museum, the Ground Zero Hurricane Katrina Museum, and beyond. Let's all take risks! Let's be Plath and Lana at once.

Brendan Vidito: I'm a short, neurotic Canadian dude who lives in Northern Ontario. I've been on a steady diet of horror films and literature for over a decade and it's rewired my brain to the point where everything appears sinister and uncanny. At least six percent of my body is made of titanium and industrial rubber. A priest might have once suspected I was possessed by a demon. And I absolutely love cheese. The bluer the better.

Stephanie Wytovich: I'm a bibliophile who spends her free time in bookstores, libraries, and tracking down rare copies of *Alice in Wonderland*. I'm addicted to coffee, but I drink tea at night, and I love to be surrounded by plants, crystals, driftwood, and candles. I love to travel, I bring up inappropriate facts in social circles, and my dog, Apollo, is attached to my hip 99.9% of the time.

WE PUT THE LIT IN LITERARY

CLASHBOOKS.COM

ALSO BY CLASH BOOKS

DARK MOONS RISING IN A STARLESS NIGHT by Mame Bougouma Diene

IF YOU DIED TOMORROW I WOULD EAT YOUR CORPSE by Wrath James White

THE ANARCHIST KOSHER COOKBOOK by Maxwell Bauman

HORROR FILM POEMS by Christoph Paul

THIS BOOK IS BROUGHT TO YOU BY MY STUDENT LOANS by Megan Kaleita

GIRL LIKE A BOMB by Autumn Christian

PRACTICE MAKES PERFECT by Jayme Karales

HE HAS MANY NAMES by Drew Chial

SEQUELLAND by Jay Clayton-Joslin

THIS BOOK AIN'T NUTTIN TO FUCK WITH: A WU-TANG TRIBUTE
ANTHOLOGY edited by Christoph Paul & Grant Wamack

THE VERY INEFFECTIVE HAUNTED HOUSE by Jeff Burk

WALK HAND IN HAND INTO EXTINCTION: STORIES INSPIRED BY
TRUE DETECTIVE edited by Christoph Paul & Leza Cantoral